"The enjoyable part of a Stone Barrington novel isn't how he solves the mystery, but instead the journey he takes to get there."*

Stone on the Rocks

Dumped by his glamorous Russian girlfriend during dinner at Elaine's and running low on cash, Stone Barrington is not having a good week. So his luck seems to be improving when he's hired to locate the missing son of a very wealthy man—lucky because the job pays well, and because the son seems to be hiding in the tropical paradise of Key West. But when Stone and his sometime running buddy Dino Bacchetti arrive in the sunny Keys, it appears that someone has been lying in wait. Stone very nearly loses his life after being blindsided at a local bar, and he realizes that the missing son he's been hired to track may have good reason for not wanting to be found. Suddenly, Key West is looking less like Margaritaville and more like the mean streets of New York. . . .

Praise for Stuart Woods's Stone Barrington Novels

Hot Mahogany

"[A] fun ride from Stuart Woods." —*Bangor Daily News*

"Series fans will find all their expectations nicely fulfilled."
—*Publishers Weekly*

Shoot Him If He Runs

"Fast-paced . . . with a whole lot of style."
—*Bangor Daily News*

"Woods certainly knows how to keep the pages turning."
—*Booklist*

Fresh Disasters

"Fast-paced, hilarious, and tragic." —*Albuquerque Journal*

"Good fun." —*Publishers Weekly*

continued . . .

Dark Harbor

"A vigilante detective in the manly-man mode . . . a rat-a-tat tone."   —*The Washington Post Book World*

"Fast pacing and an involving mystery."   —*Booklist*

Two Dollar Bill

"A smooth and solid thriller."
                    —*The News-Leader* (Springfield, MO)

Reckless Abandon

"Fast action, catchy plot, and spicy dialogue."
                    —*The Calgary Sun*

"[An] amusing, full-throttle sex-and-crime romp."
                    —*Publishers Weekly*

Dirty Work

"High on the stylish suspense."—*The Santa Fe New Mexican*

"Sleek and engaging."   —*Publishers Weekly*

The Short Forever

"A tight mystery right up to the end . . . good-guy charm."
                    —*The Palm Beach Post*

Cold Paradise

"A delightful tale of sex and violence . . . *Sopranos*-style . . . slick, sophisticated fun."   —*The Washington Post*

"Woods delivers his most riveting and glamorous Barrington novel yet."   —*Vero Beach Press Journal* (FL)

BOOKS BY STUART WOODS

FICTION

Mounting Fears[‡]
Hot Mahogany[†]
Santa Fe Dead[§]
Beverly Hills Dead
Shoot Him If He Runs[†]
Fresh Disasters[†]
Short Straw[§]
Dark Harbor[†]
Iron Orchid[*]
Two Dollar Bill[†]
The Prince of Beverly Hills
Reckless Abandon[†]
Capital Crimes[‡]
Dirty Work[†]
Blood Orchid[*]
The Short Forever[†]
Orchid Blues[*]
Cold Paradise[†]
L.A. Dead[†]
The Run[‡]

Worst Fears Realized[†]
Orchid Beach[*]
Swimming to Catalina[†]
Dead in the Water[†]
Dirt[†]
Choke
Imperfect Strangers
Heat
Dead Eyes
L.A. Times
Santa Fe Rules[§]
New York Dead[†]
Palindrome
Grass Roots[‡]
White Cargo
Under the Lake
Deep Lie[‡]
Run Before the Wind[‡]
Chiefs[‡]

TRAVEL

A Romantic's Guide to the Country Inns of
Britain and Ireland (1979)

MEMOIR

Blue Water, Green Skipper (1977)

[*]A Holly Barker Book   [†]A Stone Barrington Book
[‡]A Will Lee Book   [§]An Ed Eagle Book

LOITERING
with INTENT

STUART WOODS

A SIGNET BOOK

SIGNET
Published by New American Library, a division of
Penguin Group (USA) Inc., 375 Hudson Street,
New York, New York 10014, USA
Penguin Group (Canada), 90 Eglinton Avenue East, Suite 700, Toronto,
Ontario M4P 2Y3, Canada (a division of Pearson Penguin Canada Inc.)
Penguin Books Ltd., 80 Strand, London WC2R 0RL, England
Penguin Ireland, 25 St. Stephen's Green, Dublin 2,
Ireland (a division of Penguin Books Ltd.)
Penguin Group (Australia), 250 Camberwell Road, Camberwell, Victoria 3124,
Australia (a division of Pearson Australia Group Pty. Ltd.)
Penguin Books India Pvt. Ltd., 11 Community Centre, Panchsheel Park,
New Delhi - 110 017, India
Penguin Group (NZ), 67 Apollo Drive, Rosedale, North Shore 0632,
New Zealand (a division of Pearson New Zealand Ltd.)
Penguin Books (South Africa) (Pty.) Ltd., 24 Sturdee Avenue,
Rosebank, Johannesburg 2196, South Africa

Penguin Books Ltd., Registered Offices:
80 Strand, London WC2R 0RL, England

Published by Signet, an imprint of New American Library, a division of Penguin
Group (USA) Inc. Previously published in a Putnam hardcover edition.

First Signet Printing, December 2009
10 9 8 7 6 5 4 3 2 1

This book is for Lisa Towbin.

I

Elaine's, late.

Stone Barrington arrived at his table at the same time as his usual Knob Creek on the rocks and made a mental note to increase the waiter's tip. This generosity was blown right out of his mind as he took his first welcome sip, because entering the restaurant immediately after him, as if she had been following him in another cab, was his girlfriend, Tatiana Orlovsky.

Stone was surprised to see her, because earlier in the day he had asked her to dinner and she had declined. Her excuse had been better than the I-have-to-wash-my-hair standby, but not much, and she had declined an invitation the evening before as well. They had been seeing each other for some months, and she pleased him more and more. He stood up to greet her.

"Hello," she said.

"May I take your coat and get you a drink? I have a business dinner in a few minutes, but we have time."

She sat down without removing her coat, a bad sign. "No," she said, "I'm not staying. There's something I have to say to you."

Very bad sign: "Say to you," not "talk with you." His inference was that a response would not be entertained. "All right," he said, taking a long drag on his bourbon. He had a feeling he was going to need it.

"Henry is moving back in," she said. Henry Kennerly was her estranged husband, and in Stone's experience and from her stories, he was an unreconstructed drunk and bully.

"Tati," Stone said, as gently as possible, "are you out of your fucking mind?"

"He's been sober for ninety-one days," she replied, choosing not to address the issue of her sanity. "He's never done that before."

"And how long do you expect him to remain in that condition?"

"He's a new man, or rather an old one, the one I knew when I first met him. He has melted my heart."

Stone felt his sex life leaving his body, like a departing spirit. "Tati . . ."

"Stop," she said, holding up a hand like a traffic cop. "It won't do any good to talk about it. Our time to-gether has been wonderful, and I've enjoyed every moment of it, but it's not going anywhere, and besides, this is my marriage I'm talking about."

Stone wanted to remind her that it had been an unpleasant and abusive marriage for years, but he uncharacteristically managed to sense the obvious, that she was in no mood to talk. He shrugged.

She stood up, and he stood up with her. She walked around the table, gave him a light, sweet kiss on the lips, then walked out of the restaurant. As she made her way through the tiny vestibule, one man flattened himself against the wall to let her pass, while another held the outside door open for her. Stone could see a cab waiting with the rear door standing open; she got into it and rode away down Second Avenue into what had become a blowing snowstorm.

The two men entered the restaurant and walked toward Stone. The taller of the two was Bill Eggers, his law school buddy and currently the managing partner of the prestigious law firm of Woodman & Weld, to which Stone was of counsel, which meant that he was hired to handle the cases the firm did not wish to be seen to handle.

The other man was a stranger, shorter, heftier and squarer-shaped than Eggers. Stone did not know him but presumed he was the client Eggers wanted him to meet with.

"Evening, Stone," Eggers said, shaking his hand. "This is our client, Warren Keating."

Stone shook the man's hand and offered them both a chair. "How do you do?" he said.

"Ordinarily I do very well," the man said, sitting down, "but . . ."

"Warren has a problem I think you can help him with," Eggers interrupted.

"I hope so," Stone replied. "Can I get you a drink?"

"Scotch," Keating replied quickly. "Laphroaig, if they have it."

"Two," Eggers said.

"They have it," Stone replied, lifting an eyebrow in the direction of a waiter, who scurried over and took their order.

"And another for me," Stone said, tossing off the remainder of his bourbon.

Eggers looked sharply at Stone but didn't comment.

"How can I help you, Mr. Keating?" Stone asked.

"It's Warren," the man said. "I . . ."

"Do you mind if I sum this up for you, Warren?" Eggers said, interrupting again.

Stone reflected that Eggers did not interrupt clients without a good reason.

"All right, Bill," Keating said wearily.

"Warren runs a multigenerational family business," Eggers began.

"Elijah Keating's Sons," Keating said. "My great-grandfather started it when he got home from the Civil War."

Stone nodded, but he had never heard of it.

"This is not what you would call a mom-and-pop business," Eggers continued. "The company manufactures industrial equipment and tooling; they operate nineteen factories around the world."

"We've run out of Elijah Keating's sons," Keating said. "My only son is the most recent generation, and he . . . has no interest in coming into the business. I'm getting on, and I'm weary of the travel involved in running a worldwide operation."

"Warren has accepted an offer from a multinational company—a very, very substantial offer."

"Congratulations, Warren," Stone said.

"Not yet," Keating replied. "I need my son's consent."

"Warren's great-grandfather's will was very specific," Eggers said. "Each living heir must agree to a sale of the business."

"My father has already signed off on the sale," Keating said. "He's old, and he was initially against it, but he's finally seen the wisdom of the sale."

"I see," Stone replied. "And your son hasn't consented?"

"He doesn't know about it," Keating replied. "At least not to my knowledge."

"Warren and his son have not been in touch in recent days," Eggers said.

Stone figured he was being diplomatic. "I see," he replied, though he didn't.

Warren Keating reached into an inside pocket, produced a postcard and handed it to Stone. "This is Evan's most recent communication," he said.

Stone perused the card. On one side was a photograph of a bar, labeled "Sloppy Joe's, Key West." Stone turned it over and read the message, which was written in block capitals.

"DEAR OLD DAD," it read, "HAVING A WONDERFUL TIME. GLAD YOU'RE NOT HERE. GO FUCK YOURSELF." It was signed with a flourish, "EVAN."

Stone returned the card, and Keating handed him a photograph. It was black-and-white, like something from a college yearbook, and featured a slim, handsome young man in a blue blazer, with close-cropped hair.

"How old was he then, and how old is he now?" Stone asked.

"He was nineteen or twenty then, and he's twenty-six now," Keating replied.

"And how long is it since you've seen him?"

"Not since his graduation, and we—his mother and I—sort of missed him then. We made our way over to where his class was sitting, and there was just his cap and gown on a chair with his name on it. He had only recently come into a nice little trust fund from his mother's side of the family, which gave him a certain amount of freedom."

"I see," Stone said, seeing for the first time. "The postmark on the card was smudged; when did you receive it?"

"Five days ago," Keating replied. "I had heard he was in Miami, and when we started negotiating the sale of the business I sent a private investigator looking for him. He was contacted but rebuffed the investigator and disappeared from his hotel there. I took the, ah, tenor of his message on the card to mean that he did not wish to be contacted by me."

Stone nodded. "I should think this is a job for a skip tracer, Bill," he said to Eggers.

"No," Eggers said, pulling a thick envelope from an inside pocket and handing it to Stone. "It's a job for an attorney. This is the form of consent to the sale; I wrote it myself. His great-great-grandfather's will requires that it be explained to him by an attorney and that he be given an opportunity to engage a lawyer of his own to review it. If he chooses not to have it reviewed, there's a second document to be signed, waiving that right."

"If you can get this done for me, Stone," Keating said, "I'm prepared to be generous."

"What sort of time frame are we talking about?" Stone asked.

"A week, give or take," Eggers said.

"And that postcard is the only reason to think he's in Key West?" Stone asked.

Keating shrugged. "He could be anywhere."

"I'll leave tomorrow morning," Stone said, glancing through the restaurant's front window. "Weather permitting."

2

Eggers and Keating had just left when Dino Bacchetti, Stone's former partner in his days on the NYPD, walked into Elaine's, shucking off and shaking his overcoat. Dino was still on the force, a lieutenant now running the detective squad at the Nineteenth, the Upper East Side precinct.

"It's coming down out there," Dino said, hanging up his coat and taking a seat, while making drinking motions at a waiter, who was already in gear. He stopped and looked at Stone. "You look like you've just been dumped again."

"Again? What's that supposed to mean?" Stone asked.

"Well, you're always getting dumped," Dino said.

"I have to go to Key West tomorrow; you want to come along?"

"What about this weather?" Dino asked.

"The snowstorm is supposed to pass off the coast early in the morning, followed by clear weather."

"Yeah," Dino said, "I'd like to take a trip to Key West in the dead of winter, and I've got some time off coming."

"You're on," Stone said, sipping his drink and reaching for a menu.

Elaine got up from a nearby table, walked over and sat down. "So," she said, "Tati dumped you?"

"I knew it," Dino chimed in.

"We had a conversation," Stone said.

"It looked to me like she was doing all the talking," Elaine pointed out.

"All right, all right; she's taking her husband back."

"That ass?" Dino said, incredulous. "He's a drunk, and he beat her."

"She says he's been sober for ninety-one days, and he's a changed man."

Elaine spoke up. "When they have to count the days, they haven't changed yet. Sounds like he's in AA, though, and that can't be a bad thing."

"Forgive me if I view anything that would get him back into her house as a bad thing," Stone said.

"Don't worry," Dino said. "You haven't heard the last of her."

"What kind of job did Bill Eggers stick you with?" Elaine asked.

"Actually, it's not so bad. Dino and I are flying to Key West tomorrow morning."

"This is work?"

"This is work."

"You're a lucky son of a bitch, aren't you?" she said.

"Sometimes."

"Later," Elaine said, getting up to greet some regulars who had just wandered in.

"So what is it we have to do down there?" Dino asked. "I take it we're not going to spend all our time on the beach."

"I hate the beach," Stone said. "It's hot and sandy and uncomfortable. Have you ever made love on a beach? Sand gets into everything, and I mean *everything*. Even your ears."

"Your *ears*?"

"Trust me."

"I guess I'll have to. You know anybody in Key West?"

"I met a lawyer from there once, at a meeting in Atlanta, but I can't remember his name. Jack something, I think; nice guy."

"You remember Tommy Sculley, from the old days?"

"Yeah, he was a few years ahead of us on the squad."

"He put in his thirty and retired down there a few

years ago, but he couldn't stand it, so he got a job on the local force."

"Good. Let's look him up."

"You didn't answer my question: What do we have to do down there?"

Stone handed him the photograph. "Find this kid."

"What, he didn't come back from spring break last year?"

"That's an old picture, from his college days. He's a big boy now, twenty-six."

"So we have to throw a bag over his head and bring him home to Mommy?"

"Nope. All we have to do is get his signature on a couple of documents, notarized, and we're done. We can FedEx them back, then take a few days off and play some golf or some tennis or something." Stone explained the sale of the family business.

"What's the problem between the kid and his daddy?"

"One of them is a kid; the other one's a daddy." Stone told Dino about the message on the postcard.

"That seems pretty definitive," Dino observed.

"We don't have to get him to kiss and make up—just sign the documents and collect a big check, his share of the sale of the business. That shouldn't be too difficult."

"Not the check part, anyway."

"The kid has already got what the daddy describes as

'a nice little trust fund,' from his mother's side of the family, so I doubt if he's hurting too much."

"Still, the other check sounds like a big one, if they've got nineteen factories around the world."

"I didn't ask, but I guess so."

"You didn't read the documents?"

"Not yet."

"Read them; I'd like to know what we're dealing with."

Stone opened the envelope and flipped through the pages. "Well, the tone is a little Dickensian—I guess that's what you get when you're dealing with his great-great-grandfather's will." Stone stopped flipping. "Holy shit," he said.

"That much?"

"That much. It would be a breach of attorney-client confidentiality to tell you how much, but I think you'd be impressed."

"This is getting easier and easier. Where are we staying?"

"Good question." Stone got out his cell phone and called his twenty-four-hour-a-day travel agent. He explained himself and waited for a moment. "Sounds good," he said. "A week, I guess. What's the address?" He jotted some notes, thanked the woman on the line and hung up.

"Find something?"

"Place called the Marquesa. It sounds comfortable, and it has a good restaurant, too."

"All I'm eating is shrimp and conch."

"Conch? That spiral shell thing you find on the beach?"

"Something lives inside that shell thing, and there are lots of ways to cook it, and it's really, really good."

"If you say so."

"Native-born Key Westers call themselves Conchs, too."

"You're a mine of information, Dino; what else do you know about Key West?"

"They have nice sunsets, and you can see the Green Flash, if you've had enough margaritas."

"I can do that," Stone said.

3

Stone woke and looked out his bedroom window. The gardens inside the U-shaped row of Turtle Bay Townhouses sat, resplendent, under six inches of fresh snow, made glaring by bright sunshine. He picked up the phone and called Jet Aviation, at Teterboro Airport, in New Jersey.

"I'd like my inboard and outboard caps topped off with JetA with Prist and the airplane deiced," he said. He received an affirmative answer, then went to his computer and created two flight plans, one for each leg, for the trip south, then called Flight Services for a weather forecast, which was highly favorable, even sporting a tailwind, unusual when flying north to south.

The downstairs doorbell rang on the telephone system, and Stone picked up the phone. "Dino?"

"Yeah?"

"You have a key. Use it."

"I didn't want to come in unannounced and interrupt something."

"Fat chance," Stone said. "Put your bags in the car. I'll get a shower and meet you in the kitchen. Tell Helene what you want for breakfast."

Twenty minutes later, Stone stowed his bags in the car with Dino's, then joined him in the kitchen.

"I made you eggs and bacon," Helene said, as he took a seat.

"You're psychic," Stone said, sipping his freshly squeezed orange juice.

"How long a flight?" Dino asked.

"We have a bit of a tailwind, so around five hours, plus one fuel stop in South Carolina," Stone said, gazing out the window.

"I can stand that, I guess. You're looking at Tatiana's house."

"I wasn't looking at anything in particular," Stone lied, "just out the window."

They arrived at Teterboro Airport to find the airplane refueled and the deicing nearly complete. Stone stowed their golf clubs and tennis rackets in the forward luggage compartment and their bags in the rear. After a thorough preflight inspection and a call to Clearance Delivery, they taxied to runway 1 and were cleared for takeoff.

The departure controller turned them south and gradually gave them higher altitudes, but not until they were handed off to New York Center did they receive their final clearance to their chosen altitude, flight level 260, or 26,000 feet. Stone leveled off, adjusted the throttle and switched on the XM Satellite Radio. Dino was already doing the *Times* crossword puzzle, and Stone started on the front page.

"I hope you made a copy of the crossword," Dino said, scribbling away.

"If I hadn't, I would have already strangled you and dumped your body over Virginia."

Stone had finished reading the *Times* when they started their descent into their refueling point, a small airfield at Monks Corner, South Carolina, which offered fuel prices a couple of bucks less than nearby Charleston.

Half an hour later they were climbing back to altitude, and two hours after that they were crossing the south coast of Florida at last over open water. Key West lay, invisible, another hundred miles south. Dino was squirming in his seat.

"I've never flown over open water," Dino said.

"The life raft is on the seat behind me," Stone said, "and the life jackets are in a blue zipper bag right behind my seat. In the event of an unscheduled landing, you put on a life jacket, strap yourself into a rear seat, and when the airplane has stopped moving, open *only* the top half of the door. We'll float for a while, but if you open the bottom half, the Atlantic Ocean will join us inside immediately. You wrap the rope attached to the raft firmly around your wrist and hand, push the raft out the top of the door and jerk the cord hard. The raft will inflate. You hold it there until I can get out; then you pull the tab that inflates your life jacket and join me in the raft. I'll bring along the handheld radio and the beacon that broadcasts our position to the Coast Guard via satellite."

"Then what?"

"Then we wait for the Coast Guard to show up, remove us from the life raft, give us a cup of coffee and take us to a convenient land location."

"How long do we wait?"

"A few hours, maybe less."

"A few hours in a tiny life raft with you is all I need to complete my day."

"It's a character-building experience."

"And then?"

"We make our way to Key West by available transportation, and my insurance company buys me a new airplane. Feel better now?"

"And I lose all my stuff?"

"No, your household insurance reimburses you for your clothes and buys you a new set of golf clubs and tennis racket."

"You make it all sound so attractive," Dino said.

"Don't worry. It will scare the shit out of you," Stone replied.

First, they saw some small islands to their left. Dino looked at the chart. "The Keys don't run north-south," he said.

"You're very observant. They run northeast-south-west, and toward the end more west. Look." He pointed out the window as an island swam into view through the haze. Key West Approach had them down to 1,600 feet now.

"N123TF, Key West Approach, report Key West Airport in sight."

Stone looked to his left and saw an airplane take off in the distance. "N123TF, airport in sight."

"Fly direct Key West VOR, then enter a left downwind for runway niner. Contact Key West Tower on 118.2. Have a good day."

"Thanks, and good day," Stone replied, then switched frequencies. "Key West Tower, N123TF at the VOR, left downwind for niner."

"N123TF, Key West Tower, cleared to land."

Stone pointed as they approached the island. "We can see everything from here." The island was laid out before them, every inch of it. "You been here before?"

"Once, a weekend with the ex. You?"

"My first time."

Stone turned final at five hundred feet and lined up

on the runway. He made a smooth landing, and Ground Control directed him to parking.

They unloaded their gear, left refueling instructions and picked up their rent-a-car. Twenty minutes later they were parking in front of the Marquesa.

"Looks like somebody's house," Dino said.

But after they had checked in and followed a bellman out a rear door, they found themselves in a large courtyard with two pools, surrounded by small cottages. Stone and Dino were shown to a pair of them connected by a front porch, and were soon sitting on the porch in rockers sipping something tropical with a little umbrella in it, ogling some girls in the pool at their feet.

"So," said Dino, "when do we start looking for this kid, Evan Keating?"

"What's your hurry?" Stone murmured, sipping his drink and watching the girls. "Tomorrow is soon enough."

4

To reach the restaurant, Stone and Dino walked out the front entrance of the hotel and to the street corner, to the front door of the dining room. It was a tastefully decorated space, with a bar to the left and a dozen or fifteen tables to the right. An attractive blonde greeted them.

"You must be Mr. Barrington and Mr. Bacchetti," she said, "according to my list."

"That's us," Stone replied. "And we have another gentleman joining us."

"I'm Janet," she said. "Right this way." She seated them at a corner table and left menus.

A waiter materialized, greeted them and asked for their drinks order.

"I don't suppose you have Knob Creek bourbon," Stone said resignedly.

"You may suppose we do," the waiter replied. "We have another customer who forced us to order it."

"On the rocks, please."

Dino ordered his Scotch.

The restaurant was filling up rapidly; even all the bar stools were taken. "Busy place," Stone said.

"The food must be good," Dino replied. "Hey, here's Tommy!" He stood up to greet their old acquaintance as he entered the restaurant, and so did Stone. Shortly, Tommy had a margarita before him.

"You're drinking that tropical swill?" Dino asked.

"After a while down here, it gets to be unpatriotic if you don't," Tommy replied.

"How's retirement treating you, Tommy?" Stone asked.

"Who's retired? A week after I hit town, I was a detective again."

"Working homicide?"

"Are you kidding? You're in Paradise; we get like one homicide a year, if we're lucky, and it's nearly always perfectly clear who the killer is. He's usually standing there, holding a gun or a claw hammer in his hand, when we walk in. The only problem is getting him not to talk too fast while we're taking his statement."

"What keeps you busy, then?" Dino asked.

"Drug stuff, burglaries, mostly small-time. We get a

lot of drifters down here, especially in the winter. They at least know they're not going to freeze to death, and they can steal enough to eat. We get the usual domestic stuff, too, only more of it is gay than in New York."

"What's the job like?"

"Pretty interesting. The first thing I had to do was to train my partner, a kid named Daryl, whose acne had not yet cleared up. He was the chief's nephew at the time."

"Sounds like a drag."

"No, he was quick to learn, and he's turned into a pretty good detective. His uncle is gone now, and so is the guy who replaced him. Last week, the chief and two captains resigned over a scandal."

"What kind of scandal?"

"Fixing parking tickets, harassing gay guys on bicycles, hiring girlfriends as secretaries and fucking them in the supply room, drinking on the job—you name it. Nothing big, just a lot of continuous horseshit. I'm currently acting chief of detectives—all six of them. They offered me the chief's job, but I'm too old for the politics and the PR horseshit."

"I don't blame you," Dino said. "I'm running the squad at the Nineteenth, and that's almost more politics than I can stand."

"What's the most interesting case you've worked down here, Tommy?" Stone asked.

"Oh, that's an easy one," Tommy laughed. "We had

a big drugs, murder, sex thing right after I signed on that involved some prominent locals, among them the local tennis pro. You remember a player named Chuck Chandler?"

"The guy who choked in the Wimbledon final some years back?"

"That's the guy. The sports pages called it the Chuck Choke, and it stuck."

"I hope he didn't murder anybody."

"Nah, he was pretty much the dope in the thing. There was one very hot babe mixed up in it, though. She's doing time right now, ought to be out soon."

"What's it like living here?" Stone asked.

"Beautiful in the winter, spring and fall. Hot as hell in the summer, but no worse than New York. At least we get the breeze. You like boats?"

"Sure, who doesn't?"

"I'll take you out for some snorkeling," Tommy said. "Snorkeling and a few drinks. We got a very nice little yacht club here, and I'll take you there for dinner. To-morrow night?"

"Sure," Stone and Dino said simultaneously.

"So," Tommy said, "what brings you guys down here?"

"It's winter, isn't it?" Dino answered.

"I'm running a legal errand," Stone said. "I've got to find a guy and get him to sign some papers."

"Anybody I know?"

"I doubt it. Kid hates his father, but the old man needs his signature on some papers to sell the family business. Means a lot of bucks for the whole family, the kid, too, so it shouldn't be too much trouble to persuade him." Stone showed Tommy the old photo of Evan.

Tommy looked at it and screwed his face up. "What's his name?"

"Evan Keating," Stone replied. "Know him?"

"In a manner of speaking," Tommy replied. "I busted him in a drug case yesterday, but it ain't going to stick."

"Do you know where I can find him?"

Tommy motioned his chin in the direction of the bar. "Right over there, third stool from the left."

Stone looked toward the bar. The man's back was mostly to him, but he could catch a little profile. He was heavier than in his college photo and had longer hair, and he was dressed in jeans, cowboy boots and a flowered shirt, with the tail out, Hawaiian-style. He was talking to a beautiful girl on the next bar stool, with long, honey-colored hair, dressed in tight jeans and a leather jacket.

"Excuse me a minute," Stone said, rising and walking toward the bar. He walked up to the two people, who turned and looked at him. Evan Keating had a thin, straight nose and bright blue eyes.

"Mr. Keating?" Stone said. "I'm sorry to intrude,

but I just wanted to introduce myself." He handed the young man his card. "My name is Stone Barrington, and I've been sent by my law firm to Key West to deliver some documents for your signature."

"You must think I'm somebody else," Keating said. "I don't know what you're talking about."

"I'm aware of that, Mr. Keating, but we could get together for a few minutes tomorrow morning. I'm sure you will find our conversation greatly to your advantage."

Keating regarded him evenly for a moment without speaking; then he said, "Why don't we step outside for a moment and discuss this?"

"Of course," Stone replied.

Keating got up and led the way out, while Stone followed. Outside on the sidewalk a bench had been placed as a waiting area for the restaurant, and Keating motioned Stone to sit down.

Stone sat down next to Keating, his back to the restaurant door. "I know this will come as a surprise to you, but my law firm represents Elijah Keating's Sons, and . . ."

Something struck the back of Stone's neck, and the night exploded in stars.

5

Stone swam back into consciousness, opened his eyes, then closed them again. Some sort of bright light had blinded him. A cool hand was resting on his forehead.

"Mr. Barrington?" a woman's low voice said.

"What?" Stone replied. He tried to open his eyes again but it didn't work.

"Can you look at me, please?"

"It's too bright," Stone said. Immediately, the brightness disappeared.

"Is that better?"

"Okay, yes."

"Can you open your eyes now?"

Stone opened his eyes and found his vision filled with the face of a woman. "What happened?" he asked.

"We don't know," she replied.

Dino's face replaced the woman's, and Tommy Sculley was right behind him. "We found you facedown on the sidewalk," he said.

"I liked the other face better," Stone said and tried to sit up straighter.

"Let's get him up on the bench," the woman said, and hands gripped his arms and helped him upward.

"What happened to you, Stone?" Dino asked.

"How the hell should I know?" Stone said irritably. "I was unconscious, wasn't I?"

"Yeah, that was kind of the point," Dino said. "Do you have any idea how you got that way?"

"Well, I was sitting at a table with you and Tommy, having a drink, and then I woke up here."

"Nothing in between?" Dino asked.

"I've got a headache," Stone said, rubbing the back of his neck and finding it sore.

The woman spoke again. "He should really be in a hospital," she said.

"I don't need to go to a hospital," Stone retorted. "I need some aspirin and a drink."

She explored the back of his head and his neck with her fingers, and he winced when she got to his neck. "Seems like a blow to the back of the neck, rather than his head, so I think we can discount a skull fracture or a concussion."

"Who the hell are you?" Stone grumbled. "And where's that drink?"

"Oh, all right, give him what he wants," she said, sounding exasperated. "Get him into bed and keep him there until morning, and call me if he's still disoriented when he wakes up." She handed Dino a card. "Good night, Mr. Barrington," she said. "I hope you feel better tomorrow."

Tommy put a glass of bourbon and two aspirin into Stone's hand. "There you go."

Stone washed down the aspirin with the bourbon and took a deep breath. "That's better," he said.

"Can you stand up?" Tommy asked.

"Sure I can." He stood up and held on to Tommy's shoulder for a moment. "I'm hungry. We hadn't ordered dinner, had we?"

"No, we hadn't, but the doctor said you should be in bed."

"What doctor?"

"The woman who just washed her hands of you and left," Dino said. "Come on, Tommy, let's get him inside; he's not going to cooperate."

The three men went back into the restaurant and sat down at their table.

Stone was still rubbing his neck.

"You want some ice on that?" Tommy asked.

"I don't want to make a spectacle of myself," Stone

29

said. "People are staring at me as it is." He took another slug of the bourbon, and it began reaching the places it should, including the back of his neck. "Now, will you guys tell me what the hell happened?"

"I directed you to a guy at the bar," Tommy said. "You showed me his picture. Evan Keating?"

"I don't remember that," Stone said.

"You walked over to him and apparently introduced yourself, gave him your card. Then the two of you walked outside."

"I don't remember that, either," Stone said, sipping more bourbon.

"Tommy and I were talking for a couple of minutes, not paying attention to you. Then Janet came over and said you were lying on the sidewalk outside, and that's where we found you."

"This doesn't make any sense," Stone said. "Are you saying that Evan Keating knocked me unconscious, and that I didn't see it coming?"

"Seems like you caught one on the back of the neck," Tommy said. "Dino, did you see anybody follow them out?"

"I wasn't looking that way," Dino replied.

"Neither was I," Tommy said.

"And I don't remember any of it," Stone said.

A waiter brought menus, and they ordered, and someone brought a plate of hummus and some bread.

"I'm hungry," Stone said.

"That's probably a good sign," Tommy replied. "If you were badly hurt, you wouldn't be thinking about food and booze."

"He hardly ever thinks about anything else," Dino said, "except women."

"Speaking of women," Stone said, "who was that doctor? She looked pretty good."

Dino handed Stone her card. "I think he's going to be okay," he said to Tommy.

16

Stone woke up the following morning with his headache nearly gone. He took a couple of aspirin, ordered breakfast and found Dino on the front porch waiting for him.

"How you feeling?" Dino asked.

"A lot better. I still have a little headache, but I took some aspirin."

"You remember anything else that happened last night?"

Stone thought about that. "Yeah, I think I talked to Evan Keating at the bar, but just for a minute."

"Do you know how you got outside?"

Stone thought some more. "He suggested we talk outside, I think."

"You remember anybody following you outside?"

"No, Keating was ahead of me."

"Was he with anybody?"

"There was a girl, I think, but I thought he left her at the bar."

"Was she beefy, muscular?"

"No, she was slim and attractive."

"Then she either packs a hell of a punch or she hit you with something solid."

"I don't remember her going outside."

"She could have been behind you."

"I guess."

"What did you say to Keating at the bar?"

Stone replayed the scene in his head again. "Not much. I told him I had some business with him and suggested we get together in the morning to discuss it. I think I told him . . . that he would like what I have to say, or something like that."

"Maybe he didn't get that message and thought you were some sort of threat," Dino said.

"Didn't Tommy say that he busted the guy on some sort of drug thing?"

"Yeah, but it didn't hold up, and he was released."

"Well, maybe the cops got an address for Keating."

"I'll call Tommy," Dino said. He produced his cell phone, spoke briefly to Tommy Sculley and hung up. "Hotel La Concha," Dino said. "I think that's Spanish for 'conch.' It's on Duval Street."

Stone went and got the map the rental car agency

had given him. "Yeah, here it is," he said, pointing. "Duval is kind of the main drag, and the hotel is marked. It's only a few blocks from here."

"Then let's go see him after breakfast," Dino said.

"Yes," Stone said, "and carefully."

Breakfast arrived and they ate, then showered and dressed.

"Let's go see Mr. Keating," Stone said.

"I think I'd better watch your back this time," Dino replied.

"Good idea."

They drove over to Duval and down to the Hotel La Concha, which was a large stucco building. They found a parking place and fed a lot of quarters into a meter, then went inside to the front desk.

Stone approached the clerk on duty.

"May I help you?"

"Yes, I'd like to speak to a Mr. Evan Keating, who, I believe, is a guest here."

"You just missed him," the clerk said. "He left maybe five minutes ago."

"Do you know what time he'll be back?"

"He won't. He checked out and didn't leave a forwarding address."

"Did he say anything that might give you a clue where he was going?"

The man shook his head. "No. In fact, neither he nor his girlfriend said a word, except to ask for the bill."

"He didn't mention, for instance, the airport?"

"No."

"Do you know his girlfriend's name?"

"What's this about?" the clerk asked.

Stone handed him a card. "I'm an attorney from New York. I have some business with Mr. Keating."

"You're suing him?"

"Nothing like that. I just have some papers for him to sign." Stone showed him the envelope in his coat pocket.

The clerk went to his computer terminal and typed a few strokes. "The woman's name is Gigi Jones."

"Any home address for either of them?"

The clerk chuckled. "No, it just says 'Itinerant.' That's the first time I've ever seen that one." The clerk smote his forehead. "Oh, I remember: when they arrived, Keating said they were on a boat."

"Sail? Power?"

"He didn't say. I got the impression that they were cruising and just wanted to get some shore time. Lots of people on boats do that; they want a real shower and their laundry done."

"Did Keating get his laundry done?"

The clerk gazed at his terminal again. "Yep. Charge of $189 for laundry and dry cleaning. That's a fair amount of stuff."

"Did you have any other conversation with Keating?"

"Not really, just when he checked in and out."

"Did he get or make a lot of phone calls?"

The clerk checked his computer again. "None at all, but that's not unusual; everybody has a cell phone these days."

"Did he mention where his boat was moored?"

"Nope."

"How many marinas are there in Key West?"

The clerk laughed. "Lots."

"What's the biggest one?"

The clerk got out a tourist map and opened it, pointing at some sheltered water. "This is Key West Bight, and the biggest marina there is the Galleon, right here. But the whole bight is pretty much all marina, and there are others along the shore."

Stone thanked the man for his help, and he and Dino left. "Well, I guess we'd better start at Key West Bight," he said.

They drove down to Front Street, found a parking lot and walked to the Galleon Marina. They stopped at the dockmaster's office and spoke to a young woman at the desk. "Good morning," Stone said. "I'm looking for a fellow named Evan Keating; someone told me he's docked here."

She went to the computer. "Nope, no Keating. Do you have a boat name?"

"No."

"Boat type?"

"No."

"Then I don't think I can help you."

"Evan is about six feet, longish hair, a hundred and eighty pounds and with a pretty girl."

"That covers about half our people," the woman said.

Stone thanked her and they left.

"Time to wear out some shoe leather," Dino said.

"Yeah, I guess so."

They started to walk around Key West Bight, checking other marinas, but got nowhere.

"I think that's what we need," Stone said, pointing at a boats-for-rent sign.

"Feed me first," Dino said, pointing at a sign that said RAW BAR.

"Okay, but keep an eye peeled for Keating."

"I only saw his back," Dino said, "but if I see a familiar back, I'll let you know."

"What would I do without you?" Stone asked.

7

Stone and Dino walked into the Raw Bar, a large, open-sided barn of a place, which was rapidly filling for lunch. They were given the last free table along the waterfront, overlooking the marina area. As they sat down, Dino looked over the railing into the water and pointed.

"Hey, look at that," he said.

Stone peered into the water and saw half a dozen large fish measuring about four feet each, swimming among a lot of smaller ones. "I guess they know where to go for lunch," he said.

Dino was perusing the menu. "I want conch something," he said.

"What have they got?"

"How about conch fritters?"

"Sounds okay to me."

A fetching girl—all the waitresses were fetching—took their order and brought them glasses of iced tea.

"How long have we got to find this guy and get him to sign?" Dino asked.

"A week, give or take."

"So we're down to six days?"

"I guess. I mean, it can't be that hard. When he hears how much money is coming to him, he'll be glad to see me."

"You'd think." Dino got out his cell phone, made a call and got up. "Signal's not too good; excuse me a minute." He walked a few feet away and seemed happier.

Stone sipped his tea and looked around at his fellow diners. They all looked like tourists, but in Key West everybody was dressed like a tourist.

Dino came back and sat down. "I talked to Tommy again; I wanted to know the circumstances of the arrest. Seems his people were following a guy named Charley Boggs, who they suspected of being an importer/dealer. They tailed him around for a while. Then he parked in the parking lot of a municipal building on Simonton Street. He sits in the car for five minutes. Then Evan Keating and Gigi Jones pull up in a convertible and park next to Charley Boggs, who's in a van. Some words are exchanged between the two cars, and then Tommy's people move in and arrest everybody.

"There are traces of cocaine in the van, but Evan's car is clean. They figure Boggs's stash is near, and Evan is there to buy, so they haul everybody in. Evan's story is he's having dinner at a restaurant called Antonia's, on Duval Street, and he's just parking there. There's a walkway from that parking lot to Duval. Tommy checks Antonia's, and sure enough, Evan has a reservation there.

"Asked about what words were exchanged between Evan and Boggs, Evan says he was just asking the time, since he forgot to put his wristwatch on after showering."

"So Tommy cuts Evan and Gigi loose."

"Right. Charley Boggs, too."

"Did you ask where we could find Boggs?"

"He lives on a houseboat in Garrison Bight. You got that map?"

Stone produced the map, but their conch fritters arrived.

"Eat 'em while they're hot," the waitress said.

Stone dipped a fritter into some red sauce and took a bite. "Hey, good!"

Dino was trying one, too. "Kinda chewy, the bits of conch, but lots of flavor."

They finished the fritters and ordered key lime pie; then Stone spread out the map. "Here's Garrison Bight," he said.

"That's where the yacht club is, too, Tommy says. We're meeting him there at seven."

They ate the key lime pie.

"I could get used to this," Dino said.

Stone waved for the check. "Let's go rent that boat."

The boat was an eighteen-foot Boston Whaler, a flat-bottomed fiberglass craft, with a forty-horsepower outboard attached.

"You know how to handle this?" the renter asked, handing Stone the keys.

"Yep." Stone stepped into the boat, checked the fuel tank and started the engine. "How do we get to Garrison Bight?" he asked.

The renter spread out a chart. "You go out into the harbor and keep to your right, past the old submarine base over there. You go under a bridge and straight ahead, past some Navy family houses, and your first right turn is into Garrison Bight."

He handed Dino the chart and pushed them off.

Stone got under way slowly. "Let's stop at the fuel dock," he said. "All the boaters end up there sooner or later."

"Whatever you say," Dino said, settling into the seat ahead of the steering pedestal. They were sheltered from the sun by a Bimini canvas top.

Stone pulled up to the dock, showed the photo of Keating to the man and got a negative response. They pushed off again, then spent an hour motoring from boat to boat, hoping to get lucky.

"No luck," Dino said finally. "Let's go see Garrison Bight."

Stone took one more look at the chart, then motored past the breakwater. "Before we do, let's go take a look at the boats at anchor." There were dozens of boats of every type anchored outside Key West Bight, and their search of those yielded nothing. "All right," Stone said, "Garrison Bight it is."

They followed the boat renter's instructions and slowed for a NO WAKE sign along the row of houses, then turned through a narrow channel into the bight. The houseboats lay dead ahead.

Stone throttled back to idle speed as they drove slowly along the row of moored boats. They were pretty, most of them, with window boxes and potted palms on the decks. A man of about thirty with a full, dark beard sat on the rear deck of one, fishing.

Stone cut the engine and drifted. "Good morning," he said to the man.

"If you say so."

"You know a guy named Charley Boggs?"

"Who wants to know?"

"My name is Barrington; I just want to talk to him."

"You a cop?"

"Nope, just looking for some information."

"What kind of information?"

"You're Charley, aren't you?"

"Maybe."

"I'm looking for a guy named Evan Keating."

"Never heard of him."

"Funny, you were arrested with him the other night in the municipal parking lot."

"Was that his name? I didn't know the guy."

"You sure about that?"

"You sure about not being a cop?"

"I'm sure."

"I'm sure, too. Never set eyes on the guy before that night."

"Okay, Charley, thanks," Stone said. He started the engine, turned and started out of Garrison Bight. "That guy looks like the Unabomber, Ted Kaczynski."

"Everybody in Key West looks like Ted Kaczynski," Dino pointed out.

"Where's the Key West Yacht Club?" Stone asked.

Dino was looking at the chart, and he pointed to the east. "It's way down there in the corner of the bight."

"Nice to know that," Stone said.

"Yeah, but we don't know much else, do we?"

8

The property of the Key West Yacht Club was entered from busy Roosevelt Boulevard, and the clubhouse was an unassuming 1950s-era building, surrounded by a large parking lot and a good-sized marina. There was a party going aboard a traditional motor yacht moored near the entrance to the driveway.

Stone found a parking place, and they walked into the club, taking a left into a roomy bar sheltering a crowd of happy-sounding people. Tommy Sculley waved them over to a corner of the bar, where he introduced them to a couple.

"Stone Barrington, Dino Bacchetti, this is Jack Spotts-wood and his wife, Terry, local lawyer and real estate broker, respectively."

Hands were shaken.

"Jack, I think we met in Atlanta a few years ago," Stone said. "A real estate closing, as I remember."

"That's right, we did," Spottswood said. "Nice to see you again. I hear you and Dino used to practice the police arts in New York with Tommy."

"That's a polite way of putting it," Stone said. "We were all street detectives, and only Dino prospered in the work. Tommy and I got out when we could."

"Yeah, Stone, sure," Tommy said. "I retired in good order; you got your ass bounced by Captain Leary and the other brass."

"True enough," Stone said. "There's enough in that story for a novel. I'll tell it to you when I'm drunker."

"Speaking of drunk," Spottswood said, "we're all invited to a party on a yacht next to the club."

"The traditional one?" Stone asked.

"She's a 1937 Trumpy," Spottswood said. "A member here, the local tennis pro, Chuck Chandler, just finished restoring her."

"There's that name again," Stone said.

"Yeah, the Chuck Choke. He hasn't lived it down yet."

"Come on, let's go see Chuck's new boat," Terry said.

They walked out of the bar and around to the yacht; her name on the stern was *Choke II*. They stepped aboard into the large cockpit, which was filled with people drinking with both hands. A tall, deeply tanned man in his late thirties with sun-bleached hair made his way toward them, and Spottswood introduced them to Chuck Chandler. A pretty girl with a tray of champagne glasses came over and gave everybody one.

"She's very beautiful," Stone said to Chuck.

"Yes, she is," Chuck replied, watching the girl walk away.

"I was referring to the yacht, but I can't argue the point. She's a Trumpy, I hear. The yacht, I mean."

"Yep, 1937."

"How'd you come by her?"

"I had a client at the Olde Island Tennis Club for some years, and he died last year. I had been helping him with the finish work on the restoration, and to my astonishment, he left her to me. She already had new engines and electronics, and her hull had been painted. All I really had to do to her was a hell of a lot of varnishing."

"You did a very fine job," Stone said, touching a bit of mahogany. "How many coats?"

"Ten, and I'll give her another coat every year. It'll give me something to do in the summers, when business is slow."

"You know your varnishing, Chuck."

"I had a lot of experience restoring her predecessor, a thirty-two-foot one-off that I lived aboard. This one is forty-four feet, and, believe me, the extra room is going to come in handy."

"May I see below?" Stone asked.

Chuck led him down the companionway and into the saloon. There was a built-in dining table and a galley tucked into a corner, a chart table and seating for eight or so.

"Gorgeous," Stone said.

"There's just the one cabin, aft," Chuck said, pointing the way.

Stone found a handsome stateroom, white and mahogany, with a nice head and shower and a double berth. "Perfect bachelor quarters," he said. "How many of these were built?"

"She's a custom job," Chuck said, "the only one of her kind. She was in pretty bad shape when Jerry bought her. He replaced all the lower hull planking and then redid everything from the bottom up."

"You're a lucky man," Stone said.

"That I am. If you'll excuse me, I'd better check that my guests are drinking enough."

"Sure." Stone didn't think they would need any encouragement. He walked back into the saloon and found a woman looking into the galley cabinets and fridge.

She glanced at him. "Hello," she said. She was tall and slender, with blond hair. Late thirties, maybe.

"Good evening, Doctor," he replied.

She turned to face him and lifted an eyebrow. "Ah," she said, "my former patient."

Stone offered his hand. "My name is Stone Barrington. I'm afraid I wasn't very appreciative of your kind efforts last evening. In my defense, I plead semiconsciousness."

She shook his hand. "Yes, you were. I'm Annika Swenson."

"I know; your card is in my pocket," Stone said. "I had intended to call and thank you, but my day got busy."

"One shouldn't be too busy in Key West," she said.

"You have a point."

"Annika!" a woman's voice cried from the top of the companionway ladder. "We're leaving."

Annika turned. "Coming!" she called back. "You'll have to excuse me, Mr. Barrington," she said. "I'm with some people."

"I'm here for a few days," Stone said. "May we have dinner?"

"Yes," she replied without hesitation.

"Tomorrow?"

"Yes."

"I'll call you, and we'll arrange a time," Stone said.

"Good night, then."

He watched her climb the companionway ladder and enjoyed the view.

Dino was the next one down the ladder. "Was that the lady from last night?"

"It was," Stone replied.

"You are the only guy I know who can meet a beautiful woman while lying on a sidewalk unconscious," Dino replied. "Let's go; dinnertime."

They made their goodbyes to Chuck Chandler.

"You play tennis?" he asked Stone.

"Yes."

"Why don't you come over to the club, and we'll hit some balls." He handed Stone a card.

"If I get a moment free," Stone said.

Tommy, Dino and Stone wandered back toward the yacht club, and as they reached the door, Stone saw Annika Swenson getting into a Mercedes convertible. She waved as she drove by.

"Not bad," Tommy said.

"Yes," Stone replied, "and I like the way she waved."

9

The three men ordered drinks and were given menus.

"Everything's good," Tommy said. "I especially like the beef."

They ordered.

"Do you have a boat here, Tommy?"

"Yeah, a thirty-foot fiberglass bathtub, just big enough for my wife and me."

"How is Rosie?" Dino asked.

"Unchanged," Tommy replied. "Ornery as ever."

"Tommy," Stone said, "how are we going to find this Keating guy?"

"Well, I can't put an APB out on him," Tommy said. "It's not like he's committed a crime."

"Did you print him while you had him?"

"We didn't get that far. I ran his name, though, and he has no record."

"Keating has checked out of his hotel, and the desk clerk said he thought he was living on a boat."

"Any description of the boat?"

"No."

"Good luck on finding it, then."

"Yeah, we spent most of the day looking in Key West Bight," Dino said.

"Well, that's the most likely place for a visiting boat to be, but not the only place. They could be anchored almost anywhere, and there's also Stock Island, of course."

"Where's Stock Island?" Stone asked.

"It's the next key up," Tommy explained. "Stock Island is sort of a suburb of Key West. It has all the stuff they can't shoehorn onto this island—hospital, jail, trash dump, lower-cost housing and trailer parks, golf course—and a couple of marinas. It's worth a shot; Peninsula is the big marina."

"I think we're wasting our time without the name of the boat," Dino said. "It's like looking for a visitor to New York without an address."

"You got a point," Tommy agreed.

"Also, Keating is shy," Dino said. "He doesn't *want* to be found."

"Yeah," Stone said, "a skip tracer found him in Miami, and he left town. He's likelier to get shier after his encounter with me."

"Sounds like he's on the lam," Tommy said.

"From his father," Stone replied. "Bad blood there."

"Well," Tommy said, "at least you know what he looks like. His girlfriend, too."

"Not really," Stone said. "I didn't take a good look at her, and I'm not sure I'd recognize her on the street."

"You can always sit down with the phone book and start calling hotels," Tommy pointed out.

"That won't help us if he's living on a boat," Stone said. "The desk clerk at his hotel said that a lot of boaters check in for a couple of nights to get a decent shower and have their laundry done."

"We talked to Charley Boggs," Dino said. "He denied all knowledge of Keating, said he'd never seen him until they were all busted."

"How bad an actor is Boggs?" Stone asked.

"He's got a couple of drug busts, but nothing ever came of them."

"And why would a clean-cut rich boy with a trust fund be hanging out with a drug dealer?"

"Thrills, maybe," Tommy offered. "Do you know how big a trust fund?"

"The old man described it as 'a nice little trust fund,' but who knows what that means."

"Maybe our boy Evan has dreams of bigger, easier money," Dino said. "He wouldn't be the first rich kid to go down for dealing."

"Trouble is," Stone said, "we don't know anything about this kid—who his friends are, how he earned a living in the past."

"His old man couldn't help with that?" Tommy asked.

Stone shook his head. "Apparently, they haven't spoken since the guy was in college, and that was some years ago."

Tommy sighed. "Dealing with criminals is a lot easier," he said. "They have accomplices and parole officers, people you can talk to when you're looking for them. Rich kids just have drug dealers and maître d's." Tommy's face brightened. "Wait a minute. Your boy had a table booked at Antonia's, an Italian restaurant on Duval, the night we arrested him."

"So?" Dino asked.

Tommy was already pushing buttons on his cell phone. "Hi, it's Lieutenant Tommy Sculley, Key West PD. The night before last you had a reservation for an Evan Keating; did you get a phone number for him?" Tommy scribbled something in his notebook. "Thanks," he said; then he hung up. He ripped the sheet from his notebook and handed it to Stone. "Your boy has a cell phone number, 917 area code."

"Can your computers track cell phone numbers?" Stone asked.

"They can."

"Do me a favor, Tommy. Ask your office to wait until late tonight and see if you can locate the phone. That might tell us where Evan Keating is laying his curly head at night."

Tommy made the call.

S tone and Dino were breakfasting on their front porch when Stone's cell phone vibrated. He flipped it open. "Hello?"

"It's Tommy."

"Good morning."

"And to you. We got an overnight hit on Evan Keating's cell phone."

"Hallelujah! Where's he staying?"

"Well, you were right. He's on a boat."

"Which marina?"

"No marina; he's anchored out at the reef."

"Let me put you on speaker so Dino can hear this." Stone pressed the button. "Go."

"Key West has the only coral reef left in the continental United States. Everybody goes out there to snorkel and scuba, so a lot of moorings have been put down, to keep people from tearing up the coral with anchors. That's where we picked up Keating's cell phone, around two a.m."

"Great, I'll go out there and visit him."

"Hang on. We're not getting his phone now, not at the reef or anywhere else."

"Maybe he's charging the thing. He could still be there."

"So are a lot of other people. How are we going to know which boat?"

"Have you got coordinates?"

"Yeah, but I don't know how accurate they are. If you like, I'll take you out there. How about we meet at the yacht club in an hour? The boat's name is *Rosie,* and she's visible from the front door of the club."

"You're on," Stone said. "See you then." He hung up.

"Stone," Dino said, "here's a thought: You've got the guy's cell phone number; why don't you just call him up and talk to him?"

"I thought of that; he'd just hang up in my face, and he might stop using the cell phone or change his number, and we'd have no way at all to trace him."

"Okay, it was just a thought."

They finished breakfast and headed for the Key West Yacht Club.

*   *   *

Rosie turned out to be just as Tommy had described her: a fat, thirty-foot fiberglass bathtub, with engines, a cabin and a flying bridge up top.

Tommy welcomed them aboard; the engines were already running.

"Tell me something," Stone said. "If we all went up to the flybridge, would this thing turn upside down?"

Tommy laughed. "It looks that way, but she's well ballasted." He edged out of the boat's berth and began running along the east side of Garrison Bight, not far off the Roosevelt Boulevard sidewalk. "There's a little channel here with six feet or so," Tommy said. "All that open water to starboard is not navigable by anything more boisterous than a kayak; too shallow."

They picked up some channel markers and headed out of the bight, then under the bridge and into more open water. Five minutes later they were running at twenty-five knots, and Tommy pointed to their destination on his electronic chart plotter. "Keating's phone was right about there," he said.

They ran on for another twenty minutes; then Tommy began to slow down. "See those boats out there?" he asked, pointing.

"Yep," Stone replied.

"That's roughly where we got the location of the phone." He slowed down further as they approached the moored boats. There were a dozen or so, all but one powerboats.

"Let's get a close look," Stone said.

"Okay, we'll check every boat."

Tommy's cell phone rang. "Yeah? You're sure? Where? Thanks, keep me posted." He hung up. "We're wasting our time out here." Tommy turned back toward Key West and pushed the throttle forward.

"Why?" Stone asked.

"Because they just got another beep about a minute long from back behind us. Looks like Keating's boat is heading back to Key West. It also looks like Keating is using his cell phone only to make calls. When he finishes, he turns it off."

"Shit," Stone said. "You think he's onto us?"

"Nah, but he's sure being careful. If he was onto us he'd just buy a throwaway phone at the supermarket."

"Okay."

"I'd sure like to know what kind of boat that is," Tommy said. "It's very odd for a boat to be spending the night out at the reef. I mean, I suppose a guy might go out there to have a few drinks and get laid, then feel too drunk to drive home, but it's not a usual thing to have a boat out there at two in the morning."

"Maybe he's meeting somebody out there," Dino said.

"A drug delivery? That's possible, I suppose, but the Coast Guard might notice two boats out together and take a look. Halfway up the Keys there are two balloons moored to cables that are fifteen thousand feet long. They run them up and use down-facing radar to catch smugglers who are flying low in airplanes or doing odd stuff in boats. I think two boats out at the reef in the middle of the night might draw their attention, but probably not one boat."

"Let's make a pass at Key West Bight," Stone said. "Maybe we'll see the boat."

"Okay." Tommy ran past the cruise ship docks and the waterfront hotels and slowed as he passed the breakwater.

"Nothing but boats," Dino said. "I think it's too much to expect to get lucky doing this."

"You're right, Dino," Stone said, looking around. "We're just wasting Tommy's fuel. Why don't you let me fill up your boat on my expense account, Tommy?"

"Okay," Tommy said, aiming at the fuel dock. They spent twenty minutes there filling the tanks, then headed back toward Garrison Bight and the yacht club.

Once *Rosie* was secured in her berth, they went into the club to get a sandwich and a beer.

"Stone," Dino said, "how much longer is your law firm going to let you loiter in Key West before they pull the plug?"

"I don't know," Stone replied, "but I'm surprised Bill Eggers hasn't already been on the horn."

Stone's cell phone vibrated.

"Hello?"

"It's Eggers."

"Speak of the devil."

"Give me a report."

Stone put aside his sandwich and spent five minutes bringing Eggers up-to-date.

"You mean you're on an island that's four by five miles, you've already spotted this guy once, and now you can't find him?"

"Yeah, that's what I mean," Stone said. "It would be nice if you would call his old man and get me some background on the guy—how he makes a living, who his best friends are, anything that would give me a lead. This is a lot harder than you think."

"Okay, I'll see what I can do," Eggers said. "I'll call you when I know more, and I'll expect you to know more by then." Eggers hung up.

"Is he pissed off?" Dino asked.

"No more than usual."

"You didn't tell him about the cell phone."

"That would just have raised his expectations," Stone said, picking up his sandwich again.

"So what are we going to do this afternoon?" Dino asked. "We're sort of out of leads."

Stone brightened. "Tennis, anyone?"

11

The Olde Island Tennis Club was on the tourist map, next to and part of the Casa Marina Hotel, the first big tourist draw to Key West, built by the Standard Oil and railroad magnate Henry Flagler. Stone and Dino called Chuck Chandler, then dressed and drove over. They found Chuck in the pro shop.

"Hey, guys," Chuck said. "You want to go hit some balls? That'll give me a chance to look at your game."

Stone and Dino had played together before. Stone had the better serve and stroke, and Dino was good at the net. Chuck stood back and hit against the two of them. After a few minutes, Chuck said, "Okay, let's play a set. I'll use the singles lines."

Half an hour later, when Chuck had won six-two, they took a break and had a soft drink.

"Have you taken the boat out yet?" Stone asked.

"Just the run from the Peninsula yard on Stock Island to the yacht club. It's tough to get much time off during the winter season—I'm so booked up with students."

"Are you living aboard?"

Chuck laughed. "That's the only way I can afford the boat. I can't buy a house, too, not with real estate prices the way they are down here. I'm comfortable, though. The old boat was a lot more cramped, and every time I bought a piece of clothing, I had to throw one away."

"What did you do with the old boat?" Stone asked.

"I sold it to the first guy who looked at it. I think I may not have asked enough."

"I've heard about the Peninsula Marina. Is that where you did the work?"

"Yeah, I rented a shed in the yard."

"Did you ever run into a guy named Evan Keating in the marina there?"

"Sure did; I sold him my boat."

Stone broke into a broad smile. "Finally!" he said.

"Finally what?" Chuck asked.

"We came down here to find Keating; I've got some documents for him to sign. I saw him once, but he got away from me, and we haven't been able to find him. Do you have an address for him?"

"No, but as far as I know, he's living aboard my old

boat. At least that's what he told me he was going to do."

"Where is he berthed?"

"I don't know. I know the Peninsula didn't have a berth for him."

"Where did you keep the boat?"

"In the same slip at the yacht club where the new boat is."

"Did you get an address from Keating or any other information that might help me find him?"

"No. It was a cash deal, so I didn't need an address, and, like I said, he was planning to live aboard." He dug into a pocket of his shorts for his cell phone. "I've got his cell number, though," he said, and he read it from his phone. It was the number they already had.

"Do you remember what bank his check was written on?"

"No bank. He showed up at the club with a paper bag with a hundred and thirty thousand in hundreds in it. I'd never seen that much cash before."

"How long ago was this?"

"Yesterday."

"The same day he checked out of his hotel," Dino said. "At least we know what boat to look for now. What's the name?"

"*Choke,*" Chuck said.

"Can you describe the boat?"

"Sure. Thirty-two-footer, white hull, mahogany superstructure, twin screws."

"That's pretty small for twin engines," Stone said.

"They're small engines, but they give you a lot more maneuverability than a single."

"Gas or diesel?"

"Gas."

"Anything else you can tell us about it?"

"Prettiest boat in Key West, except for *Choke II*."

"Do you know anything at all about Keating, besides that he bought your boat?" Stone asked.

Chuck thought about it. "He has a pretty girlfriend, name of Gigi."

"Anything else?"

"He saw me play at Wimbledon, the year I, ah, finished second. Seems like half the world saw me fuck it up."

"Was Keating driving a car when you met him?"

"Oh, yeah, he was driving a Chrysler convertible; that's a common rental here."

"Color?"

"Ummm, silver—no, white. Oh, and he brought a guy with him to help him move the boat. I spent an hour showing them around it. The girl drove away in the convertible."

"Can you describe his helper?"

"A little under six feet, I guess, fairly scrawny. Full beard. Oh, and Keating called him Charley."

"Aha," Stone said, "Boggs lied to us."

"What did you expect?" Dino asked.

"Want to play another set?" Chuck asked.

"I think we have to go see Charley Boggs," Stone said.

They drove back to Garrison Bight, parked near the sport fisherman fleet and walked over to Boggs's houseboat. Nobody home. Stone and Dino looked through the windows. The boat was sparsely furnished.

"Can I help you?" a voice said from behind them.

They turned to find a woman on the next boat looking at them.

"We're looking for Charley Boggs," Stone said.

"Haven't seen him since yesterday," the woman replied. "A couple came and got him in a boat, and he hasn't come back yet."

"What kind of boat?"

"Old, pretty; white hull, mahogany everything else."

"Right. Do you know Charley well?"

"Well enough to know that he doesn't seem to do anything to make a living. Most of the time, he's fishing off the back of that boat."

"Has his houseboat been moored here long?"

"He bought it from the previous berth holder a few months back. That's how you get a houseboat berth in Key West—you buy the houseboat."

"Had you seen the couple in the boat before?"

"I saw them once having a drink with Boggs up on the top deck."

"Do you have any idea where they live?"

"No idea at all. You want me to give Boggs a message when he comes back?"

Stone wrote his cell number on his card. "There's a hundred in it for you if you'll call me when he returns— or if you see the couple again."

"I can always use a hundred," the woman said, stretching out between the boats to take the card.

Stone and Dino drove back to the Marquesa.

"Evan Keating is . . . what's the word?" Dino asked.

"Elusive," Stone replied.

12

Stone, as earlier requested, picked up Annika Swenson at a small, pretty conch house on South Street. She was dressed in white—lacy top, linen pants—with a yellow sweater thrown over her shoulders. Stone put her in the car.

"I booked us a table at Louie's Backyard," she said. "Straight ahead, I'll direct you."

Louie's turned out to be a large clapboard house on the beach with a big deck out back overlooking the water. They took a table on the deck, ordered mojitos and asked the waitress to call them when their dinner table was ready. The sun was going down.

"The light is beautiful here," Stone said.

"Always," Annika replied.

"What brought you to Key West?"

"A job in the ER here. I was a late finisher from med school—Johns Hopkins—and by the time I finished my internship and residency, I was already thirty-five. I had had enough of cold winters, so when I got the Key West offer I jumped at it."

"Were you born in this country? I think I detect a slight accent."

"No. I was born in Stockholm. My parents moved to Miami when I finished college, and I came with them and applied to Johns Hopkins."

"Do you prefer the United States to Sweden?"

"Yes, I think so. At any rate, I never think about moving back to Sweden. I do miss some of the Swedish attitudes."

"Attitudes about what?"

"Sex, mainly. Americans have so many hang-ups about sex. Things are simpler in Sweden."

"I've heard that, but I haven't encountered it."

"You have now. For instance, what would you say if I told you that I find you attractive, and that after dinner I would like to take you back to my house and make love to you?"

"Are we speaking hypothetically?"

"Not necessarily."

"I would be flattered and pleased," Stone said.

"Then you have a Swedish attitude," she said.

Then there was some sort of scuffle at the bar, and Stone turned to see a man take a swing at another. The swinger was a compact, muscular man with blood in his eye; the one scrambling to his feet was Charley Boggs.

Two men came running down the stairs from the main restaurant and pulled the fighters apart. There was some discussion, which Stone couldn't hear. Then Charley Boggs stalked away from the deck and out of the restaurant, while the shorter man returned to his table and his drink.

"Why are you so interested in this argument?" Annika asked.

"I'm sorry. I'm a great deal more interested in you, but I know one of the men."

"Which one?"

"The one who got thrown out. His name is Charley Boggs, and the local police suspect him of being a drug dealer."

"And why are you acquainted with a drug dealer?" she asked, not unreasonably.

"I've met him only once; he's apparently an associate of a man I'm trying to find."

"Do you want to follow him?"

"No, I want to have dinner with you, then take you back to your house and make love to you."

She smiled. "Thank you. I would prefer that, too. Who is the man you're looking for, and why?"

"His name is Evan Keating, and I need to get his signature on some legal documents."

"Are you a lawyer?"

"Yes, in New York."

"Does your work often bring you into contact with drug dealers?"

"No. Keating's father wants to sell the family business, and they need the agreement of the young man. The company is a client of a law firm I'm associated with."

"Well, if you are sent to Key West on business, then you lead an interesting life," she said.

"Sometimes it's interesting; sometimes it's too interesting."

"What do you mean?"

"I mean it's interesting if I meet someone like you during the course of my business, and it's too interesting if I'm knocked unconscious outside a restaurant."

She smiled. "Well, you are the first man I've ever met when he was lying facedown on a sidewalk."

"Did you see whoever hit me?"

"No. I turned a corner, and there you were. A car was driving away."

"What kind of car?"

"A white convertible with a man and a woman inside."

"That would have been Evan Keating and his girlfriend, Gigi Jones."

"The man you're looking for?"

"Yes. I had approached him at the bar in the Marquesa and asked to speak with him. He suggested we go outside."

"Isn't that what American men do when they wish to fight? Go outside?"

Stone laughed. "Sometimes. I wasn't expecting a fight on that occasion, though."

"She must have hit you with something heavy," Annika said.

"Why do you think the girl hit me?"

"She was with the man. Was there any other man present?"

"No."

"Then it must have been the girl. You should not turn your back on strange women."

"That's good advice," Stone admitted. They were called to their table, where they ordered another mojito and dinner.

After dinner, they returned to Annika's house, as previously discussed, and she led him upstairs to her bedroom. She undressed and hung up her clothes, and Stone draped his over a chair. She pulled the bedcover off the bed and onto the floor.

"You're very beautiful," Stone said.

"You're beautiful, too," she said. "I think we will be good lovers together."

They lay on the bed and came into each other's arms.

"First, we will do the missionary position," Annika said, pulling him on top of her. "I love that name. Then we will rest and we will do it a different way."

"All right," Stone said. "Should we discuss which way now?"

"You are laughing at me," she said, taking his penis in her hand and sliding it inside her. She did not need a lubricant.

"Only a little," Stone said. "And suddenly I can't remember why."

"Good," she said. "You must think only of now."

She was right, he decided.

13

Stone was wakened by a buzzing noise that he did not immediately recognize. It took him a moment to see that his cell phone, vibrating, was doing a little dance on the glass top of Annika's dressing table. He gently removed Annika's blond head from his shoulder, tiptoed naked across the room and picked up the phone. "Yes?" he whispered.

"Where the hell are you?" Dino asked. "As if I didn't know."

"I'm at Annika's. What do you want?"

"That figures. This whole thing is blowing wide open, and you're in the sack with a blonde."

"What do you mean, it's blowing wide-open?"

"I mean that Charley Boggs was found floating facedown in Garrison Bight this morning, not far from his houseboat, dead as a mackerel."

"I saw him get into a fight last night at Louie's Backyard. He lost."

"Was he alive after the fight?"

"Yes, he left under his own steam."

"You might want to pass that news on to Tommy Sculley," Dino said. "I expect he'd want a chat with the other fighter."

"I'll call him in a few minutes," Stone said.

"What, after you've fucked the blonde again?"

"None of your business. And don't worry, Charley Boggs isn't going anywhere."

"Okay, you fuck the girl, and I'll call Tommy. Give me a description of the fighter."

"White male, five-nine, a hundred and seventy, dark hair, lots of stubble. Built like he labors for a living."

"That'll do. Go get back in bed." Dino hung up.

Stone got back in bed, and Annika snuggled up close to him. "I like it that we're both blond," she said. "I mean blond all over. That must be very rare in this country."

"Now that you mention it, it is rare, at least for me." He kissed her and their tongues played with each other.

"I hope you are fully rested from last night," she said, "and ready to make love again."

"I think I might just manage it," Stone replied, "if you do most of the work."

"All right," she said, cheerfully. "We did the missionary position and the doggie position last night; now we will do the blow-job position. Lie on your back."

"Yes, ma'am," Stone said, following instructions.

She glanced at the clock. "You mustn't take too long to come, because I must go to work."

"Yes, ma'am," he replied. "I'll be as quick as I can."

Stone got back to the Marquesa in time to see Dino's breakfast dishes taken away.

"Have you eaten anything?" Dino asked. "I'm referring to the like of bacon and eggs."

"Nothing like that," Stone said. He picked up the phone and ordered.

"As soon as you can get yourself together, we should go over to Boggs's houseboat," Dino said.

"Why?"

"Well, don't you think we might find something there that could tell us more about your Evan Keating?"

"I suppose we might."

"You don't think very clearly first thing in the morning, do you?"

"I do, but I wasn't thinking about Charley Boggs."

"Oh."

"Yeah."

"I take it you had a pleasant evening."

"That is an inadequate description of my evening."

"I think I'm going to have to call Genevieve and get her down here," Dino said, referring to his girlfriend.

"If that will keep you from exploding with envy, by all means. She can ride back with us."

Dino went inside to use the phone, and Stone had his breakfast.

They arrived at the Garrison Bight houseboat of Charley Boggs an hour later, with Stone freshly shaved and showered. Tommy Sculley was sitting in a teak chair on the rear deck reading the local newspaper.

"Take a pew," Tommy said. "My crime scene people will let us in there in a few minutes."

"This is your idea of working a scene?" Dino said, sitting down.

"First, they work it and show me any evidence. Then I work it. Like that, we don't get in each other's way."

"This is where Charley Boggs liked to do his fishing," Stone said, sitting down. "You think he fell in and drowned?"

Tommy nodded. "I think he could have fallen in and drowned right after he caught the bullet in the back of the head. He might have lived long enough to drown."

"Any luck on the guy he fought with at Louie's last night?" Stone asked.

Tommy nodded. "Guy name of Billy Guy." He jerked a thumb behind him, toward the row of charter fishing boats. "He skippers a fisherman parked over there. My guy Daryl is talking to him now."

"That's quick work," Stone said.

"It's Key West; nobody who lives here can go into a restaurant or bar without being seen by somebody who knows him. It makes life simpler when you want to find a guy."

"Any news on what the fight was about?"

"Daryl will bring us up-to-date after he pumps Billy. He's already talked to a couple of witnesses; you're next."

"Sounds like he won't need me," Stone said.

"You could be right," Tommy replied, turning the page of his newspaper.

"Anything worth reading in there?" Dino asked.

"Nothing about Charley Boggs," Tommy said. "He was found only a couple of hours ago."

"Do a lot of people in Key West get shot in the back of the head?" Stone asked.

"Remarkably few compared to, say, New Orleans or Chicago. Last execution-style killing I can remember here was year before last. This one is the first gunshot killing of any kind this year. Hope it's the last."

Daryl appeared on the gangplank. "Permission to come aboard, skipper?"

"Get your ass aboard," Tommy called back.

Daryl, clad in jeans and a splashy shirt with a lot of tropical fruit on it, came onto the rear deck and seated himself on the railing, since all the chairs were occupied by his elders.

"So?" Tommy asked. "Are we charging Billy Guy with Charley's murder?"

"Probably not," Daryl said.

"What was the fight about?"

"Charley made an unkind comment about Billy's girl. Billy took exception and put a fist in Charley's face."

"I got sort of a sideways look at that," Stone said. "The management separated them before it got any farther."

"Was Charley's remark unkind enough to make Billy want to kill him?" Tommy asked.

"Nah," Daryl replied, "and his girl wasn't even along. She was back on his boat with PMS. He got home about nine and stuck."

"Is that just Billy's story, or did she confirm it?"

"She confirmed."

"It's not very far from over there to over here," Tommy pointed out.

"I know Billy," Daryl said. "I don't think he has a murderous streak."

"If you say so, Daryl," Tommy said.

A Boston Whaler putted by with Charley Boggs's corpse covered and strapped to a stretcher.

"You have a decent medical examiner down here?" Stone asked.

"Yeah, but he ain't going to find anything, except a bullet in Charley's brain. This one ain't rocket science."

"Then somebody tell me who offed Charley Boggs," Stone said. "And tell me if Evan Keating had anything to do with it."

"All in good time," Tommy said, turning to the sports page.

14

The inside of Charley Boggs's houseboat looked like he hadn't lived there for very long. There was a sofa, a big flat-screen TV and an expensive-looking audio system and a lot of CDs.

"Pretty easy to see where Charley's interests lay," Tommy said.

"Yeah, and his interests make the place easy to search," Dino agreed.

"Let's look at upstairs," Stone said. "I predict a bed and another TV."

Stone turned out to be right.

"Look, there's a bedside table, too," Dino said.

"They must love Charley at the furniture store," Tommy opined. He opened a drawer in the bedside table and pointed. Inside was a new-looking semiautomatic pistol.

"SigArms P229," Stone said. "Charley lived simply, but he liked the best of everything—at least, the best of everything he owned: TVs, stereos and weapons."

Tommy pulled on a pair of latex gloves, popped the magazine from the gun and racked the slide, spitting a round onto the bed. He sniffed the barrel.

"Cordite?" Dino asked.

"Gun oil," Tommy replied. "The deed didn't get done with Charley's own gun." He put the round back into the magazine and bagged the works.

Tommy checked the closet, which contained some jeans and Hawaiian shirts. "He'd blend right in in Key West with that wardrobe," he said.

They checked the bathroom medicine cabinet, which contained a toothbrush and a razor, and the toilet tank, which contained water.

They went downstairs and checked the kitchen. There were two cases of Bud in the fridge, along with a jar of peanut butter and some leftover Chinese in cartons. In a drawer they found some utensils, and in a cabinet a few glasses.

"That's it," Tommy said. "Do you believe it? I mean, everybody collects a little of life's detritus, but not Charley."

"How long did the neighbor say he'd lived here?" Stone asked Dino.

"Since last year. She didn't say when last year."

"Did he own a car?" Stone asked.

"There was a motorcycle chained to the electrical post on the dock," Tommy said. "I reckon that's his."

"Was it searched?" Stone asked.

"Search a motorcycle?"

Stone walked up the dock and found the motorcycle, a light Honda. "Do you have the keys?" he called back to Tommy.

Tommy produced a plastic bag containing some items and found some keys. He tossed them to Stone. "These were in his pocket."

Stone found the right key and unlocked a little storage compartment on the cycle. "Hey, hey!" he yelled and held up a ziplock bag with two fingers. "That's half a key, I reckon."

Tommy walked down the dock, took the bag, opened it and tasted a sample. "Cocaine," he said, "and my guess is it's uncut."

"That's a lot of product to be walking around with," Stone said, "and there were no smaller bags, so I guess he wasn't hawking it on the street."

"More like a delivery," Tommy said, "one that didn't get made."

"Enough to get killed for," Stone pointed out.

"I guess the killer asked Charley for it, and when he didn't give, the guy got pissed off."

"It wouldn't have taken long to search the house-boat," Stone said, "but he didn't search the motor-cycle."

Dino had joined them. "Let's take another look at the boathouse," Dino said.

They did, and this time they looked *everywhere*.

Dino stood in the little wheelhouse, holding a floorboard in his hand. "Take a look at this," he said to Tommy.

Tommy looked and found an empty compartment with a trace of white powder at the bottom. "Maybe the shooter didn't go away empty-handed after all."

"You could get half a dozen kilos in there," Dino said.

"Yeah, and that's *more* than enough to get shot for. Anybody know what a key goes for these days?"

"I don't know," Dino said, "maybe twenty-five, thirty thou? I guess it would depend on availability."

"There's no way he could sell five or six kilos of uncut cocaine in Key West," Tommy said. "If that much was in there, it was bound for somewhere else, like Miami."

"Tommy, if you had half a dozen kilos of pure coke and you wanted to get them to Miami, how would you do it?"

"Well, I wouldn't drive it," Tommy said. "There's only one road, and if you get stopped for a broken taillight and get searched, well . . ." He looked thoughtful. "Boat or light aircraft," he said. "And there's a lot more boats around here than light aircraft."

"How long to Miami in a boat?" Stone asked.

"Well, in something that could do twenty-five, thirty knots, one long day. Any faster than that might attract the attention of the Coast Guard."

"The right boat sounds like a good investment in time," Dino said.

"We got two questions to answer here," Tommy said. "Where did he get it, and how was he going to move it?"

"He got it from South America or Mexico, like everybody else," Stone said. "And there's no shortage of means to move it."

"Evan Keating has a new boat," Dino said, "and he was chummy with Charley Boggs, at least for a while."

"And his boat was parked all night out at the reef," Tommy pointed out. "Another boat could have handed something off."

"Or an airplane could have dropped it," Stone said. "As I recall, it isn't very deep out at the reef."

"Not deep at all," Tommy agreed. "You could pick something off the bottom with a snorkel; you wouldn't even need scuba gear."

"Well," Dino said, "I guess we've solved this crime. Except for the part about who killed Charley and where the cocaine is now."

"Yeah, except for that part," Tommy said.

"I don't think Evan is our guy," Stone said.

"Why not?" Dino asked. "I like him for it."

"Okay, let's say that Evan bought Chuck Chandler's

boat for the purpose of picking up packages at the reef and delivering them to Miami. Was Chuck's old boat good for that, Tommy?"

"Yeah, I know the boat, and it was pretty fast. It also doesn't look like something a drug dealer would use, it being an old classic and all."

"But why would Evan hide the coke on Charley Boggs's houseboat? Why wouldn't he pick it up at the reef and just keep going until he got to Miami? Why trust Charley with a hundred and fifty grand worth of powder? Charley didn't look all that trustworthy to me. And if Evan and Charley were in business together, why would Evan have to kill him to get the product?"

"Partners can disagree," Dino pointed out.

Tommy sighed. "I don't think we've solved this crime yet."

15

The three of them had lunch at the Raw Bar. Dino looked across the table at Stone. "Why are you looking so glum? Are you sad that Charley Boggs is dead?"

"Well, yeah, since he was our only connection to Evan Keating."

"We know what kind of boat Evan is driving now. How about that?"

"Dino, you remember the whole afternoon we spent in a rented boat looking for Evan?"

"Well, yeah."

"Do you recall seeing anything that answered the description of *Choke*?"

Dino thought about it. "Now that you mention it, no."

"That's because ninety-nine percent of all boats in Key West are white plastic tubs. There aren't that many 1930s craft around."

"But at least we have a boat name now."

"Probably not," Tommy said. "It's awful easy to change the name on a boat these days. You don't have to wait for a guy to paint it on—you just go to a graphics shop and they print it out on a sheet of polyethylene, and you slap it on the stern of your boat. The whole thing takes maybe a couple of hours, and that includes lifting the old name off with a hair dryer. If Keating doesn't want to be found, you can bet he's changed the name of his boat."

"Now *I'm* feeling glum," Dino said.

"You'll feel better when Genevieve gets here," Stone said.

"She isn't coming; she couldn't get the time off."

"Okay, so we're both glum."

"I don't know why *you're* glum; you've got the Swedish doctor."

Stone brightened. "That's right, I do. We've already made dinner plans for tonight."

"Where are you going?" Tommy asked. "You need a recommendation?"

"Nope, she's cooking."

"What's she cooking?" Dino asked.

"Who cares? I'm sure it will be delicious, and if it isn't, she will be."

"I'd call that an evening with no downside," Tommy said. "What's her story, anyway?"

"She's Swedish," Stone explained.

"Oh."

"You seem to have gotten over Tatiana pretty easily," Dino said. "I thought you were all broken up."

"I was," Stone replied, "and more than I'd realized at first. But it's easier to pick up the pieces if there's somebody to help rearrange them."

"And he isn't talking about you, Dino," Tommy said.

"You think I didn't know that? It's a pity, really. This Tati was a beautiful woman. And the killer is, she went back to her awful ex-husband."

"They'll do that," Tommy said. "No guy can ever understand why a woman would go back to her ex."

"Do you have an explanation for that phenomenon?" Stone asked.

"Nope. I'm a guy."

"Don't worry," Dino said. "It'll end badly. She'll come back after he goes off the wagon a couple of times and breaks her china."

"Let's not talk about Tati anymore," Stone said. "There's nothing I can do about her. I'm in Key West."

"With a Swedish beauty," Dino added.

"That too."

"What happens to her when we find Keating and go back to New York?"

"I'll throw a sack over her head and take her with me."

"Now you're talking!"

"I've thought of a way we might find Evan Keating," Tommy said suddenly.

"Speak to me," Stone replied.

"I'll have somebody at the station call the twenty best restaurants in town and alert them to call us if Keating makes a reservation."

"That's brilliant," Stone said. "He looks like the kind of guy who's eating out at the best places every night."

"He's gotta eat," Tommy said, reaching for his cell phone and pressing a speed-dial button. He gave the instructions and hung up. "It's done; all we've gotta do is wait, then meet him at the restaurant. It helps that he's now a person of interest in the death of Charley Boggs."

"Did Charley have any visible means of support?" Dino asked.

"Not so's you'd notice," Tommy said.

Dino sighed. "One more dead end."

"I like the restaurant idea," Stone said.

"It occurs to me," Dino said, "that maybe, in light of what happened to Charley Boggs, we should be packing."

"The State of Florida is okay with cops from other jurisdictions packing," Tommy said.

"How about retired cops?" Stone asked.

"We'll cut you some slack."

Stone's cell phone buzzed, and he flipped it open. "Yes?"

"It's Eggers."

"Oh, hi, Bill."

"Don't hi me; where's that signed paperwork?"

"We're working on a new way to track the guy down."

"Working? Why haven't you already worked?"

"Bill, it's tougher than you think. A friend of Evan's turned up dead, so we've got the local cops on our side now; they want to talk to him as much as we do."

"I don't care if they talk to him or not," Eggers said. "I just want those papers back—signed, sealed and delivered."

"That's what I want, too, Bill, but I'll understand if you'd rather send somebody else down here to find the kid."

"Don't hand me that crap. You know I don't have time to start over with somebody else."

"Then leave it with me, and let me get the job done, okay?"

Eggers made a harrumphing noise and hung up.

"He's not happy?" Dino asked.

"What do you think?"

"I think he's not happy."

"Good guess. I can't say that I'm happy, either."

"Except for the Swedish doctor."

"Except for the Swedish doctor; I'm happy about her. You want me to see if she has a friend?"

Dino thought about that. "Nah, Genevieve would find out and nail me with it."

"How would she find out? I wouldn't tell."

"She'd find out, believe me. Sometimes I think she has some sort of ESP girl-to-girl network that constantly broadcasts my whereabouts and my company."

"That's a scary thought," Stone said.

16

Stone knocked on Annika's door, clutching a bouquet of flowers. She opened the door, kissed him, took the flowers and led him inside.

"Can I get you a drink?" she asked.

"Do you have any bourbon?"

"I don't know," she said, pointing at the bar. "Look through those bottles."

To Stone's surprise, he found a bottle of Knob Creek, unopened. "My favorite," he called to her, holding up the bottle. "How'd you know?"

"I didn't," she called from the kitchen. "Most of those bottles were brought by other people as gifts."

Stone was opening the bottle when his cell phone vibrated. "Yes?"

"It's Tommy. Evan Keating has a reservation at Louie's Backyard."

"When?"

"Five minutes ago. I'm going over there myself."

"Will you give me a couple of minutes with him before you barge in?"

"Yeah, sure, but move your ass."

Stone hung up and went into the kitchen, where something smelled good. "I have to go out for a few minutes. It's business. Will you forgive me?"

"If you hurry," she said.

He kissed her and ran for his car. Five minutes later he was walking into Louie's. He looked around the restaurant but didn't see Keating. Then he walked outside to the bar area and saw him seated, alone, at a table by the water. He walked over to the table and sat down.

"Now listen . . ." Keating said.

"No, you listen." Stone took a card from his wallet and wrote his cell phone number on the back. "Here's how you can get in touch with me."

Keating looked at the card on the table but didn't pick it up. "I don't want to get in touch with you. Now, leave."

"How would you like to have twenty-one million dollars?" Stone asked.

"You're going to give me twenty-one million dollars?"

"I think I told you this before, but your father is selling the company, and that's your share of the proceeds."

"That's what my father says my share is?" Keating asked.

"It is."

"Then it's the wrong amount. My father is a liar and a thief, and if he's offering me that much money, he owes me a lot more."

"Why do you think that?"

"Why don't you ask my uncle Harry?"

"I didn't know you had an uncle Harry."

"I don't anymore; he's dead."

"What are you talking about?"

"Mr. Barrington, my uncle Harry is the one who made the company into what it is. My father had nothing to do with its success, and now that Uncle Harry is dead, he's cashing in."

"What about your grandfather? Can he still run it?"

"My grandfather has Alzheimer's; he's in a home."

"Do you have any interest in running the company?" Stone asked.

"Not in the least."

"Then why don't you just take the money?"

"I told you, my father is a liar and a thief. He made a drunk of my mother, and he probably murdered my uncle Harry."

"Do you have any evidence of that?"

"No, but I understand the police are looking into it."

"When did your uncle Harry die?"

"Three months ago. I saw his obituary in the *New York Times*."

"So you're not going to sign the papers okaying the sale?"

"No, I'm not. That will royally screw my father, and I'll enjoy that."

Shit, Stone thought. "Then I'm wasting my time?"

"Yes, you are. By the way, I owe you an apology. I'm sorry you got socked in the neck the last time we met."

"Why did that happen?"

"My girlfriend is sometimes a little overprotective. Apparently she thought you meant me ill."

"Where is she now?" Stone said, looking behind him.

"Relax, she's in the ladies' room."

"Good. By the way, did you know that Charley Boggs is dead?"

Keating's face fell. "What are you talking about?"

"I saw them fish his body out of Garrison Bight this morning. You'll read about it in tomorrow's paper."

"Oh, shit," Keating said.

"Well, yeah. The police want to talk to you about it."

"Me? I would never hurt Charley. We've been friends since prep school."

"Prep school? I thought Boggs was just some Key West drug dealer."

"He may be that, but it wasn't a part of our relationship. When I came to Key West, he was the only person I knew here."

"The police found a bag of cocaine in his motorcycle storage locker and a hiding place on his houseboat where more drugs were probably stashed."

"I wouldn't know anything about that," Keating said. "How did Charley die?"

"Bullet to the back of the head. Do you own a nine-millimeter pistol?"

"No."

"Why was your boat out at the reef in the middle of the night a couple of days ago?"

"I don't know what you're talking about," Keating said.

"It was spotted there." Stone didn't tell him how. "The police are going to want to talk to you about that, too."

"I've only driven the boat once, the day I bought it. It's been at anchor ever since."

"Could Charley Boggs have used it without your knowledge?"

"Well, yes. He knew where the keys were stashed."

"Could Charley have used your cell phone?"

"I lost my cell phone the day I bought the boat; it must have gone overboard."

"You may need a lawyer soon," Stone said. "You've got my number." He got up and left by the exit directly from the bar deck to the street and saw Tommy Sculley and Daryl getting out of their car. "He's out back," Stone said, jerking a thumb in that direction.

Stone drove back to Annika's house and found her setting the table.

"Smells good," he said. "What are we having?"

"Swedish meatballs," she replied. "What else?"

"Sounds great."

"Did you conclude your business?"

"Not really," Stone replied. He had the feeling there was more business to do, but he wasn't sure what it was.

17

Stone woke up the following morning in Annika's bed, exhausted. They had made love until they fell asleep after midnight, and she had wakened him in the middle of the night for more. He didn't have another round in him, so he got out of bed, slipped into his clothes and tiptoed out of the house.

He was halfway back to the Marquesa when his cell phone vibrated. "Hello?"

"Where did you go?" Annika said.

"I have a breakfast meeting," he lied.

"I want you. Let's have dinner tonight?"

"I'm not sure what's going on yet. Let me call you this afternoon."

"All right, but you better."

"I will." He snapped the phone shut and returned it to its holster.

Dino wasn't up yet. Stone showered, shaved and dressed and walked out to their porch. Dino was sipping coffee from the pot in his room.

"I ordered breakfast for you," Dino said.

"Good."

"You look a little peaked."

"You could say that," Stone agreed.

"Is the Swede turning out to be too much for you?"

"Don't ask." Stone looked at his watch. Eggers would be at his desk momentarily.

"Any news on any front?" Dino asked.

"Yes, and I'm going to call Eggers in a minute. You can listen in, so I won't have to repeat myself."

"I'll try and contain myself," Dino said drily.

Stone pressed the speed-dial button on his phone, and it began to ring. He pressed the speaker button so Dino could hear the conversation.

"Eggers," the phone said.

"It's Stone."

"God, you're up early; I hope it's good news."

"Is there such a person as Harry Keating?"

"Yes, or rather, there was."

"Was he Warren Keating's brother?"

"Yes, he was the man I dealt with until his death."

"What do you know about Warren Keating?"

"That he was Harry's brother. He wasn't in the business until Harry died, doesn't know anything about it, really. He's a chemist, or at least he has a chemistry degree. I don't think he had much of a career; he just took a monthly check from Harry."

"I finally pinned Evan Keating down last night, and he won't sign the papers."

"What?"

"He says his father is a liar and a thief."

"We're talking twenty-one million dollars! Is the kid nuts?"

"Do you know more about the family than the kid does?"

"Well, no."

"Who negotiated the deal for the sale of the business?"

"I initiated the talks, but the buyer had to retain another lawyer, since I represent him, too."

"How was Evan's share of the proceeds determined?"

"As the managing partner, Warren has the authority in the will to allocate the funds, and he has his father's agreement."

"Do you know the father?"

"Yes, he was still running the company when they became our clients. He retired a good ten years ago, and Harry ran the company since then. Grew it a lot."

"Do you know the old man?"

"Sure."

"When was the last time you saw him?"

"At Harry's funeral, about three months ago."

"Did you have an opportunity to talk with him then?"

"For a few minutes. He was crushed about Harry's death."

"Did he seem all right to you at the time?"

"No, I told you, he was crushed."

"I mean mentally all right."

"Oh. Yeah, I guess."

"Evan says his grandfather has Alzheimer's and that he's in a home."

Eggers was silent.

"Are the pieces falling into place, Bill?"

"What are you suggesting?"

"How did Harry Keating die?"

"I don't know, exactly. He fell ill and died a couple of days later. What are you getting at, Stone?"

"Me? Nothing. But Evan says his father killed Harry."

Eggers was silent again.

"Bill, are you weighing what our ethical obligations are in this matter?"

"I'm weighing everything," Eggers replied.

"I can't force Evan Keating to sign the documents. You'd better tell Warren that."

"He's going to be livid," Eggers said.

"Then he'll just have to be livid. By the way, Evan says the police are looking into Harry's death. You did say that Warren is a chemist, didn't you?"

"Yeah, yeah, I get it, Stone. But you and I don't have any grounds for calling the police in. Warren and his son have been estranged for years; we can't just accept the boy's theory of Harry's death. If Evan has suspicions, then he should share them with the local police."

"I'll mention that to him, if I see him again."

"What do you mean, *if* you see him again?"

"Well, I don't have any further plans to contact him. He may be contacting me, because a friend of his here got himself murdered, and the local cops want to have a chat with Evan. I don't think he had anything to do with it."

"God, what a nest of snakes this is turning into."

"Bill, why don't you make a few phone calls and check into Warren Keating's background. It may be that if he's trying to screw his son on this deal, you'll want to resign the account."

"I'm not in the habit of resigning accounts," Eggers said.

"If Evan should decide to sue his father over this, the law firm could get dragged into it as a defendant. And frankly, I don't think Evan is going to be bought off easily. Maybe you'd better broach the subject with Warren and get him to divide the sales proceeds equally."

"This is all very distasteful," Eggers said.

"You want me to talk to Warren? If he goes nuts, you can always blame it all on me."

"I'll talk to the man," Eggers said.

"And you'll get back to me?"

"Give me a day or two."

"You want me to hang here until then?"

"Yes. I want somebody near Evan Keating, if we need to negotiate with him. You won't mind working on your tan for a little longer, will you?"

"I'll tough it out," Stone said, then hung up.

"I'll tough it out, too," Dino said.

18

They finished breakfast, and Stone called Tommy Sculley. "Hey, Tommy."

"Hey, Stone."

"What happened with Evan Keating?"

"We brought him in for a chat. He said he didn't know Charley Boggs was dead until you told him. He seemed upset about it."

"Yeah, he said he and Charley had known each other since they were in prep school."

"It's hard to think of Charley in prep school, but we're checking with the school now to confirm all this."

"What's your take on Keating's possible involvement?"

"I'm inclined to think he's not involved, but I've been burned before, so I'm not going to form an opinion until I've checked everything out."

"Did he tell you about Charley using his boat?"

"I didn't ask him about his boat."

"Evan denies having spent a night on his boat out at the reef, and he says he lost his cell phone the day he bought the boat. For what it's worth, Charley helped him move the boat the day he bought it, so he could have filched Evan's cell phone and taken the boat out to the reef without Evan's knowledge."

"Yeah, I guess. That would support the contention that Evan wasn't involved in the drug trade with Charley."

"Something else makes me think Evan is clean of all this," Stone said.

"What's that?"

"This is between you and me, Tommy; it involves client confidentiality."

"Okay, it goes no further."

"Last night I offered Evan Keating twenty-one million for his share of the family business, and he turned me down."

"He *turned down* twenty-one mil? Holy shit! Why?"

"Because he thinks his father owes him a lot more and is trying to cheat him. Doesn't sound like he'd be a candidate for a quick buck dealing drugs, does it? I mean, he's already living on one trust fund that seems to be supporting him in comfort."

"You got a point," Tommy said.

"One other thing, and this doesn't sound so good:

when Evan bought Chuck Chandler's boat, he paid for it with a hundred thirty thousand in hundred-dollar bills."

"Why?"

"I don't know. Why don't you ask him?"

"I mean, a guy who's got that kind of money would run it through a bank, wouldn't he?"

"Could be some sort of tax dodge."

"Yeah, that could make sense."

"Did you release him?"

"Yeah, we talked for about two hours. Then I cut him loose."

"Did you get an address?"

"Yeah, he's staying at the Gardens, which is a block or two from the Marquesa. It's just as nice, but more expensive."

"Be interesting to know if he's paying cash," Stone said.

"I'll find out."

"Will you let me hear from you about that and the check with the prep school?"

"Sure. See you later."

Stone hung up. "Evan is staying at the Gardens, just up the street from here."

"I saw the sign," Dino said.

"Oh, it was Evan's girlfriend, Gigi Jones, who slugged me outside the restaurant. He says she's sometimes overprotective."

"Well, at least that resulted in your meeting the Swede. Was the blow to the neck worth the roll in the hay?"

"I think it's going to take me longer to recover from the roll in the hay," Stone said. "I'm supposed to call her about dinner tonight, but I'm not sure I'm up to it."

"Take a nap; you'll be fine."

Stone's cell phone vibrated. "Hello?"

"Hi, it's Evan Keating."

"Good morning."

"I didn't call you last night, because I got the feeling I didn't need a lawyer."

"Evan, let me explain something to you: cops do everything they can to make you feel like you don't need a lawyer. Then they can nail you for something you said. If they call you in again, take along a lawyer."

"Well, okay, but I didn't kill Charley, and I don't think I'm a suspect."

"You'll be a suspect until they can hang it on somebody else, or until they can prove to themselves that you didn't do it."

"How did my father react to my turning his offer down?"

"I haven't spoken to him, just to my law firm's managing partner. He'll break the news to your father."

"Expect an explosion," Evan said. "Old Dad has always exploded easily."

"Do you think he'll want to renegotiate?"

"He won't have a choice; he can't sell the business without my agreement, and it's my guess that he's already figured out that he's not equipped to run the place."

"Is there anyone in your family who is qualified?"

"No. So selling is the right thing to do. Do you know what he was offered for it?"

"No, and if I knew I couldn't tell you. There's nothing stopping you from demanding to see the contract, though."

"Good point. Tell your office that I want to see the contract, and that I won't discuss it further until I see it."

"I'll do that. Where can I reach you?"

"I'm at the Gardens."

"How about a cell phone number?"

"I've got to buy a new one; I'll call you when I get it. In the meantime, you can leave a message at the Gardens."

"Okay, Evan, I'll request the contract."

"Bye." Keating hung up.

Stone redialed Bill Eggers.

"Eggers."

"Evan Keating just called me. He wants to see the sales contract for the business."

"Warren doesn't have to show it to him," Eggers said.

"He does if he wants Evan's assent to sell. He says he'll have nothing else to say until he sees the contract."

"You haven't been giving him legal advice, have you, Stone?"

"Me? I'm not his lawyer."

"Exactly, so be careful what you say to him."

"I won't be speaking to him again, unless he sees the contract."

"I'll talk to Warren, and if he's agreeable, I'll FedEx it to you."

Stone gave him the Marquesa address and hung up.

"Now negotiations get interesting," he said to Dino.

"Take your time," Dino said.

19

Stone turned to Dino. "How about some tennis?"

"Okay," Dino replied, "but is this tennis business or business business?"

"A little of both," Stone said.

They changed clothes and drove to the Olde Island Tennis Club. Chuck Chandler was working with a student, a very pretty girl in a tiny tennis dress. He stood behind her, holding her arm as she swung.

"I like the teaching position," Dino said.

Stone went into the pro shop, found the reservation book and led Dino to a vacant court. They hit balls for a few minutes; then Chuck finished with his student and joined them.

"You need more backswing in your serve," he said to

Stone. "You could pick up another ten miles an hour of ball speed."

"I'll work on that," Stone said.

"And Dino, you need to turn your body more when you hit the ball; you're using too much arm and not enough full body."

"Okay," Dino replied.

"You guys want to play a three-handed set?"

"Sure," Stone said. He and Dino played Chuck, and Chuck beat them six-four. They sat down for a break.

"Chuck," Stone said, "when Evan Keating paid you the hundred and thirty grand in cash for your boat, what did it look like? New bills or old?"

"A mix, I guess. It was all neatly wrapped, some of it with rubber bands, some with bank wrappers."

"What was the bank name on the wrappers?"

"I don't really remember, except that it was in Miami. Something Security."

"Think hard."

"South Beach Security, that's it."

"Never heard of it," Stone said.

"I've never heard of half the banks in Florida," Chuck said. "I'd never heard of any of the banks in Key West until I moved here."

"May I ask what you did with all that cash."

"Well," Chuck said, "I had a yard bill at Peninsula

Marina for around forty thousand, mostly materials and shed rental; I paid off about twenty thousand in personal debts, I bought a T-bill for fifty thousand, and I put the rest in my safe. Sometimes you can do better deals for stuff if you've got cash."

"Yes, you can," Stone said. "Did you fill out the federal forms for big cash deposits at your bank?"

"Yeah, and at my brokerage house, too. I thought I might expect a visit from the feds, but my banker told me the feds are inundated with those forms, and they never get around to checking most of them."

"Don't forget to pay your taxes on the sale of the boat," Stone said.

"I actually had a small loss; my basis was more than Keating paid. Did you ever find him?"

"Yep."

"Good. You seemed a little stressed about it the last time we talked."

They played another set; then Stone and Dino went back to the Marquesa and showered. Stone called Tommy Sculley.

"Tommy, do you know a bank in Miami called South Beach Security?"

"That has a familiar ring," Tommy said, "but I can't place it. I've heard somebody talking about it, though. It'll come to me. Why do you ask?"

"Some of the hundred and thirty grand Evan Keating paid Chuck Chandler for his boat had South Beach Security bands wrapped around it. The rest had rubber bands."

"Let me look into it. By the way, I talked to the headmaster's office at the Groton School, and Evan and Charley Boggs were in the same class there for three years. They were described as inseparable. The office gave me a next-of-kin address for Charley, too. His parents are still alive, and I had to tell them their son was dead."

"That's never fun."

"His old man said he was only mildly surprised; the only news he had had of him in years was that he was still drawing on his trust fund. He didn't want the body; he said to have it cremated and disposed of and to send him the bill. He also said that Charley's mother has thought he was dead for a long time, so he's not going to tell her."

"I wonder if trust funds make father-son relationships worse," Stone said.

"I guess they make the kids more independent. What is it they call a trust fund?"

"Fuck-you money?"

"That's it. Independence means they don't have to be nice to the folks anymore."

"Kind of sad, isn't it?" Stone asked.

"I still talk to my old man a couple of times a week," Tommy said. "He's in a retirement home in Boca. He comes down here for Christmas, or we go up there. But then I don't have a trust fund."

"My folks are gone," Stone said, "and I miss them."

"I'll bet you didn't have a trust fund, either."

"Nope."

"Hang on a minute," Tommy said. "Hey, Jim, have you ever heard of a bank in Miami called South Beach Security? Pick up the extension, line three."

"Hello?" another voice said.

"Stone, this is Jim Pierce; he's the worst kind of fed: an FBI man."

"Hi, Jim."

"Hi, Stone. How'd you get tangled up with this reprobate?"

"Beats me."

"Jim, tell Stone about South Beach Security."

"Tell you what I know, Stone. The bank is less than five years old; majority stockholder is one Max Melfi. I'm told he's from old sugarcane money in the Glades, but I can't prove it. I can't prove the bank is dirty, either, but the name keeps coming up in investigations. You might say it's red-flagged with us. Why do you want to know about South Beach Security?"

"Friend of mine sold his boat for a bunch of money, and the deal was done in cash, some of it with wrappers from South Beach Security."

"Sounds like whoever bought your friend's boat is in the drug business."

"Possible, but unlikely. The guy told me he had sold

a previous boat for cash and that's why he had so much on hand."

"Then the guy who bought *his* boat is probably dirty. In my experience honest people don't do business in large sums of cash, unless they're dodging the IRS, and that's dishonest, too. You want to tell me who the three parties in this two-boat transaction are? I'll check it out."

"Not yet, but maybe later."

Pierce gave Stone his cell phone number. "You can get me there 'most anytime, unless I'm doing business, and if that's the case, I'll call you back."

"Maybe we'll talk later, Jim. Nice to talk to you, Tommy. See you later."

Stone hung up. "You get the gist of that?" he asked Dino.

"Pretty much. Maybe Evan Keating is in deeper than he thinks."

"Maybe."

20

Stone was getting out of the shower when his cell phone vibrated. "Hello?"

"It's Eggers."

"Hey, Bill."

"Okay, I'm FedExing you the sales contract for Elijah Keating's Sons. I had a hard time getting Warren Keating to let me do it, but I convinced him the sale won't go through until Evan sees the deal. I can tell you now that when he does, he won't like it."

"Okay, I'll get it to him tomorrow, then. Bill, was Warren telling me the truth when he said he has no idea what Evan has been doing since his college graduation?"

"Stone, after what you've learned about that family the past few days, I can't tell you to believe anything

116

Warren says, and if I were you, I'd be damn careful about believing anything Evan tells you, too. I did a little checking and found out what nursing home Warren's dad is in, and I'm having that looked into."

"Good. What's the old man's name?"

"Elijah, like his ancestor; he's called Eli."

"Warren said, or maybe you said, that he hired a skip tracer, who found Evan in Miami."

"I hired him. Do you know Wally Millard?"

"Sure, from Elaine's." Wally was a retired cop, now a private investigator.

"I gave it to him, and he got it done."

"I'll call Wally."

"Tell him I said it's okay to talk to you and to call me for confirmation if he wants."

"Okay. Talk to you later." Stone hung up and called the Gardens and left a voice mail for Evan Keating. "The contract will be here by noon tomorrow. Call me in the morning, and I'll buy you lunch."

Stone looked up Wally Millard's number in his address book and called him.

"Hey, Stone."

"Hey, Wally. Bill Eggers asked me to call you about a skip trace you did for him."

"If I call Eggers, will he tell me that?"

"Yes."

"I'll take your word for it. What do you want to know?"

"It was a guy named Evan Keating. Apparently, you found him in Miami, but he skipped again."

"Jesus, I'm getting too old to go running off to Miami on a skip. I called a guy named Manny White, ex-NYPD, who's a PI down there, and he put somebody on it." Wally gave him White's number. "Took him a couple of weeks, so finding the guy wasn't a piece of cake. Tell him I said to call."

"Thanks, Wally. Say hello to Elaine."

"Sure." Wally hung up.

"How's Wally?" Dino asked.

"He's okay."

"I'm hungry, let's get out of here. You can call Manny White later."

"You know him?"

"Old-timer, Wally's generation. I had some dealings with him on a case when I was still in a rookie uniform, and he busted my chops every chance he got."

"Obviously, he knew you well."

"What do you mean? I was a great rookie."

"Yeah, I remember."

"Remember what?"

"Everything."

"Oh."

They went to the Raw Bar for conch fritters, third time. They were halfway through lunch when Stone's cell phone went off. A Miami number.

"Hello?" Stone put it on speaker; it was easier than repeating everything to Dino.

"Is this that little Barrington shit who worked out of the Nineteenth, until they kicked his ass down the stairs?"

Dino broke up. "It's Manny White."

"No," Stone said, "this is the Barrington who was a very smart detective at the Nineteenth and who walked down the stairs on his own."

"I didn't know there was one like that."

"There was."

"Wally called me. What the fuck do you want?"

"Wally gave you a skip trace on a guy named Evan Keating."

"Yeah, I know that."

"He said it took you two weeks to find him. What was so hard about it?"

"You think I hoof it up and down the streets looking for guys at my age? I put an agent on it. Took two weeks to check every hotel in South Beach, locate the guy and put a tail on him."

"I hear you lost him."

"So? People lose things all the time. Anyway, my *agent* lost him. What's it to you?"

"I need background on the guy; there's a hundred in it for you, if you can give me something I need."

"What do you need?"

"Like I said, background. What was he doing in South Beach? Did he work? Who were his friends?"

"He was doing what everybody else in South Beach was doing—looking pretty, drinking, snorting powder and spending money they don't have, except he had the money. That'll be a hundred bucks."

"Come on, Manny, give me something about the guy, not about everybody else."

Manny thought about it for a moment. "He had a boat. He left in it—that's why my agent couldn't figure out where he went."

"I already knew he had a boat. Give me something worth the hundred."

"He was staying at the Delano, which, if you don't already know, is a hotshot hotel for the young and stupid. They got a pretty bar, but the rooms look like underfurnished cells in an insane asylum. The people who stay there think this is stylish."

"Did he have a girl with him?"

"A different one every night. At least one."

"How long was he there?"

"A month, give or take, and in a suite, too."

"Where'd he come from?"

"His mama's belly, where do you think?"

"Where did he live before South Beach?" Stone could hear some papers shuffling.

"Santa Fe."

"In New Mexico?"

"No, in Alaska. A very hot spot, I hear."

"How long was he there?"

"A month, give or take. Same thing with the girls. I hear he's cute. Lemme give you my P.O. box for the hundred, which you've used up." He gave the number and zip code. "You want to start on a second hundred?"

"You got anything else?"

"No, but I'll take the second hundred."

"Thanks, Manny, you're a prince." Stone hung up.

"Was he always like that?" he asked Dino.

"Always. Did you call the Swede? You promised."

Stone sighed and got out his cell again.

21

Stone lay on his back, panting. The ceiling fan was a blur above him. For the past two hours, off and on, he and Annika had explored every nook and cranny, every orifice, every nerve ending in both their bodies. To his credit, even she seemed tired.

"Tell me, Stone," she said, "what do you do?"

They were going to have the first-date chitchat *now*? "Do you really want to know?"

"I don't ask what I don't want to know."

"I'm an attorney."

"Why do lawyers always say they are attorneys, instead of lawyers?"

"Because lawyers have a bad name with a lot of people."

"And attorneys don't?"

"Oh, no. Attorneys are a different class of people altogether. Much higher up the totem pole."

"They are Eskimos?"

"Just a figure of speech."

"Americans use a lot of figure of speeches."

"Yes, we do. You will, too, when you've been here a little longer."

"What possible business could an attorney have in Key West?" she asked.

"I was looking for a man."

"Did you find him?"

"Finally."

"Why was it so hard?"

"You know, today I asked the same question of another man who took a while to find him."

"It was hard for him, too?"

"Yes."

"Who is this man?"

"His name is Evan Keating."

"Oh, Evan."

Stone lifted his head from the damp pillow and looked at her. "You know him?"

"Of course."

"What do you mean, of course?"

"It's just a figure of speech."

"How could you possibly know him?"

"All sorts of people come through an emergency room," she replied. "We get drunks, criminals, brand-new quadriplegics and . . ."

"Hang on, what's a brand-new quadriplegic?"

"A drunken college student who, during spring break, dives off the White Street Pier into shallow water and breaks his neck. We get about one a year."

"Good God."

"Exactly. And there's a big sign saying, 'Don't Dive Off the Pier, Because the Water Is Shallow, and You'll Break Your Neck.' Or words to that effect."

"How do you treat a brand-new quadriplegic?"

"You pack him onto a helicopter and send him to Miami, where they know better how to deal with these things."

"What else do you deal with?"

"We treat a few gunshot wounds now and then."

"Yeah?"

"Usually in the foot, which is where people often shoot themselves. If somebody else shoots them, they're often dead."

"I know. I used to be a cop, and in New York people shoot each other somewhat more often than in Key West."

"It must be interesting to be an emergency room physician in New York," she said.

"I used to go out with one, until she married a doctor."

"Is her job still open? I'm thinking of moving on."

"As far as I know, she didn't leave her job. You're thinking of moving to New York?"

"Why not? I was there once, and I liked it."

"Annika, if you moved to New York, I would be dead in a month."

She laughed. "No, I would keep you alive," she said, fondling him. "I would chain you to the bed and fuck you until you were at the edge of death. Then I would revive you with Swedish meatballs until you were ready again."

"That's pretty much what you're doing here," he said.

"I suppose it is. Oh, look, you're coming up again."

"I don't need to look; I can tell."

"Where would you like me to put it this time?"

"You choose."

"I choose everywhere."

"Again?"

"Again and again."

Stone groaned.

"It's just a figure of speech," she said, throwing a leg over him.

"Wait a minute," he said, but it was too late; he was already inside her. "How do you know Evan Keating?"

"I treated him in the emergency room," she said, moving slowly.

"For what?"

"He said it was some sort of boating accident, but it was a knife wound." She began moving faster.

"Who cut him?"

"That wasn't one of the questions on the admitting form," she said, then exploded in climax.

Stone hung on for dear life, though that was just a figure of speech.

22

Stone and Dino were lounging by the pool when the FedEx lady arrived. Stone signed for the package and thanked her.

"Aren't you going to open it?" Dino asked.

"It's addressed to Evan, in care of me," Stone said.

"So?"

"I don't think I should open a package addressed to somebody else."

"Give it to me," Dino said. "I'll open it."

"That's very kind of you," Stone said. "Why are you so curious about a contract?"

"I want to know what Evan's old man is getting for the company."

"But it's none of your business."

"What the fuck difference does that make?"

"I mean, it's my business, sort of, but I'm not opening the package. Are you accustomed to reading other people's mail?"

"Every chance I get," Dino replied.

Stone's cell phone rang, and he answered it.

"It's Evan Keating. When do you expect to have the contract?"

"It came about ninety seconds ago."

"Have you read the contract?"

"It's addressed to you. If I have your permission to open the package and read it, I'll be glad to do so."

"No. Your message said something about lunch?"

"Do you know the Raw Bar?"

"Yes."

"Forty-five minutes?"

"Fine." Evan hung up.

"He wouldn't let you open the package," Dino said. "Serves you right."

"No, it confirms my judgment," Stone said.

Stone sat in the Raw Bar, gazing out over the marina and smelling the frying seafood. He glanced at the front entrance and saw Evan Keating and Gigi Jones arriving, and he waved them over.

Evan came over; Gigi went and sat at another table. "Good afternoon," Evan said. "May I see the contract, please?"

A waitress approached.

"Shall we order first?" Stone asked.

"A pound of stone crab claws and a Heineken," Evan said.

"Conch fritters and iced tea," Stone said, and the waitress left.

"Now may I see the contract?"

"Not yet; I want to ask you some questions."

"Questions?"

"How do I know you're Evan Keating?" Stone said. "I would hate to deliver a confidential document to the wrong person. How about a picture ID?"

Evan took out a wallet and handed Stone a Florida driver's license. The face matched the name. "Now may I see the contract?"

"I'm not finished with my questions."

"What else could you possibly want to know?"

"How did you get the knife wound?"

Evan rarely seemed to register anything, but at the question he registered surprise. "How the hell did you know about that?"

"That's not pertinent," Stone replied. "How'd you get the knife wound?"

"From a knife."

"Who was holding it?"

"A bad person."

"You don't really want to see the contract, do you?"

"A drug dealer. I was buying a little cocaine, and we disagreed over the quality and price."

"And why do you know enough about cocaine to be able to judge quality and price?"

"Experience," Evan said. "On widely separated occasions."

"What happened after he knifed you?"

"Gigi rendered him unconscious, and we left."

"Gigi is a handy girl to have around, isn't she?"

"Sometimes. At other times she's just a pain in the ass."

"Or the neck," Stone said, rubbing his own at the memory. "Did you pay for the cocaine?"

"Gigi stuffed the money in his mouth."

"Are you likely to meet up with him again?"

"I certainly hope not. Gigi might kill him next time."

"He might kill you *and* Gigi next time," Stone said. "You should consider that before dealing with the criminal element again. Did the hospital report the knife wound to the police?"

"I told them the cut was from a gaffing hook while fishing. How did you know I went to the hospital?"

"It's where I would go, if somebody knifed me."

"Now may I see the contract?"

"Give me an account of your whereabouts and activities since you graduated from college."

"You really are a very curious guy," Evan said. "Why do you want to know?"

"Because I'm a very curious guy," Stone replied.

"Maybe I should sic Gigi on you."

"You may tell Gigi for me that if she ever again approaches me from any angle, I'll break her pretty face."

Evan burst out laughing. "I'd like to see you try that," he said.

"How did you meet Gigi?"

"We hooked up in Miami."

"In South Beach?"

"How did . . . Never mind. Yes."

"How much business have you done with South Beach Security?"

"I had an account there when I lived in South Beach," Evan said warily.

"Did you do any illegal business with them?"

Their food arrived, and Evan used it as an excuse not to answer the question. They ate in silence for a while.

"Do you really think your father poisoned your uncle Harry?" Stone asked finally.

Evan regarded him evenly over a crab claw. "I think it's well within the realm of possibility. If I ever see that contract, I can give you a better answer."

Stone handed him the FedEx envelope.

Evan ate the crab claw, wiped his hands carefully on a paper towel from the roll on the table and ripped open the package. He seemed to be speed-reading, flipping the pages rapidly. Then he stopped halfway through and read more slowly.

"Well?" Stone said.

Evan stuffed the contract back into the envelope, ate another crab claw and sipped his beer. "Yes," he said. "I think my father poisoned Uncle Harry, and you can pass the word to him: no deal." He tossed a fifty-dollar bill on the table, then got up and left without another word, taking the contract with him.

23

Stone arrived back at the Marquesa to find Dino still by the pool, eating an enormous club sandwich, accompanied by a fruity-looking drink with an umbrella in it.

"So did he read the contract?" Dino asked.

"Yes."

"How much is the business being sold for?"

"I don't know; he didn't tell me, and he took the contract with him." Stone's cell phone vibrated, and he glanced at it. "Eggers; he's going to love this."

Stone put the phone on speaker. "Yes, Bill?"

"Did you get the contract?"

"Yes."

"Did you show it to Evan Keating?"

"Yes."

"And?"

"He said to tell Warren, no deal."

"Shit!" Eggers said.

"You were hoping he would take it?"

"It sure would have made my life a lot simpler," Eggers said. "This was supposed to go like clockwork; you were supposed to find Evan, get his signature and everybody would have been happy."

"Everybody except Grandpa Eli, who's locked in the nursing home, Uncle Harry, who's dead, and Evan, who thinks, not without cause, that he's being cheated out of his share of the business."

"It's a snakepit—that's what it is," Eggers moaned.

"Bill, what's the sales price for the business?"

"Didn't you read the contract?"

"No, it was addressed to Evan, care of me, and when I gave it to him he didn't read it aloud."

"What did he say?"

"He said, 'No deal,' and when I asked him if he thought his father poisoned Uncle Harry, he replied in the affirmative."

"And you think I should go to the police?"

"From what Evan said the other day, the police are already looking into Harry's death. What could you tell them?"

"That I have reason to believe that Harry Keating was poisoned by his brother."

"And what reason do you have to believe that?"

"Warren Keating is a chemist; his brother died under mysterious circumstances; Warren stood to gain from his death."

"Don't you think the police have already figured out that much? In addition, they've probably searched Warren's house, garage and toolshed for ant poison, or whatever the hell is poisonous these days, and they surely took fluid and tissue samples from the corpse."

"Then why haven't they arrested Warren?"

"Maybe because toxicology screens seem to take one hell of a long time to come back, especially in small towns like— Where is it Warren and Harry live?"

"Torrington, Connecticut."

"Like Torrington, Connecticut."

"Yeah," Eggers said, "and did I mention that Harry's body was cremated?"

"Before or after they took samples?"

"I'm not sure. Can a crime lab get toxicology reports from ashes, or whatever's left after a cremation?"

"Maybe, in the case of heavy metals, like arsenic, but if Warren is a chemist I should think he'd use something more sophisticated than arsenic."

"Like ant poison?"

"Some of those insecticides have cyanide in them—at least I think that's the case; I'm not an expert on poisoning. Somebody once told me that there are two common household fluids that, when mixed, form a poison that can't be analyzed."

"I didn't know there was *anything* that can't be analyzed."

"I'm not a chemist, Bill. Did Harry have any family other than Warren, Eli and Evan?"

"No, he was a lifelong bachelor, didn't even have a girlfriend," Eggers said.

"Then has it occurred to you that Evan's share of the proceeds of the sale would be even larger with Harry's death?"

"I suppose so. Warren's, too."

"And, Bill, has it occurred to you that the remaining split would be larger still if Eli kicked off?"

"You mean . . ."

"That maybe dutiful son Warren, when visiting his father, might bring along a treat like a box of chocolates or a bottle of Scotch?"

"Oh, my God." Eggers groaned.

"Maybe you ought to have a chat with the Torrington police after all," Stone said.

"I'm Warren's lawyer, Stone, and so are you."

"You have a point."

"And don't go getting Dino to call the cops, either; that would be like telling them yourself."

"Yeah. What are you going to do?"

"Think about it," Eggers said. "And I have to call Warren and tell him what Evan said."

"You'd better tell him to do the right thing, Bill."

But Eggers had already hung up.

Stone looked at Dino, whose eyes had narrowed and who appeared to be in deep thought.

"What?" Stone said.

"I'm just thinking about your problem," Dino said. "We could probably get somebody else to approach the Torrington cops in a roundabout way."

"Somebody like Wally Millard?" Stone asked.

"Maybe, but he's connected with Eggers, who hired him to find Evan Keating. That might be too close."

"Manny White?"

"Still too close."

"If I'm going to do something about this, I'd better do it fast," Stone said.

"I know a detective on the Connecticut State Police," Dino said.

"Yeah, but you're too close to this to talk to him."

"Maybe, but I know somebody who has every right to express his concern to Connecticut law enforcement."

"Who's that?"

"Evan Keating."

Stone smote his forehead. "Why didn't I tell him at lunch to do that?"

"Because you're so fucking dumb," Dino said.

Stone dialed the Gardens. Evan's room didn't answer, so he left a message.

"And we still don't know what the contract price is," Dino pointed out.

"It's not as though we really need to know that, is it?" Stone said.

"Still," Dino replied, "a big number is motive."

"It's going to be a very big motive," Stone said.

24

Stone and Dino left their hotel to play tennis, and Stone kept his cell phone in his pocket, but it never rang.

"I'm worried," Stone said as they were taking a break between sets.

"I suppose you've got visions of Warren visiting Eli and stuffing something down his throat?"

"Something like that." Stone called the Gardens again and still got Evan's voice mail.

"You're doing all you can do," Dino said.

"I keep thinking there's something else."

"You could call the nursing home, pretend to be the cops and tell them not to let Warren anywhere near Eli."

"That's a wonderful idea, Dino. What's the name of the nursing home?"

"I don't know."

"Neither do I."

"Oh. Let's play another set."

They played another set.

"Come on," Stone said, "let's go to the Gardens. Maybe he's just not answering his phone."

"Okay," Dino said, "but I was winning."

"The hell you were."

They drove to the Gardens and went inside.

"May I help you?" a young woman at the desk asked.

"Yes, I'd like to see Evan Keating," Stone said.

"I'm afraid Mr. Keating just checked out," she replied. "Not more than fifteen minutes ago."

"Did he leave a forwarding address?" Stone asked.

She checked her records. "Miami, Florida," she said.

"What hotel?"

"No hotel, just Miami."

"Do you have a cell phone number for him?"

She checked again. "Yes, we do." She gave him the number.

Stone was about to dial it when Dino spoke up.

"That's his old cell number, the one that went overboard."

"Shit," Stone said in disgust.

"What do you want to do now?"

"You want me to call my guy on the Connecticut State Police?"

Stone thought about that. Somebody's life was at stake. "Yes," he said, "call him."

"What do you want me to tell him?"

"You know what to tell him, but tell him not to tell anybody the call came from you."

They got into their car, and Dino went through his address book and found the number. "You're sure you want me to call?"

"Yes, dammit!"

Dino dialed the number and put the phone on speaker.

"Robbery Homicide, Lieutenant Hotchkiss."

"Dan, it's Dino Bacchetti, NYPD, remember me?"

"How could I forget?" Dan replied. "I bet you want me to solve another homicide for you."

"I don't need your help in solving homicides, Dan, but . . ."

"I know a perp who would still be a free man if . . ."

"I need help in *preventing* a homicide."

"Anybody I know?"

"I doubt it; it's an old man from Torrington named Eli Keating."

"Elijah Keating's Sons? That Keating?"

"That Keating."

"Harry Keating's father?"

"The *late* Harry Keating's father."

"Harry Keating is dead?"

141

"You hadn't heard? I hear the Torrington police are looking into the cause of death."

"What do they suspect?"

"I don't know how smart the Torrington cops are, so I can't tell you. Suffice it to say that Harry's brother, Warren, and his son inherit the business, along with old Eli, and Warren is a chemist."

"You mean . . ."

"I don't mean anything; you're going to have to draw your own conclusions, and you can't tell anybody I gave you any hints."

"Okay, hang on while I draw some conclusions: You think Warren poisoned his brother?"

"I don't think anything; you're drawing your own conclusions."

"And that he might be going to poison his father as well, to get a bigger chunk of the business?"

"That's an interesting conclusion, Dan; why don't you follow up on it?"

"I need more."

"Old Eli is in a nursing home, ostensibly with Alzheimer's, though somebody who talked with him at Harry's funeral says he seemed just fine."

"So you think that Warren locked the old man up to get him out of the way?"

"I don't think anything, but it's interesting that you have drawn that conclusion."

"I still need more."

"Then why don't you conclude that you ought to call the Torrington cops and see what they know about all this? Maybe *they* would like to get the credit for solving one homicide and preventing another."

"Dino, you think there's really something to all this?"

"Dan, when you answered the phone, you spoke the words, 'Robbery and . . .' What was that other word? Try and remember it."

"Okay, okay, I'll make some calls."

"I think you should conclude that you'd better hurry; it might be visiting day at the nursing home."

"Okay, Dino."

"I don't know who that is, but call me at this number and let me know what you find out." Dino gave him his cell phone number.

"You're in New York?"

"I'm in Key West."

"What are you doing in Key West?"

"Loitering."

"That's what I would do if I were in Key West," Dan said.

"It's one of the things I do best," Dino said; then he hung up. He turned back to Stone. "Let's see if that gets him to move his ass."

"It ought to," Stone said.

"Now, where the hell do you think Evan has gone?"

"I don't know, back to his boat?"

"And what's the name of that boat?"

"I don't know."

"You didn't ask him? You had lunch with the guy, and you didn't ask him?" Dino slapped Stone on the back of the head.

"I needed that," Stone said.

25

Bill Eggers drove across the Harlem River Bridge and headed north, toward Connecticut. He was going there against his better judgment, but his conscience had been bothering him. Stone had been making a lot of sense, and as far as he could tell, he was the only person who could do anything about this. Harry Keating was dead and Evan Keating had dropped out of sight again, so who else was left?

Two hours later Eggers arrived in Torrington, and he consulted the map his secretary had printed out from the Internet. It took him another fifteen minutes to find the nursing home, out on the east side of town, toward Hartford.

The Happy Hills Care Center was perched, true to its name, on a low hilltop. There were big oak trees on the front lawn and the building, with its colonial columns, was freshly painted. The reception area was newly decorated, with comfortable chairs. All of this was encouraging. He began to feel better. He approached the front desk, where a well-coiffed middle-aged woman gave him a warm smile.

"Good morning," she said. "May I help you?"

"Good morning. My name is William Eggers, and I'd like to visit with Mr. Eli Keating."

The woman turned to her computer and tapped a few keys. "I'm sorry, Mr. Eggers, but your name isn't on the authorized visitors' list. Are you a family member?"

"No," Eggers said, producing his business card, "I am Mr. Keating's attorney."

"I'm sorry," she said, still smiling sweetly. "I cannot allow anyone who is not on the authorized visitors' list to see a patient without a written order from Mr. Keating's guardian."

"Guardian? And who might that be?"

She consulted her computer screen. "Mr. Warren Keating."

"Who is the director of this institution?" Eggers inquired.

"The medical director or the administrative director?"

"Who's *in charge*?"

"One moment, please." She picked up the phone and tapped in an extension. "Mr. Parker? There's a gentleman at the front desk who *insists* on speaking with someone in authority. Could you come out here right away, please? Thank you so much." She hung up. "Mr. Parker will be right with you," she said.

"And what is Mr. Parker's position here?"

"Mr. Parker is the administrative director."

"And who is the medical director?"

"That would be Dr. Parker."

"Would Mr. Parker be the son of Dr. Parker?"

"That would be correct."

"Ah, a family business." Eggers was too agitated to sit down, so he paced. After a few minutes a skinny young man in an ill-fitting blue suit appeared.

"I'm Mr. Parker," he said. "How can I help you?"

"Mr. Parker, I am the attorney for Mr. Eli Keating, who is an inmate of your institution."

"A *patient*," Parker said.

"We'll see. I wish to see Mr. Keating at once."

"He's not on Mr. Keating's visitors' list," the receptionist said.

"Then I'm afraid it will not be possible for you to see Mr. Keating," young Parker said.

"Mr. Parker, you'd better get your daddy out here right now," Eggers said in a low voice, "and I mean *right now*."

The young man's eyes widened slightly, and he turned to the receptionist. "Call Dr. Parker, code three."

The receptionist called another extension and repeated the message. Half a minute later, a gray-haired, gray-skinned man in a starched white lab coat presented himself at the front desk.

"This man wants to see Mr. Keating," young Parker said to his father. "I've explained that that is not possible, since he is not on the visitors' list."

"Who are you?" Dr. Parker asked.

"I am Mr. Keating's attorney," Eggers said, digging out another card, "and I have a pretyped court order in my pocket that I can have Judge Carter's signature on in ten minutes, so my advice to you would be to present Mr. Keating *now*."

Dr. Parker regarded him for a slow count of about five, then picked up a phone and tapped in an extension. "This is Dr. Parker. Give Mr. Keating his medication and bring him to the dayroom immediately."

"If you medicate that man, I'm calling the police as well as the judge," Eggers said.

"Never mind the medication," Parker said into the phone. Then he hung up. "The dayroom is right over there," he said, pointing to a double door. "You may have five minutes with Mr. Keating, no more."

"I'll take as long as I like," Eggers said; then he turned and strode toward the doors. The dayroom was as pleasant as the rest of the place, and Eggers took a seat. Ten minutes passed, and he was about to go looking for Dr. Parker when a door swung open and a beefy orderly pushed a wheelchair into the room.

Eli Keating looked thinner than when Eggers had

seen him at the funeral, and his stare was vacant. Eggers stood up. "Eli, it's Bill Eggers. How are you?"

"All right," Keating said sleepily. "I think."

Eggers turned to the orderly. "We won't be needing you."

"I got my instructions," the orderly said.

Eggers drew himself to his full six feet, four inches and took a step toward the orderly. "Get out."

The man blinked a couple of times, then retreated the way he had come, and began staring through a glass panel in the door.

Eggers sat down. "Eli, why are you here?"

"That's what I'd like to know," Keating said in a manner more himself. "You'd have to ask my son."

"Listen carefully to me. What is my name?"

"Bill Eggers."

"Who am I?"

"You're my lawyer, or at least you were. Where the hell have you been?"

"When did you hire me?"

"When you joined Woodman and Weld. I knew your daddy."

"How old are you?"

"Eighty-two next week."

"What are your sons' names?"

"Harry and Warren. I've got a grandson, too, Evan. Harry's dead, and I don't know where the hell Evan is. I wish he'd come and get me out of here."

"Would you like to leave this place now?"

"You're goddamned right I would. I want to go back to my house and see my own doctor."

Eggers pulled out his cell phone and pressed the speed-dial button for his secretary. "It's Eggers," he said. "Plan B now." He hung up. "You just sit tight, Eli, and I'll have you out of here in less than an hour. My secretary is making a call to a lawyer in Torrington, who is ready to have a court order signed. Do you need an ambulance, or would you rather ride with me in my car?"

"Bill," Eli said, "if you can stop them from giving me another one of those injections, *I'll* drive *you*."

26

Late in the afternoon, Stone and Dino were back in a rented Boston Whaler, patrolling the marinas, looking for Evan Keating's boat, whatever its name might be.

"There's a period piece over there," Dino said, pointing at a motor yacht.

"Too big," Stone replied. "Evan's boat is a thirty-two-footer, and that one is at least forty feet long."

"Oh," Dino said, settling himself on the front bench under the canvas top and sipping a cold beer from a cooler. "You want a beer?"

"I'll wait awhile," Stone said, gazing at row after row of motorboats.

Stone's cell phone vibrated on his belt, and he answered it.

"It's Eggers."

"Hey, Bill. Listen, we're looking for Evan Keating's boat right now. He checked out of his hotel, and we think we'll find him aboard."

"You can forget about Evan Keating," Eggers said.

"What, you got the signed papers?"

"I did not, and I do not expect to," Eggers replied.

"What's going on?"

"I've got a lot to tell you," Eggers said, "so relax and enjoy."

Stone cut the power and let the boat drift. He motioned to Dino for a beer. "Shoot." He pressed the speaker button on his phone.

"After some of our conversations, I got more and more worried about what's going on in this deal. For a start, and I'll tell you this just once and deny I ever said it, the offer for Elijah Keating's Sons is eight hundred million dollars."

"Holy shit!" Stone gasped. "And he was offering Evan only twenty-one million of that?"

"I don't have any more to say about the deal," Eggers said. "Last night I hatched a plan: I made a phone call to a law firm we've dealt with in Torrington, one that has done no business with the Keatings. Then I dictated some documents by phone that were typed up this morning. Then I went to Torrington."

"To resign the account, I hope."

"Shut up and listen, Stone. I'm enjoying telling you about this."

"Sorry. Go on."

"I went out to the Happy Hills place that Warren had stuffed his father into, and I brazened my way in and got to see Eli Keating."

"How was he?"

"A little woozy from whatever they've been dosing him with, but pretty sharp. Once I ascertained that, I put my plan into motion. First, my secretary faxed a letter of resignation to Warren Keating, specifically stating that I would continue to represent Eli until the old man fired me."

"Bully for you!"

"Then a call went in to the Torrington law firm, and one of their attorneys hotfooted it to the courthouse, armed with a court order freeing Eli and negating Warren's guardianship, and barged in on the local judge. He also took an affidavit from me, saying that Eli is compos mentis and desires to leave Happy Hills immediately.

"Then I went down to Eli's room, which was little more than a cell, really, stuffed his clothes into a suitcase and drove him to his home. By this time, Warren had found another lawyer and was arguing with the judge, but by the time we got to Eli's place, the judge had signed off on it, a little late perhaps, but Eli is back in charge of his life."

"Hallelujah!" Stone shouted.

"Eli called his old secretary, got her out of retirement and over to his house, and she's taken charge of running his life. Warren will never get hold of him again, if I have anything to say about it, and Eli has withdrawn his permission for the deal to go through. In fact, he says he never signed it, so that means that Warren or somebody who works for him forged the document."

"What happens now?"

"Eli likes the sale, but he's going to be dealing directly with the buyers, and distribution of the proceeds will be made according to the original will of Elijah Keating."

"I hate it that Warren will still get a bundle."

"I'm going to see what I can do about that," Eggers said.

"I'm really delighted to hear all this, Bill."

"I'm pretty delighted with it myself," Eggers said. "Warren may sue the firm, but with everything we've got on him, we'll have him for lunch."

"I'll be very happy to testify to my part in this," Stone said.

"Now, this is the sad part, Stone," Eggers said. "Tonight is your last night in Key West on my dime. You get your ass out of there tomorrow or start using your own credit card, you hear?"

"I hear you, Bill." Then he thought about that. "Dino and I may stick around for a couple more days and start enjoying ourselves, instead of working so hard."

Dino had to put a hand over his mouth to keep from hooting.

"Do whatever you like," Eggers said. "Oh, you might spend the rest of your time today trying to find Evan Keating and telling him to get in touch with his grandfather."

"I'll do that," Stone said.

"Now I have to get back with Eli and paper over any cracks in all this," Eggers said. "So bye-bye." He hung up.

"Isn't that great?" Stone said to Dino.

"Couldn't be better," Dino said. "We're going to stick around for a couple more days?"

"Have you got the time?"

"I've got the days, and my captain is on vacation in the Bahamas, so he can hardly squawk. You still want to find Evan, don't you?"

"Yes, I do. I'd like to wrap this up neatly before we abandon ship."

"Nah, you just want to see the Swede a couple more times," Dino said.

"Well," Stone replied, "there is that."

27

Stone and Dino were enjoying a drink on their front porch when Stone's cell phone buzzed. "Hello?"

"Stone, it's Wally Millard."

"Hey, Wally, how are you?"

"I'm okay, but I don't think everybody else is."

"What do you mean?"

"What's this kid's name you're looking for?"

"Evan Keating."

"That's the one. I got a call from Manny White in Miami, and he was steamed, which isn't unusual for Manny."

"I guess not. What's his problem?"

"Well, Manny doesn't like to hear from people who want to have some dirty work done."

"Okay. Who asked him to do what?"

"Somebody called him and hinted that he needed somebody hit."

"I can see how that might steam Manny. Who was the caller?"

"He's not positive, but he thinks it was the guy who hired him to find Keating."

"He thinks it was Warren Keating?" Stone didn't like the sound of this.

"That's right. He wanted Manny to find his son. I passed it on to him after Eggers called me."

"Why does he think it was Warren Keating?"

"He had an upper-class New England accent; Manny doesn't get many calls from people who talk like George Plimpton. That's who Manny said he talks like."

"When you referred Keating to Manny, did you make the call, or did he?"

"I did."

"Then how can Manny recognize his voice?"

"It was the accent. Manny can't think of anybody else who would call him who has an accent like that. And George Plimpton is dead, God rest his soul."

"Okay, I get all of that."

"Did you find the Keating kid?"

"Yeah, but I've lost him again. Why?"

"Well, Manny cut the guy short, but after he hung up, it occurred to him that what might have been going on was that old Keating wanted young Keating taken out."

"Given the circumstances," Stone said, "that's not an outrageous assumption, even though Manny's evidence for it is pretty slim."

"Manny always had good instincts," Wally said. "I wouldn't dismiss this out of hand, if you want the kid to stay alive."

"I wouldn't like to see anybody take a hit," Stone said, "so I'll try to find the kid and let him know what's going on."

"That's all anybody can do," Wally said. "Just tell the kid to watch his ass."

"I'll do that, if I can find him, Wally. Thanks for letting me know."

Stone hung up and turned to Dino. "The short version: Somebody who sounds like George Plimpton called Manny White and intimated that he wanted somebody popped. Manny hung up on him, but he inferred—and I know this is a leap—that Warren Keating wants Evan dead."

Dino thought about this for a minute. "The second part of that makes perfect sense, if you consider that a guy who is getting eight hundred mil in a business deal and who is supposed to share it with his father and son might want both of them dead."

"Yeah, but what about the first part? He didn't give Manny his name before Manny hung up on him."

"Manny's kind of weird like that. I remember a time when we had a robbery to deal with, and before Manny looked at any of the evidence, he named the perp. We all thought he was crazy, but he turned out to be right, and we would have saved a lot of man-hours if we had just busted the guy right away. So I think you should let Evan Keating know that something might be afoot."

"I'd love to, Dino, but I don't know where he is, and I don't think we're going to find him by puttering around the marinas in a Whaler."

"Then we'll have to find another way, won't we?"

"Suggest one, please."

"Didn't Evan tell you he was going to buy a new cell phone?"

"Yes, but you can't call information and get a cell phone number."

"Maybe Bob Cantor can find it."

Stone thought about this. Bob Cantor was a techie whom Stone had used for years for all sorts of electronic, computer and surveillance and phone problems. "Dino," he said, "that is a very good idea." Stone called Bob Cantor, got his voice mail and left a message.

"Dino, do you think Evan might really be in Miami? I mean, he did leave that as a forwarding address."

"Who knows? I guess it's possible."

"I think I'm going to call Manny White."

"This is going to be entertaining. Can I listen in?"

"Sure." Stone called Manny White's number and put the phone on speaker.

"Yeah?"

"Manny?"

"Yeah?"

"It's Stone Barrington. Do you always answer the phone that way?"

"I do on my private line," Manny said. "How'd you get this number?"

"You called my cell phone on this line. Did you get the hundred I sent you?"

"Yeah."

"Would you like some more hundreds?"

"Maybe. How many and what for?"

"Five hundred to find Evan Keating again. I think he may be in Miami, maybe South Beach."

"That's going to run you at least a thousand," Manny said. "I have to start from scratch."

"Why? You've already done this once."

"Yeah, but the agent I used is no longer available. I'll have to start with a new one."

"All right, Manny, start a new guy on the job, and call me when we get to a thousand, and I'll decide whether I want to go further."

"I'll need five hundred up front," Manny said.

"Manny, for old times' sake, could you start right now? I'll send the money today."

"What old times' sake? It's not like you and me have got some kind of warm, fuzzy history."

"Manny, we have the NYPD in common. That's a basis to start on."

"If you FedEx the money, I'll have it first thing tomorrow."

Stone sighed. "Give me the address."

28

Stone and Dino were with Tommy Sculley when Bob Cantor called back.

"Hey, Bob," Stone said. "You okay?"

"I'm okay. Are you in New York?"

"No, I'm in Key West."

"That's almost as good as St. Thomas, which is where I am."

"Not bad, Bob. Can you get me a cell phone number from there?"

"Maybe. Old number?"

"New number, maybe only a day or two old."

"Do you know where the caller is based?"

"Key West, I should think."

"What's the name?"

"Evan Keating." Stone spelled it for him.

"I'm going to need to do some work on the computer," Bob said. "I'll call you back."

"Today?"

"Give me a few minutes."

"Okay, thanks, Bob." Stone hung up.

"What else can we do?" he asked Dino.

"I think this is our best bet," Dino replied. "Let's wait to hear from Bob, before we start patrolling the streets, which seems like our last remaining option."

Stone's cell phone buzzed. "Hello?"

"It's Manny. Did you send the money?"

"I haven't had a chance yet, Manny, but I'll get it to FedEx before the day is out, okay?"

"Terrific. When I get it, I'll give you what I've got."

"You've got something on Keating?"

"Yes, I have."

"Come on, Manny, you'll get the money."

"This is business, Barrington. Why should I trust you?"

"Jesus Christ."

"I wouldn't trust him, either. Tell you what: You go send the money, then give me the tracking number, and I'll check it out. If it's on the way, I'll tell you what I've got."

Stone sighed again. "All right, Manny." He hung up.

Tommy spoke up. "Is this the same Manny White from the Nineteenth?"

"I'm afraid so."

"He was always a pain in the ass. Sit tight; I'll be right back." Tommy got up from the table and disappeared through a door. A moment later he was back with a FedEx envelope and waybill. "Here you go; they'll call it in from the office."

Stone put five hundreds in the envelope, addressed it and made a note of the tracking number; then Tommy took it to the office.

Stone called Manny White.

"Good day, Manny White Investigations," Manny said.

"Isn't this still the private line?" Stone asked.

"Yes. Who's this?"

"It's Stone Barrington."

"What do you want?"

"Manny, it's what *you* want. The FedEx tracking number, remember?"

"Yeah, gimme it."

Stone recited the number. "Okay?"

"Okay."

"So what's your information?"

"I haven't had a chance to call FedEx and track it yet. I'll call you back."

"Manny, the package is in the office of the Key West Yacht Club, waiting for FedEx to pick it up."

"So it's not in the system yet?"

"I guess not, but it will be."

"I can't track 'will be.'"

Tommy and Dino were laughing so hard they couldn't eat.

"Look," Tommy said, pointing out the front window. A FedEx truck was leaving the parking lot.

"Okay, Manny," Stone said, "the truck just left; it's in the system."

"I'll call you back." Manny hung up.

"It would have been easier to go to Miami and look for the guy myself," Stone said. His cell phone buzzed. "Hello?"

"Is this Barrington?"

"Yes, Manny."

"Your package checked out."

"Good, Manny, now what's the information you have?"

"Here it is—after a thorough search, the name Evan Keating does not appear on any hotel register in South Beach."

"That's it?" Tommy and Dino were in new paroxysms of laughter.

"That's it."

"That's what you call information?"

"It's what I call very hard-won information," Manny replied. "My agent had to go to every hotel to get it."

"Okay, Manny," Stone said, "cancel the rest of the search."

"Whatever you say," Manny said, and he hung up.

Tommy spoke through his tears. "You gotta admit, it *was* information. Now you know where the guy is not."

Stone's cell phone went off. "Hello?"

"It's Cantor."

"Good. What've you got for me?"

"Zip, I'm afraid. Nobody by that name has gotten new cell phone service in Key West for a week."

Stone thought about that. "Anybody named Gigi Jones on the list of new customers?"

"Lemme see." Cantor was shuffling papers. "Nope, nobody by that name, either."

"Okay, Bob, thanks. Send me your bill."

"In Key West?"

"Nope, in New York."

"See ya." Cantor hung up.

"Stone," Tommy said, "if Evan Keating lost his old cell phone and is getting a new one, why would he get a new number?"

Stone smote his forehead. "Right! He'd just cancel the old phone and transfer the number to the new phone!"

"Why didn't you think of that?" Dino asked.

"I don't know. I should have."

"Your brain is Swede-addled," Dino said.

"Is this the doctor?" Tommy asked.

"Yeah. Stone has been sacrificing himself on that altar every night."

"Some sacrifice," Tommy said.

Stone ignored them; he was looking for Evan Keating's old cell number in the list of calls in his phone's memory. He found it and pressed the send button.

"Hello?"

"Evan?"

"Yes. Who's this?"

"It's Stone Barrington."

Long pause. "What do you want?"

"I need to see you. There have been developments at home that you need to know about."

"Where are you?"

"At the Key West Yacht Club."

"Funny, so am I," Evan said. "I'm parked within sight of the bar, which I figure is where you're calling from."

"Don't move," Stone said. He got up and started walking toward the door.

29

Stone burst out the door and saw a beautiful little thirty-two-footer moored at the end of the outer dock. Evan Keating was standing in the cockpit, looking at him.

Stone hurried over and stepped aboard. Evan pointed at a cockpit seat, and Stone sat down. "How long have you been here?"

"Just a couple of minutes. I came in for fuel, but they don't have fuel here."

"I guess you'll have to go down to Key West Bight."

"What's up?"

"First of all, the managing partner of my law firm got your grandfather out of the nursing home where your father had imprisoned him. He's at home and being taken care of by his old secretary."

"Hey, that's great," Evan said, without much enthusiasm. "What else?"

"It appears that your father may be trying to hire somebody to kill you."

This got Evan's full attention. "Why do you think that?"

"Because someone sounding like him, New England accent and all, called a private investigator of my acquaintance and inquired about having a dirty job done. Earlier, your father had hired him to find you."

"That sounds like the old man," Evan said. "Any details of who he hired and how he plans to do it?"

"No, the PI hung up on him when it became obvious what he wanted."

"And you don't know if he found somebody else?"

"You know your father better than I—is he the sort of man who would stop with one attempt?"

Evan thought about that. "No, he isn't."

"Then, if I were you, I'd start watching my back."

"That's my job," a female voice said.

Stone looked up to see Gigi Jones stepping out of the cabin, almost dressed in a tiny bikini that showed everything to great effect. "Yes, I've had some experience of that," he said. "I'm glad I'm seated with my back to the water."

Gigi giggled. "Don't be nervous, Mr. Barrington. It appears we're on the same side, both dedicated to keeping Evan alive."

"I guess," Stone said; then he turned back to Evan. "There's more: Your grandfather likes the idea of selling the company, so he's taking over negotiations himself. He'd like very much to hear from you. Will you call him?"

"Sure," Evan said. "I've got nothing against him. Why do you think my father wants me dead?"

"You've seen the number on the sales contract," Stone said. "Do you think he would kill you for your third of eight hundred million dollars?"

Evan shrugged. "I guess that's motive enough. He'd kill my grandfather for that, too."

"But then why would he bother to put him in a nursing home? Also, if you're right about his poisoning your uncle Harry, then he might hesitate to kill your grandfather, too."

"Too many deaths by poisoning in one family, huh?"

"Yes, but if he had somebody put a bullet in you in Key West, he's going to be far removed from the crime scene, isn't he? You'd just be another rich boy who mingled with the wrong people, nothing to do with him."

"I guess that would work for him," Evan said.

"Tell me something: Do you think it's possible your father had something to do with the killing of your friend Charley Boggs? Could a hit man have gotten the two of you mixed up?"

"I doubt that," Evan said. "Charley had a beard, remember?"

"Maybe you've been in Key West for too long," Stone said. "Maybe you'd be more comfortable in a different state."

"Maybe," Evan said. "How about it, babe?" he said to Gigi. "You ready to move on?"

"I like it here," Gigi replied.

"As a matter of fact, so do I," Evan said. "I guess I'll take my chances."

"Well, Evan," Stone said, "you're the only guy I know who, upon being told there was a contract out on him, would just sit tight and wait for a hit man to show up."

"Stone, you had a pretty hard time finding me, didn't you?"

"Yes, I did."

"Well, why do you think some stupid ex-con would have an easier time of it?"

"If he's as stupid as you think, then he might not find you. Or he might get lucky. Or if he's a real pro, he might find you faster than I did and you won't see him coming."

"Gigi will," Evan said, smiling at her.

"I hope you're right," Stone said. "You've got your grandfather's phone number?"

"I don't expect it's changed."

"Then I'll be saying goodbye, Evan; my work here is done." Stone stood up.

"I guess it is, at that," Evan said, offering him a hand. "Please don't worry about me."

Stone shook the hand. "I'll try and put the whole business out of my mind," he said. "But I'll watch the business pages to see how the sale of Elijah Keating's Sons turns out."

"So will I," Evan said. He went to the helm and started the engines.

"I'll cast you off," Stone said.

"Thanks."

Stone walked down the dock and untied the bow line, the springs and the stern line, coiled them and tossed them to Gigi.

He watched them ease out of the berth and turn toward the channel, and he noticed that there was no longer a name on the boat's stern. He supposed Evan hadn't thought of one yet.

Stone walked back into the yacht club and to Tommy's table.

"Your food's getting cold," Tommy said.

Stone tucked into his burger.

"So you all square with young Mr. Keating?" Dino asked.

"I've told him all the news from home," Stone replied.

"And the news from Manny White?"

"Yep."

"How'd he take it?"

"Like a champ," Stone said. "Hardly batted an eye."

"You know," Tommy said, "if somebody told me

there was a hit man coming for me, I think I'd be upset."

"Upset enough to leave town?" Stone asked.

"Oh, yeah."

"Well, Evan isn't upset at all," Stone said, "and he says he isn't going anywhere. Maybe you'd better save him a slab at your morgue."

"Oh, we've always got a vacant slab," Tommy said. "And the rates are better than at the Gardens."

"Cooler, too, I'll bet," Dino chimed in.

"Sometimes in summer," Tommy said, "when the heat and the humidity are up and there's no breeze, I've thought that a slab of marble might make a cool bed."

"Brrrr," Stone said, shivering. "Say, have you made any progress on the homicide of Charley Boggs?"

Tommy shook his head. "It was a clean crime scene, and the canvassing of the neighboring houseboats turned up nothing."

"Not even the talkative lady next door?"

"Nope. Apparently, she sleeps well. One of these days we'll bust somebody on a drug charge or something, and he'll want to give us Charley's killer in exchange for a walk."

"That often happens," Dino agreed.

"I guess," Stone said.

30

That evening Stone drove slowly to Annika's house, taking in Key West as he went. He felt oddly let down, having concluded his business with Evan Keating. He had no real purpose in Key West now, and he thought he might as well head home the next day. His business with Annika Swenson, however, did not seem to be concluded, and he was beginning to wonder if her idea of moving to New York mightn't be a good one. As long as he paced himself.

The front door was open, and the sounds of good jazz wafted from somewhere in the house. "Hello!" he called out.

"Hello! I'm in the kitchen!" she shouted back.

He found her there, stirring something in a pot,

wearing a wraparound apron. "Smells good," he said. "What are you cooking?"

"A venison ragout," she replied.

"And where would you find venison in Key West? I hope you didn't go out and shoot one of those lovely little Key deer; they're protected, you know."

"Of course not; I got it on the Internet, like anything else. You want Japanese blowfish? You want Iranian caviar? It's all on the Internet, for delivery the next day."

"I never thought of the Internet for food."

"Oh, you can order all your groceries on the Internet," she said. "The freshest foods, all delivered to your door."

"I wonder if you could order a hit man on the Internet," he mused.

"What?"

"A hit man, an assassin."

"Oh, I'm sure. I'll bet there's a Web site called hit man dot com or something."

"If there is, you can be sure it's operated by the FBI or a police department."

"Why?"

"Don't you see all these news stories on TV where somebody, a husband or wife usually, tries to hire a hit man to off the spouse, and he turns out to be a cop?"

"Yes, I have seen that story, now that you mention it. How can people be so stupid?"

"What's stupid is trying to murder someone," Stone said. "Even if you got lucky and found a competent pro, it would always come back to bite you on the ass."

"How do you mean?"

"I mean that people in jail solve an inordinate number of homicides."

"How do they do that?"

"Let's say you want to have me knocked off . . ."

"Knocked off what?"

"Knocked off my perch, capped, murdered."

"Okay, let's say."

"Let's say you wander into the right bar and somebody offers to buy you a drink, and the evening passes and you learn that this guy is willing to do unusual work for a price. You hire him to kill me . . ."

"How much would that be?"

"Almost anything: five hundred, ten thousand, whatever the traffic will bear."

"Traffic?"

"The free market."

"Okay, I hire him to kill you, then what?"

"Then he kills me. He hangs around outside my house until I get home; then he shoots me and runs, gets away with it. You pay him off, and he's happy, you're happy."

"But you're not happy."

"No, I'm not happy, I'm dead. Then some time

passes—a year or two or five—and your hit man gets arrested on a completely unrelated charge."

"Unrelated to what?"

"Unrelated to making me dead. Let's say he gets caught trying to rob a liquor store, or maybe he makes a deal to kill somebody else, but the dealmaker is a cop."

"Okay, let's say."

"So they've got him down at the police station, and they convince him that they've got him dead to rights, that they have all the evidence necessary to send him to prison for many years. But suddenly he says, 'What if I could solve a bigger crime for you? A murder, maybe? Remember a guy named Barrington who was shot outside his house a few years back? I could give you the murderer, if you'll give me immunity from prosecution.'"

"Prosecution for what?"

"For any crime he has committed."

"The police will do that?"

"They do it all the time. They'll say, 'Okay, you've got immunity; who killed Barrington?' 'I did,' he'll say, 'but Swenson hired me to do it; I was only a tool.' And they can't prosecute him. They can prosecute you, though."

"They would do that?"

"Of course. All over the world, in every society, the greatest taboo of all is murder. We place a very high value on human life—that's why we devote so much of our police resources to solving murders. That's why there's no statute of limitations. Once you've murdered someone—or paid to have someone murdered—you're never safe again. They can always come and get you when the evidence turns up."

"Well, that is very sobering," Annika said. "Perhaps I won't have you killed after all. What if I fuck you to death? Can they get me for that?"

Stone laughed. "Only if they could prove you intended to kill me, that maybe I had a heart condition and you knew I couldn't stand the strain."

"But not if I were just fucking you for several hours and you finally, ah, turned up your toes, I believe the expression is?"

"Annika, I think you've found a way to commit the perfect murder."

"Well," she said, taking off her wraparound apron and revealing herself to be naked from the waist down, "let's get started now, and I can finish killing you after dinner, for dessert."

And she nearly did. Much later Stone was lying in the fetal position, trying not to whimper, when his cell phone vibrated on the bedside table. "Humpf," he managed to say.

"It's Dino."

"Who else?" Stone responded weakly.

"Take a couple of breaths and see if you can generate some adrenaline," Dino said.

Stone did not take this advice. "I'm listening," he said.

"Tommy called. Evan Keating is in the hospital; he's been shot."

Stone sat up on the side of the bed. "How bad?"

"I don't know. Pick me up at the hotel in ten minutes; we'll go together."

"Right." Stone closed the phone and looked at the sleeping Annika. It was just as well he got out before she woke up.

31

Dino was standing out in front of the Marquesa when Stone drove up. Following Tommy's directions, they drove up to Stock Island and found the hospital. A hint of dawn was in the eastern sky.

Stone asked for Evan at the admitting desk.

"Are you a relative?" she asked.

"I'm his attorney," Stone lied. "He asked for me."

Tommy came out of a room down the hall and waved them in.

"Oh, go ahead," the woman said.

Stone and Dino walked down the hall and stopped outside the room. "How is he?"

"He seems to be resting comfortably," Tommy replied, "since the painkillers kicked in."

"How bad?"

"He took it through the left shoulder. Somehow the angle allowed the slug to miss the heart and lung. He's stable."

"What kind of weapon?"

"Looks like a .223."

"Sniper?"

"He was sitting in the cockpit of his boat with the Gigi dame, anchored off Key West Bight, having a late drink. The shot probably came from the shore, near one of the big hotels."

"Telescopic sight?"

"We found the weapon in some bushes: M16 assault rifle, well used. The sort of thing you'd find at a gun show."

"Sounds like a pro. Anybody get a look at him?"

"Nope. Gigi emptied a nine-millimeter magazine in the general direction, scaring the hell out of everybody. I'm sure the guy looks like every other tourist in Key West. I mean, he wasn't dressed all in black or wearing camos."

"You think he's still on the island?"

"We've alerted the state cops and the locals along Route One North, but more than likely he flew in, rented a car or scooter, and he'll leave tomorrow the same way, along with five hundred other visitors. If we had the man-power to interview every one of them, we might be able to narrow it to a dozen, but of course we don't. He'll walk."

"Or stay around for another shot?"

"Who knows?"

"People who hire hit men don't pay for near misses," Dino said. "If he feels safe, he'll try again. He might be in this hospital right now."

"I'll put a uniform on the door until they discharge him in the morning," Tommy said. "Is there anybody to call?"

"I'm sure the shooter has already called Evan's father," Stone said wryly. "I'll see that his grandfather hears about it. Can I see him?"

"It's okay with me. Gigi's with him, so watch your back."

"That'll be Dino's job." Stone knocked on the door, got a response and walked in, with Dino following. Evan was sitting with the bed cranked up, and Gigi was holding his hand.

"Good evening," Evan said.

"Morning," Stone replied. "How are you feeling?"

"Just swell," Evan replied wanly. "Never better."

"I hope you've reconsidered your position on relocating," Stone said.

"Yes, but not just yet. I have some business to conclude. When do you plan to return to New York?"

"Soon. There's nothing to keep me here now."

"I'd like to keep you here for a few days," Evan said. "I want to retain you as my attorney."

"I'm not licensed in Florida," Stone said.

"It won't require any courtroom appearances," Evan said. "Or if it does, I'll hire somebody else. I want you here for a negotiation. I'll pay you thirty thousand dollars for three, four days of your time. If it runs beyond that, I'll pay you another thirty."

Stone looked at Dino. "Can you hang around? I'll pick up the hotel bill."

"Why not?" Dino said.

"All right."

"Gigi," Evan said.

Gigi picked up a shoulder bag that had been lying on the floor beside the bed, rummaged in it and came up with a stack of notes and handed it to Stone. It was three bundles of hundreds, in South Beach Security wrappers.

"Is this money clean?" Stone asked.

"It is."

"I'll have to fill out the relevant federal form when I deposit it in my bank."

"I understand."

"What do you want me to do now?" Stone asked.

"I've got your cell number. I'll call you when we need to talk."

"Have you spoken to your grandfather?"

"Not yet."

"If you like, I'll have someone notify him about this."

"No, it would just worry him. He's better off not knowing. I'll tell him about it when this is over."

"And when will that be?"

"Soon, I hope."

"All right," Stone said, stuffing bundles of cash into his pockets. "I'm your lawyer. If the police ask you any more questions of any kind, refer them to me. Talk to you later." He and Dino left the room.

Tommy was standing outside talking to a uniformed officer.

Stone took him aside. "Tommy, Evan has just retained me as his lawyer. I'm not entirely sure why, but in the meantime, please don't ask him any more questions unless I'm present."

"What's the problem?" Tommy asked. "He hasn't done anything."

"I know, but in his condition I can't go into all this with him. I assume you have both Evan's and Gigi's statements about the shooting?"

"Yeah."

"That'll have to do you for the moment. I'll know more when I've had a chance to sit down with him when his head is clear."

"Okay, Stone."

"Thanks for having a cop out here."

"Don't mention it."

Stone and Dino left the hospital and went back to their car.

"There's an IHOP on our way back; you want to get some breakfast?"

"Sure."

"You're buying," Dino said.

32

Stone sat thinking, picking at his enormous break-fast. Dino, untroubled, was stuffing his down.

"All right," Dino said, pausing for a sip of coffee, "what's on your mind?"

"Doesn't it bother you that it was real hard for us to find Evan in Key West, but an assassin found him from a standing start in less than twenty-four hours?"

"It's certainly interesting."

"I mean, you and I were pretty good cops, weren't we?"

"I still am. I'm not so sure about you."

"Tommy bothers me, too."

"Tommy?"

"A cop like Tommy in a town this size ought to know everybody moving, but he had a hard time with Evan."

"Have you forgotten that Tommy put a finger on Evan five seconds after you mentioned his name? At the Marquesa restaurant?"

"Oh, yeah. I take it back."

"And he's been nothing but helpful ever since."

"You're right; Tommy's a great guy, and he's been nothing but helpful. My mind's a little fuzzy, that's all. Lack of sleep."

"Too much sex," Dino said. "It always wears you down."

"It does not," Stone protested. "I thrive on it."

"You've been eating like a pig ever since we got here. Gained any weight?"

"I don't know."

"I'd say you've lost a couple of pounds," Dino said. "It's the Swede; she's sapping your life force."

"Nonsense."

"Otherwise, why would you let Evan Keating hire you in about a second?"

"An excuse to stay here for a few days. The money's good, too."

"It smells funny," Dino said, and he took a big bite of an English muffin.

"Why do you think that?"

"What could he possibly have for you to negotiate?"

"I don't know. Maybe he's buying a house or something."

"He'd hire Jack Spottswood if he were buying a

house, or somebody else local who knows the market. You'd be useless."

"I can read a contract."

"But what's to negotiate? And why the hell isn't Evan getting his ass out of Key West? He didn't go when you warned him, and now he's been shot, nearly killed, and he's still hanging around. It doesn't make any sense."

"I guess he has some unfinished business."

"The guy is in line for whatever a third of eight hundred million bucks is, and he's got business in Key West? What does he need with business here?"

"All right, it's screwy. I'll give you that."

"Gee, thanks."

"It's also intriguing, and I want to see how it plays out."

"Well, while it's playing out, I hope you don't end up between Evan and whoever took that shot. From what Tommy says, it was a damn fine shot, and if the guy left the rifle there, it only means that he's got something else to shoot with."

"I like the private airplane thing," Stone said.

"It's one way to travel."

"It's an ideal way to travel, if you don't want your luggage X-rayed or searched," Stone pointed out. "After all, it's how you and I got here armed."

Dino stuffed the last piece of sausage in his mouth. "Okay, you want to go to the airport, right?"

"Right."

"Then let's do it; we'll sleep later."

Stone and Dino walked into Island City Flying Service, the fixed base operator for private aircraft at Key West International. Stone could see his own airplane through the window. They found Paul DePoo, who ran the place, and introduced themselves.

"What can I do for you?" DePoo asked.

"Can I see a list of all the private airplanes that've landed here in the past twenty-four hours?" Stone asked.

DePoo handed him a clipboard that held two sheets of paper. "That's yesterday's landings," he said. "We haven't had anything today yet; it's still early."

Stone looked through the list slowly, eliminating the jets and big twins.

"What are you looking for?"

"One guy in a light aircraft, probably a single, some luggage, maybe something like a shotgun case."

"Nobody comes to Key West to hunt," DePoo said.

"Then a shotgun or rifle case would make him stand out, wouldn't it?"

DePoo picked up a phone and punched in an extension. "You see anybody come in here from an airplane yesterday carrying something like a rifle or shotgun case?" He laughed. "You're kidding! What's the tail number?" He jotted something down and hung up. "How about that? There was such a guy." He ran a finger down the list on the clipboard. "There's his tail number; he's one Ted Larson, from Fort Lauderdale."

Stone looked at the clipboard. "Can you access the FAA list of registered aircraft from your computer?"

"Sure," DePoo said. He went to the Web site and typed in the tail number. "Cessna 182 RG, 1984 vintage, registered to a Frank G. Harmon, Sarasota."

"Can we take a look at it?" Stone asked.

DePoo looked at the clipboard. "We hangared it for him, come on." He got up and led Stone and Dino out of the building and across the tarmac to a big hangar containing half a dozen airplanes of different types.

"That's it," Dino said, pointing to a red Cessna parked in a corner, behind two other airplanes.

The three men approached the airplane.

"Nice paint," DePoo said. "Couldn't be more than a year old."

Stone looked in the pilot's window. "Nice interior, too—all leather. Hey, nice panel!"

"Glass cockpit," DePoo said. "You don't see that on old Cessnas. This guy has spent a hundred and fifty grand on a twenty-five-year-old airplane."

"Yeah," Stone said, "but even if he stripped it and replaced the engine and everything else, he probably only has two-fifty or three hundred in it, and a new one would cost, what, double that?"

"About that," DePoo said.

"Does your clipboard say when he plans to leave?"

"Ten o'clock this morning."

Dino was looking through the window into the rear seat. "Have a look at this," he said.

Stone looked through the window and saw an aluminum briefcase on the rear floor. "He could get four guns in there."

"And a silencer or two as well," Dino said.

"Hey, you guys," DePoo said, "are you cops?"

"He is," Stone said, jerking a thumb at Dino, "and I used to be, but we're going to need some local talent for this. Dino, will you call Tommy and tell him we think we've got a lock on his shooter." Stone tried the airplane door, but it was locked. "I don't suppose you've got a Cessna passkey?"

DePoo shook his head. "No, and I'm not in the habit of breaking into customers' airplanes."

"I understand," Stone said. "Let's wait for the local cops."

33

They hung around the hangar looking at airplanes for the half hour it took Tommy to get there.

"What's up?" he asked.

Stone crooked a finger. "This way." He led Tommy to the corner of the hangar and the bright red Cessna. "The guy who flew this in yesterday carried a shotgun or rifle case and gave a name different from the registered owner of the airplane. Also, if you'll cast your eye toward the rear floor, there's an aluminum case commonly used to carry handguns."

"Okay," Tommy said, "now what?"

"I don't know. I just thought you might like to get a search warrant."

"On what evidence?" Tommy asked. "The guy hasn't done anything illegal."

"Maybe he stole the airplane, since it isn't registered in his name, which he gave as Ted Larson, of Fort Lauderdale. The registered owner is one Frank G. Harmon, of Sarasota."

"Maybe he borrowed it or rented it."

"This airplane has had a ton of money spent on it; it's not the kind of thing an owner would lend to a friend, let alone rent out."

"Come on, Stone, how many times have you stood in front of a judge and been told to take a hike? I don't like to do that around here, because I get the same judge or two every time I go for a warrant, and I want to protect my reputation for having real evidence."

"Tommy, you've got an assassin in your town."

"Yeah, and if I arrest him, I want to get a conviction, not get the case thrown out for an illegal search."

"He's scheduled to leave at ten this morning," Stone said. "You want to stick around and see what he has to say for himself?"

"Sure, I'll do that."

"You fellows want some coffee?" Paul DePoo asked.

"Sure, why not?"

"Tell you what," Paul said, "I won't pull his airplane out of the hangar; that'll delay him for half an hour while we move the two others blocking him."

They all walked back into the air-conditioned building and got coffee.

193

"Are you guys always this lucky?" Tommy asked. "'Cause I'm not. You stroll into an airport hangar a few hours after a shooting and find a guy who landed with a rifle case and a handgun case in his backseat? That never happens to me."

"Then you're not working hard enough, Tommy," Dino said. "I find that the harder I work, the luckier I get."

"Just how much work have you done this morning, Dino? You and Stone had a chat over breakfast and decided to amble out here? That kind of work?"

"There's a certain amount of instinct involved, too," Dino said, blandly.

Tommy burst out laughing. "It's a pity vaudeville is dead," he said. "You'd make a great duo on the stage."

"I didn't say anything," Stone pointed out.

"You didn't need to; I was supplying all the straight lines."

DePoo's desk phone rang. "Yes? Did he mention what hotel he's in? Okay, thanks." He hung up. "This Ted Larson, or whoever he is, just called and said he'd be staying a day or two longer."

"Please ask her to describe the man," Stone said.

DePoo called back to the desk, asked and hung up. "White guy, middle-aged, medium height and weight, wearing a yellow baseball cap."

"Well," Tommy said, "I choose not to wait for him

to show up or to institute a manhunt for a guy answering that description. Paul, will you call me the minute he shows up?"

"Sure," DePoo answered. He wrote down Tommy's cell number.

"Take mine, too," Stone said, handing him a card.

The three men walked outside to the parking lot.

"You two sticking around?" Tommy asked.

"Yeah, for a few days," Stone said.

"You really think you're onto something here?"

"Well, I guess we'll have to wait until Evan Keating gets shot at again before we'll know for sure. I hope he doesn't get dead in the process."

"I'd put a police guard on him, if he didn't have the lovely Gigi to watch his back," Tommy said.

"At least she knows how to shoot back," Dino said.

"Tommy," Stone said, "do you know if Evan is being discharged this morning?"

"Looks like he's going to be there another day," Tommy replied. "Apparently, he's running a fever, and they've got him on intravenous antibiotics. Best guess now is tomorrow. My uniformed guy is still on him, though, so he'll be okay."

"See you later, then," Stone said, and they went to their respective cars.

"So you want to go looking for Ted Larson or Frank Harmon or whatever his name is?"

"What's the point? If I were a hit man, I'd fly in here and give a false name, then register in a hotel under another false name and give anybody I met another false name."

"I'm glad he doesn't know who we are," Dino said.

34

Stone and Dino went back to the Marquesa, and Stone got into a shower, thinking about the events of that morning. When he came out onto the porch, Dino was at the pool with a vividly colored drink in his hand, chatting with two young women. Stone was about to join him when his cell phone buzzed.

"Hello?"

"It's Eggers."

"Good morning. How's it going up there? And by 'up there' I mean Connecticut."

"Well, let's see: Eli has filed a lawsuit against Warren Keating, asking that he be barred from any participation in the sale of the company and that the disposition of the proceeds be put in Eli's hands. That ought to keep

Warren busy for a while, I guess. What's going on down there?"

"Warren has been busier than you think. The day before yesterday he apparently called a Miami PI of my acquaintance and inquired about having some slightly illegal work done."

"What kind of slightly illegal work?"

"My acquaintance hung up on him before he could spit it all out, but the trend of the conversation seemed toward the hiring of somebody to kill his son."

"C'mon, Warren's not that stupid."

"No? He's not only stupid but fast-acting. Last night Evan Keating was shot while sitting in his boat, anchored off Key West."

Eggers made an odd noise.

"That was pretty much my reaction, too."

"Is he dead?"

"No, just shot through a shoulder. He's in the local hospital under police guard, in case the hit guy tries again. He should be out tomorrow, if his fever goes away."

"I'm having a pretty hard time getting my mind around this," Eggers said. "I can't believe Warren is that evil."

"You can't? The man is under suspicion for having murdered his brother by poisoning, he locked up his healthy father in a nursing home on phony grounds, and he's tried to cheat both his father and his son out of their rightful share of the proceeds of the business sale. Isn't that evil enough for you?"

"Okay, I'll admit it. I misjudged the man. Even when I was prying Eli out of that home, I never thought Warren had poisoned his brother, but now I've reconsidered. I think I should go to the police."

"I understand the Connecticut State Police are already investigating him, and I'm sure they'll get around to you eventually. Just sit tight."

"Are you coming back to New York soon?"

"No, not for a few days. Evan has hired me."

"For what?"

"He says for a negotiation, but I have no idea what that means. I intend to ask him again as soon as he's out of the hospital."

"Well, I guess we're enough legally clear of Warren for that to be all right."

"I'm glad to hear it," Stone said.

"Can you find out how the investigation of Warren is going?" Eggers asked. "You seem to have an in."

"I'll ask questions of somebody who can ask questions, that's all I can do."

"Keep me posted," Eggers said; then he hung up.

Stone strolled over to where Dino was sitting. "Sorry to interrupt," he said, "but can you call your guy in Connecticut and find out what's happening?"

"I guess," Dino said. "Excuse me a minute, ladies."

The girls tittered and wandered away.

Dino dialed the number and put his phone on speaker.

"Robbery Homicide."

"Lieutenant Dan Hotchkiss, please."

"This is Lieutenant Hotchkiss."

"Hey, Dan, it's Dino."

"I could have predicted that."

"What did you find out about the Warren Keating thing?"

"I found out that it's hard to analyze the ashes of a corpse for traces of poison."

"You ever heard that tale about there being three common household substances—or maybe it's two—that, when combined, make an unanalyzable poison?"

"Dino, how am I going to look for an unanalyzable poison?"

"You can get a search warrant for Keating's house and look for the ingredients."

"What are the ingredients?"

"I told you, two or three common household substances."

"You're a big fucking help, Dino."

"Well, the people who know about these things don't like to mention the names of the substances, for fear of setting off a nationwide epidemic of dead husbands, but Warren Keating has a chemistry degree, and you know what college kids are like: Something of that sort would be talked about in lab classes."

"So what do I do, ask a college chemistry major?"

"Why don't you ask the FBI lab? If anybody knows about this poison, they would."

"Okay, say I call the FBI lab, or get somebody at our lab to do it, and they tell me that the three secret ingredients are toilet cleaner, bug spray and a decent Scotch. Half the people in the state have those things in their houses, so they'd be just as good for the crime as Warren Keating, wouldn't they?"

"Dan . . ."

"You think a judge, a sober one anyway, would give me a warrant to search for those three items? I'll bet the judge has them at home, too."

"I take your point, Dan. Now, can you tell me what, if anything, is being done in this investigation?"

"Right now, it's in the hands of the lab, and they won't give me an ETA for their results."

"They've probably laid it off on the FBI lab, anyway," Dino said.

"I wouldn't be surprised. Anything else, before I go back to fighting crime?"

"There has been a development. Warren Keating may have hired a hit man to kill his son."

"Have you got anything more than three secret ingredients to back that up?"

"Well, his son is in a Key West hospital with a bullet wound to the shoulder."

"That's certainly an interesting development, Dino, but how do I tie that to Warren?"

"A guy with a New England accent, like Warren's, called a Miami PI I know and made inquiries."

"Did the PI recommend anybody?"

"No, he hung up when he saw which way the conversation was leading."

"I'm really happy that the crime is out of my jurisdiction, Dino. Let me know if something happens that I can actually arrest Warren Keating for." Hotchkiss hung up.

Dino turned to Stone. "For this kind of abuse, I lose the company of two attractive women?"

35

Stone had become accustomed to being awakened in the mornings by his cell phone while in Dr. Annika Swenson's bed, and this morning was no exception.

"Hello?"

"Stone? It's your client, Evan Keating."

Stone looked at the clock. Seven a.m. "Good morning, Evan. You're up early."

"Aren't you?"

"Not exactly."

"I'm being discharged from this place at ten o'clock this morning. Can you pick me up here and take me to police headquarters?"

"I suppose so, but why do you want to go to police headquarters?"

"I'll explain that when we're on the way. Will you

make an appointment with Lieutenant Sculley and ask him to have a representative of the district attorney there, too?"

"Why do we need the DA there?"

"Again, I'll explain on the way. Just tell him I'm going to solve Charley Boggs's murder for him. And when you come here, there's a second entrance, two doors beyond the emergency room. Please meet me there at ten sharp."

"All right, Evan. See you then." Stone hung up and, with nothing to do until nine, when Tommy Sculley would be at work, he turned his attention to Annika, who was lying on her stomach, pretending to sleep. He ran a finger lightly down the crack of her ass.

"Mmmmm," she said.

"You're not asleep, are you?"

"Nooooo."

He deployed the finger again.

"More," she said.

He could deny her nothing.

Shortly after nine, after finishing breakfast, he phoned Tommy Sculley.

"Lieutenant Sculley."

"Tommy, it's Stone Barrington."

"Good morning, Stone, and what request do you have for me today?"

"Only a request for a meeting with you and somebody from the DA's office."

"For what purpose?"

"My client says he can solve the Charley Boggs murder for you."

"Which client?"

"I have only one in Key West."

"Well, that's very decent of him. What evidence does he have?"

"He has not yet informed me. I'm picking him up at the hospital at ten o'clock, so we can be there shortly after that."

"Hang on a second." Tommy put him on hold and came back two minutes later. "Okay, the assistant county attorney, Jim Rawlings, will be here. In my office."

"Thank you, Tommy. See you then." Stone hung up, thinking this must have something to do with some drug deal that Evan and Charley had collaborated on.

Stone pulled up to the specified hospital door at ten o'clock, and Evan stepped out, his left arm in a sling, looked around furtively and got into Stone's car.

Stone drove away. "Evan, let me give you a tip: When you're leaving a building while worried about being shot at, don't pause and look around; just dive into the car."

"Thanks, that's a good tip," Evan said.

"How are you feeling?"

"A little sore, but the drugs are good."

"Temperature gone?"

"Yes, my head is clear."

"Good. We have a meeting with Tommy Sculley and Jim Rawlings, the assistant county attorney. Now perhaps you can tell me why you want the meeting?"

"I'm going to solve Charley Boggs's homicide for them."

"Yes, you mentioned that. How do you plan to do it?"

"You'll find out at the same moment they do, Stone. What I want you to do is to negotiate an immunity agreement for Gigi and me with the county attorney before I tell them."

"What do you wish to be immune from?"

"Prosecution for any crime or knowledge of a crime committed in the state of Florida."

"That's kind of broad, isn't it? Why don't we narrow it down to the specific circumstances?"

"I like the idea of broad," Evan said. "And remember, it has to include Gigi, too."

"Why Gigi?"

"Stone . . ."

"I know, I know. I'll find out when you tell them."

"Yes. I just want a clear and enforceable understanding with the prosecutor, before I tell them what I have to tell them."

"And speaking of the lovely Gigi, where is she?"

"Grocery shopping for the boat. I don't want her included in this meeting."

"Just in the immunity agreement?"

"Exactly."

"Evan, tell me why you think they will agree to give you immunity from all crimes? After all, you could have robbed a few banks or something."

"I haven't robbed any banks. They'll give me the agreement because it's the only way they can solve Charley's homicide."

"How can you be sure of that?"

"Trust me, Stone. All will be revealed after we have the immunity agreement."

Stone sighed and continued to drive. They reached police headquarters and parked the car and Stone hurriedly walked Evan inside.

"Don't worry about my being shot," Evan said. "That problem is going to go away after this meeting."

Stone stopped and faced Evan. "Listen to me. If I'm going to effectively represent you in this meeting, I'm going to have to know in advance of it what you're going to say."

"You don't need to know that, Stone," Evan replied. "All you need is the immunity agreement."

Stone threw up his hands and got on the elevator. "I warn you, you could get into trouble by not confiding in your lawyer."

"No," Evan replied, "I won't."

Stone checked in with the receptionist, and he and Evan were directed to a small, glassed-in conference room across the hall from Tommy's office. The two men stood up to greet them, Tommy made the introductions, and they all sat down.

"Now," Tommy said, "what's this about solving the Boggs killing?"

Stone held up a hand. "First, Tommy, Jim, we're going to need immunity for Evan and his girlfriend, Gigi Jones."

"Immunity from what?"

"From any possible criminal involvement in any crime."

"Hang on," Rawlings said. "From *any* involvement in *any* crime?"

"That's what my client needs to feel comfortable discussing the homicide with you."

"I don't know about that," Rawlings said. "Will you excuse us for a moment?"

"Of course," Stone replied. He and Evan walked out of the office and took chairs in the hall. They could see Tommy and Rawlings arguing. Arms were being waved. Finally, they were told to come back into the conference room.

"All right," Rawlings said, "I'll offer immunity from prosecution for any crime associated with the death of Charley Boggs. That's the best I can do."

"All right," Evan said.

"We're going to need that in writing," Stone said.

Evan interrupted. "That won't be necessary, Stone. I trust Mr. Rawlings and Lieutenant Sculley."

"Evan . . ."

"I'm ready to speak on this subject," Evan said.

Stone shrugged. "All right, but remember, Mr. Rawlings, I'm holding you to this agreement, and Tommy is a witness."

"Yeah, I'm a witness," Tommy said. "Now spit it out, Mr. Keating."

And Evan spat it out.

36

Evan Keating regarded the two men across the table calmly. "Charley Boggs is not dead," he said.

Rawlings looked at Stone. "For this we came? The guy is still alive?"

"Wait a minute," Tommy Sculley said. "I have the feeling there's more. Go on, Evan."

"I'm Charley Boggs," Evan said.

Tommy screwed up his face. "*You're* Charley Boggs?"

"Yes."

"Then who was the guy we found floating in Garrison Bight?"

"That was Evan Keating."

Stone decided to keep his mouth shut, since he was as baffled as everybody else.

"Let's see some ID," Tommy said.

"My ID was in Evan's pocket," the new Charley Boggs said. "Do you still have it?"

"No," Tommy said, "it was sent to his parents."

"Then I'm afraid I can't help you with ID; I only have Evan's."

"Mr. Keating," Rawlings said. "I'm sorry, Mr. Boggs. Who killed Char . . . Evan Keating?"

"I did," Charley said.

"Why?"

"It was self-defense. I'm sorry. I mean it was in defense of another's life."

"Whose life?" Tommy asked.

"Gigi's. Evan was about to kill her, and I shot him in the head. I was afraid that if I shot him anywhere else, his gun would go off."

"We found Charley's gun," Tommy said. "I mean your gun. Whosever gun it was who lived in the boathouse. It hadn't been fired."

"Evan's gun," Charley said. "He had two of them. I shot him with the other one."

"And where is the other one?"

"I ditched it in the sea, off Key West."

"Can you point out the spot?"

"I don't think so; it was a dark night."

"Why did . . . the other guy want to kill Gigi?"

"Because Gigi had stolen his drugs from a hiding place in the wheelhouse of his boat. Oh, and some from his motorcycle, too."

"And what did Gigi do with the drugs?"

"I dropped them into the sea, along with Evan's gun."

"How much drugs?"

"I'm not sure; seven or eight bags, I think. I didn't want to be involved in the drug business, so I got rid of the stuff."

Tommy picked up a phone and dialed an extension. "Bring me a fingerprint kit," he said.

A moment later a female officer came into the conference room and fingerprinted Charley, while the others watched silently. She finished, and Charley went into an adjoining bathroom to wash his hands.

"We have an earlier set of prints on Evan Keating," Tommy said to the woman. "Bring them to me, please."

She left, and Charley returned and sat down.

"Tell me how you got to be Charley and the other guy got to be Evan," Tommy said.

"Evan and I traded places nearly a year ago. I knew my father would try to find me at some stage, and I didn't want that to happen, and Evan didn't want to hear from his father, either. We did it to confuse anybody who might be looking for us."

Tommy seemed to run out of questions. Then the woman returned with the two fingerprint cards. Tommy examined them both with a loupe. "These two sets of prints are identical," Tommy said to Charley. "You're Evan Keating."

"No, I'm Charley Boggs; the card just has Evan's name on it instead of mine. We did that when your people picked us up a couple of weeks ago."

Tommy looked at the female officer. "Get me the prints of Charley Boggs we took from his corpse."

She went away.

"Stone," Tommy said, "do you have anything to say about this?"

"Not a thing," Stone said. "This is as much a surprise to me as it is to you. Evan—sorry, Charley—refused to tell me anything he was going to say when we were on the way here, except that he was going to clear up the Charley Boggs homicide, and I guess he's done that."

The woman came back. "We didn't take prints from the Boggs corpse," she said. "The body was identified by two people."

"Who?"

"The woman who lived on the houseboat next to Boggs's."

"And the other one?"

"That would be you."

"Thanks, that'll be all," Tommy said. "Wait a minute. Go pull the Florida driver's license photos of Charley Boggs and Evan Keating."

She left again.

"Lieutenant Sculley," Charley said, "I think I should tell you that Evan and I strongly resembled each other, before he grew the beard. In school, most people thought we were brothers. Once, we even attended each other's classes for a day, and nobody noticed."

The woman came back with the two photos, and Tommy and Rawlings looked at them.

"May I see them?" Stone asked, and Tommy pushed them across the table. Stone looked at the two photos. "Damned if he isn't right; I might be able to tell them apart if they were sitting next to each other, but not if I saw them in different places."

Rawlings was shaking his head. "I don't know what to make of this," he said.

"Gentlemen," Stone said, "it appears that no crime has been committed here, so will there be anything else?"

Tommy and Rawlings looked at each other, and Rawlings shook his head.

"I guess not," Tommy said.

"Well, then," Stone said, "if you'll excuse us." He stood up, and so did the new Charley Boggs. "Please send the completed immunity agreement to me at the Marquesa today." Rawlings nodded. Stone half expected to be stopped, but he and Charley walked out of the building unmolested and got into Stone's car.

"Well," Stone said, "that was the damnedest thing I've ever seen in my law practice."

"I guess it was kind of strange," Charley said. "Thanks for negotiating the immunity agreement. It's a load off my mind, and it will be for Gigi, too."

"I'm going to assume you told them the truth," Stone said, "and if you didn't, I don't want to know."

"Of course not," Charley said, "you're a lawyer."

"Where to?"

"The Marquesa; I took your advice."

Stone drove there and parked the car in the guest garage.

"Oh," Charley said, "I almost forgot."

"What?"

"Will you get word to Warren Keating that Evan is dead? I'd like his man to stop shooting at me."

37

Stone walked back to his cottage and watched Charley Boggs walk to his own, directly opposite. Gigi was waiting for him on the front porch, and she stood up to kiss him, laughing when he apparently told her the news.

Dino was sitting on their porch, rocking. "What's going on?"

Stone got out his cell phone. "I may as well tell you and Eggers at the same time," he said, pressing the speed-dial number and the speaker button.

Eggers answered, and Stone gave him a blow-by-blow account of the meeting. Eggers was silent.

"Bill?" Stone said.

"I'm still here. At least, I think I'm still here. I'm feeling a little disoriented."

"I know the feeling," Stone said. "Are you in touch with Warren Keating at all?"

"I've spoken to his attorney a couple of times. There was a lot of shouting."

"I think you'd better give the attorney the news, so that he can transmit it to his client. Charley Boggs wants Warren to stop trying to kill him."

"I can understand that," Eggers said.

"Sooner, rather than later, please."

"I'll call him now."

"Thanks, Bill."

"You coming back to New York now?"

"In a couple of days, maybe. I want to see what it's like in Key West when I don't have anything to worry about."

"Bye, then." Eggers hung up.

Stone turned to Dino. "Any questions?"

"Seems like all my questions have been answered," Dino said. "All that I can think of at the moment, anyway."

Stone got a soda out of his refrigerator and sat on the porch, sipping it. "I feel kind of let down," he said.

"Not me," Dino said. "I feel just great."

A young man came down the path and stopped at their porch. "Is one of you Mr. Stone Barrington?"

"I'm Barrington," Stone said.

"I have a letter for you from the county attorney's office," the man said, holding out an envelope.

Stone pointed at the cottage across the way. "See that cottage?"

"Yessir."

"Knock on the door and give the letter to Mr. Boggs; he's expecting it."

"Okay." The young man did as he was told, and Charley Boggs received the letter. He opened it, read it, waved at Stone and went back inside.

"Business concluded," Stone said.

"It's not too early for a drink, is it?" Dino asked.

"Of course it's too early. Let's go to the Raw Bar and get some conch fritters."

"I'm game," Dino said.

They were halfway through their fritters when Dino broke the silence. "There's something I don't under-stand," he said.

"Tell me," Stone replied.

"What did these two guys get out of switching identities?"

"They made it harder for their respective fathers to find them."

"My recollection, from what Tommy said, was that Charley's father's response to being told his son was dead was that he wasn't surprised, that he'd thought he might be already dead."

"Yeah, that's what Tommy said the elder Mr. Boggs said."

"Which means that Charley Boggs's old man wasn't looking for him."

"Yeah, I guess you're right."

"So what's in it for him to switch identities with Evan?"

"I've got two answers for you: the first, not much; the second, maybe Charley was just doing Evan a favor. After all, we know that Evan's father was looking for him, because he hired Manny White and me to find him, and Evan and Charley had been close friends since prep school, so it's the sort of thing one friend might do for the other."

"Yeah, okay," Dino said, "but I think there's another reason we don't know about."

"What's that?" Stone asked.

"I don't know. We don't know about it. I just think there's more to this story than we've been told."

Another voice spoke. "That's what I think."

Stone looked up to see Tommy Sculley standing next to the table. He shoved onto the bench next to Dino.

"I'm willing to believe that," Stone said. "But from my point of view, I know all I need to know. So do you, Tommy. You cleared a homicide, and you know what happened to Charley's—excuse me, Evan's drugs. Aren't you happy?"

"No," Tommy said, "and I don't know why. Did Charley ask you to let Evan's old man know he's dead?"

"Yes, he did, and for a very good reason: He wants Warren Keating to stop trying to kill him."

"That's what I figured," Tommy said. "That's a good reason, also, for him to come in today and tell his story."

"Yeah, I guess so. But he didn't have to do that; he wasn't a suspect, was he?"

"No."

"So he could have gone right on being Evan Keating, if he'd wanted to."

"Yeah, I guess he could have. And gone right on getting shot at. Doesn't it bother you guys that this all wrapped up so neatly?"

"I like it when things wrap up neatly," Dino said. "It's just that they never do."

"Sure they do," Stone said. "Sometimes. All right, rarely."

"There are always loose ends," Tommy said. "Only this time, there aren't."

The three men sat and contemplated that in silence.

"You're a troublemaker, Tommy," Stone said.

"Sorry about that; I'm just not satisfied."

"Try this," Stone said. "If you find out Evan—ah, Charley—did commit some other crime associated with the murder, Rawlings has already given him immunity for it, so there's nothing you can do, anyway."

"Yeah, that's very clever of what's-his-name," Tommy said. "I think Rawlings and I were snookered."

"Now, wait a minute, Tommy. I haven't snookered anybody. I didn't know what Ev . . . what's-his-name was going to say until I heard him tell you."

"I believe you, Stone. That means you've been snookered, too. Doesn't that bother you?"

"It would," Stone said, "if I *knew* I had been snookered, but I don't know that."

"Well," Tommy said, "when you find out you've been snookered, would you let me know how?" He got up and left, without waiting for an answer.

38

Stone spent yet another happily exhausting night with Dr. Annika Swenson but got up early and returned to the Marquesa for breakfast with Dino, who was already having his on the front porch. Stone ordered, then sat down.

"You missed Charley and Gigi from across the way."

"They left?"

"They checked out last night, luggage and all."

"Maybe they were planning a cruise," Stone said. "Charley said yesterday that Gigi was shopping for groceries for the boat."

"Maybe so," Dino said. "Think we'll ever see them again?"

"Who knows? I don't particularly care."

"Are you starting to get free of this business, then?"

"Annika makes it hard to think about anything else when you're with her."

"Yeah, I know what you mean. Genevieve can be like that. I've been late to work a few times."

"When do you think we ought to get out of here?"

"I'm good for another day," Dino said. "Tommy invited us for lunch and a boat ride to nowhere."

"Sounds good," Stone said. "I'll ask Annika to join us; it's her day off."

"Tommy and I will protect you from her."

"Let's get an early start tomorrow. It'll take us about five flying hours, plus a fuel stop in South Carolina, and I'd like to get to Teterboro by three or so, before rush hour starts."

"I'm fine with that," Dino said.

Stone's breakfast arrived, and he dug in.

A little before noon Stone dropped Dino at the yacht club, then went to pick up Annika. She wasn't quite ready, and he took a chair in her bedroom and watched her get dressed. It wasn't as much fun as watching her get undressed, but it wasn't bad.

"Annika?"

"Yes?"

"You remember, you said you treated Evan Keating for a knife wound at the hospital?"

"Yes, I remember."

"Do you remember how he paid his bill? I mean, did he have medical insurance?"

"I don't know; that's not my department."

"Where was the knife wound?"

"He was raked across the ribs on the left side. The ribs protected the internal organs."

"How long was the cut?"

"Perhaps twelve centimeters."

"That's what, five inches?"

"A bit less."

"Can you find out if he had insurance and, if not, how he paid his bill?"

"Yes," she said. She picked up a phone, called the hospital's billing department and spoke for a couple of minutes, then hung up. "He didn't have medical insurance," she said. "He paid with his American Express card. The cashier remembered it, because it was black, and she had never seen one before."

"A black American Express card? That's the one you have to spend a lot of money to get, isn't it?"

"I think so; I've never seen one. Why are you interested in this?"

"Idle curiosity. Did Evan Keating have a beard?"

"No, he was clean-shaven. There was a girl with him, I remember—very pretty."

Stone's cell phone buzzed on his belt. "Hello?"

"It's Tommy; Dino and I are on the way to the airport. Paul DePoo called, and the guy with the red Cessna is there, waiting for them to get it out of the hangar."

"I'll be right with you," Stone said, and he hung up. "Annika, are you ready?"

She presented herself in an outfit that showed off her long legs and considerable cleavage. "I am ready," she said.

Stone made it to the airport in record time. "Annika, do you mind waiting in the lounge for a few minutes? I have to do this."

"All right," she said, and she went inside.

Stone followed her, then found Tommy and Dino in Paul DePoo's office.

"The guy's in the waiting room," Tommy said. "Did you notice him?"

"No, I wasn't looking for him, I guess."

"And he's getting impatient," Paul added.

"Give us a one-minute head start," Tommy said to Paul. "We'll wait for him in the hangar."

The three of them hotfooted it to the hangar, where a lineman with a tow was just clearing the doors with the red Cessna.

"Okay," Tommy said, "let's just be looking at the airplane, until he gets close enough to talk to. Dino, are you carrying?"

"Yep," Dino said.

"Nope," Stone said.

"Then stay behind us, Stone, and let me do the talking."

"He's coming," Dino said, pretending to inspect the airplane, "and I don't believe it, but he's got the gun case slung over his shoulder."

The man approached. As the counter woman had said, he was medium everything, and his yellow baseball cap was his only distinguishing feature. "Can I help you gentlemen?" he asked, unslinging the gun case and setting down a leather duffel.

"We were just admiring your airplane," Tommy said. "Are you Frank Harmon?"

"No," the man replied, "Frank Harmon is the man I bought the airplane from. I'm Jim Vernon."

Tommy showed him a badge. "May I see some ID, Mr. Vernon?"

The man looked slowly around the group. "For what purpose?"

"For the purpose of identifying you," Tommy replied. "Please don't make me ask you again."

The man dug out a wallet and handed Tommy a driver's license.

Stone watched him like a hawk, expecting trouble.

Tommy looked carefully at both sides of the license. "Is this your current address, Mr. Vernon?"

"Yes, it is."

"Do you have any documentation for the airplane with your name on it?"

"I have a bill of sale in the backseat," Vernon replied. "I'll get it for you." He unlocked the pilot-side door.

"Allow me," Dino said, stepping between Vernon and the airplane. He reached into the rear seat and brought out the aluminum briefcase. "Heavy," Dino said, weighing it in his hand. "Shall I open it for you?"

"That's all right," the man said. "I'll do it. It has a combination lock."

"Why don't you give Lieutenant Bacchetti the combination and let him open it?" Tommy said. "We'd feel more comfortable."

Again, Vernon looked at the three strangers. "It's one-two-three," he said.

Dino spun the combination on the two locks and opened the case.

Stone leaned forward and looked over Dino's shoulder. There were some papers in the case, and Dino lifted them to reveal half a dozen camera lenses underneath.

Vernon took the papers from Dino and handed Tommy one of them. "That's the bill of sale," he said. "Harmon's phone number is on it, if you'd like to call him. The FAA is a little slow in issuing new registrations."

Tommy looked the document over. "Mind if we have a look in the gun case?" he asked.

"What is this?" Vernon asked. "Some kind of drug thing?"

"If you wouldn't mind," Dino said, relieving him of the case. "I assume the combination is the same." He set the case on the ground and opened it. Inside were three fly-fishing rods and reels.

"I'm down here for the bonefishing," Vernon said, "not running drugs. You want to search the airplane?"

"Thank you," Tommy said, and he and Dino began looking inside the cabin.

"Beautiful airplane," Stone said.

"Thanks," Vernon replied, watching the cops work.

"I used to own one, but it wasn't as nice as this."

"Frank Harmon does nothing but restore old airplanes," Vernon said. "He does good work."

Tommy closed the airplane door and approached Vernon. "Thank you," he said. "Now may I have a look in your duffel?"

"There's a handgun in there," Vernon said. "And I'm licensed to carry it." He handed over the duffel.

Dino and Stone gathered around to watch Tommy go through the bag.

"Well, look what we've got here," Tommy said, holding up a rifle barrel and a silencer. "Mr. Vernon," he said, "you're under arrest."

The three men turned to look at him, but Jim Vernon was gone.

"Over there," Stone said, pointing. Vernon hit the

chain-link fence with a foot, grabbed the top and vaulted over it. He hit the ground on the other side and ran like a frightened deer.

Tommy, Stone and Dino began to run. They reached the fence. "Give me a leg up," Tommy said. "Then go get your car."

Stone and Dino tossed Tommy over the fence, then ran for the parking lot.

39

Annika was standing at the watercooler, sipping from a cup, when Stone grabbed her arm and hurried out the door.

"He ran," Stone explained.

"Do we have to run, too?" she asked.

"We just drive," Stone said. He, Annika and Dino got into the rental car; then they drove to the main road, turned right and drove along the beach.

"Why do you think he went this way?" Dino asked.

"Look at all the people and cars," Stone replied, driving slowly. "It's camouflage."

They made their way along the beach, and when they saw Tommy, Stone and Dino got out.

"Any sign of him?" Stone asked. He heard police whoopers in the distance, approaching.

"Nope, but help is on the way. He's got to be in this beach crowd somewhere. You stick with me."

A couple of squad cars screeched to a halt, and Tommy gave them Vernon's description and dispatched them in different directions.

Stone happened to look back toward the airport. "Hang on, Tommy!" he shouted. "You're not going to need the help." He pointed at the red Cessna, climbing, then turning north.

"The son of a bitch doubled back!" Tommy cried.

"Call the tower and see if he filed a flight plan," Stone said.

Tommy had to call information for the number, but he got connected and asked his questions. He hung up. "No flight plan. They don't even know his tail number; he took off without contacting the tower. Also, he didn't have his transponder on."

"That means air traffic control can only track him as a primary target, which is harder," Stone said. "Call Paul DePoo. He'll have the tail number from when Vernon checked in, and he'll probably have a credit card number for his fuel."

Tommy called, spoke to DePoo, then hung up. "I've got the tail number, but he paid cash for his fuel."

"Then call the state police," Stone said. "They must have aircraft that can start looking for him. But first call the Navy base. They're ATC for the area. See if they have a course and altitude for him; that will make the search easier."

After several minutes of trying to get the right number, Tommy finally got a controller on the line. "He's headed due north, and he leveled off at eight thousand feet," Tommy said. "Then they lost him."

"Eight thousand is the best-speed altitude for that airplane, and he probably has a stiff tailwind. He can do 155 knots true airspeed, and with, say, twenty knots of wind he can reach the mainland in half an hour or so. Ask the state police to try and alert as many South Florida airports as they can, especially Fort Lauderdale, where Vernon says he's from."

Tommy got the state police on the line and talked for several minutes. Finally, he hung up, looking discouraged. "They've got only one aircraft available, and it's in Orlando, but they're sending it south."

"He'll be on the ground somewhere by then," Stone said. "Best thing is for your department to start calling airports and see if anybody spots him. Then at least you'll know what city you're looking for him in."

"I expect he took his duffel with him," Tommy said, "so we don't have the rifle. All in all, I'd say this is a total disaster."

Jim Vernon descended to a thousand feet over the water, then crossed the mainland coast, flying over the Everglades. He tapped a code into the GPS for a location he had defined by longitude and latitude; then he set up an instrument approach he had defined as well; then he set the autopilot for the approach. Soon he was flying along a line that was an extension of the runway centerline, watching the GPS count down the miles. When he was three miles out, he spotted the clearing. Nobody would spot it who didn't know where it was. He brought back the throttle and began his final descent.

He landed softly on the grass and taxied the airplane back toward the cabin he had built there. Next to the cabin he had erected a ramada, which amounted to poles and a roof, a hangar without sides, which would make it impossible to spot the red airplane from the air. Once under the ramada, he spun the airplane around and shut down the engine.

He walked over to where a dozen fifty-five-gallon steel drums sat, picked up the hose attached to one of them and refueled the airplane, using a hand pump. Best to have a full load of fuel if he needed to get out of there in a hurry.

He went into the cabin, switched on the generator and the TV and opened a can of chili for lunch; then he sat down and watched a news channel while he ate. Then it came.

"South Florida airports have been alerted by the state police to be on the lookout for a small airplane, described as a red Cessna 182. The pilot, whose name is

Jim Vernon, is alleged to be a hired killer who shot and wounded a man in Key West two days ago."

That was it. As long as he didn't land the airplane at a South Florida airport, they'd never find him. The rest of the country was his oyster, but he wasn't ready to leave Florida just yet. He burned all his Vernon identification in the woodstove, then opened a small safe hidden under the floorboards and took out a packet of IDs. He selected a driver's license and cards with a new name, Thomas Sutherland, and put the wallet in his pocket.

He was cleaning up after his lunch when his cell phone rang. It was a throwaway, with no GPS chip, so he had no qualms about using it. "Yes?"

"Are you aware that the man you were sent to deal with is still active?" a voice said.

"I am. I'll have to make another attempt."

"The person who issued the contract has canceled it," the voice said. "You can keep the first payment, but it's over. Is there any reason to believe the police know who you are?"

"None," he replied. "I've taken care of that."

"I have another assignment for you, in the Northeast. Can you depart immediately? It pays better than the last one, and I already have the first half."

"I can't leave until tonight," he replied. "The airplane is hot in Florida. I'll change the registration number this afternoon and get started after dark."

"Good. Here are your instructions."

He wrote down all the information.

"The subject lives alone and dines at home every evening around eight o'clock. A dining room window will give you the access you need, and there is considerable foliage on the property. You can drive within fifty yards, then approach the house."

"Understood. I'll call you when the job is complete." He hung up and went to work. Using a hair dryer, he removed the registration number from the airplane, then affixed new numbers. He went back into the house and, consulting his collection of state and city maps and his aviation charts, he found an unmanned airport called Johnnycake, only a few miles from his target city, then mapped out his route. He would also take along a portable GPS unit.

He packed fresh clothes and put his soiled ones into the washing machine; then he put everything he needed into the airplane. He had only to wait until dark, and he used the time to phone his wife in nearby Jupiter.

"How did your trip go?" she asked.

"Not perfect, but not bad. I had to settle for half the fee."

"We've got some ripe bills, you know."

"Don't worry, I have a new job, and our man will deliver some cash tonight."

"Are you coming home?"

"I have to leave as soon as it's dark, so it will be a couple of days."

"Oh, all right. I guess we need the money."

"I love you. Take care of yourself."

"I love you, too." They both hung up.

He waited until dusk, then started the airplane's engine and taxied to the end of the short runway while he could still see without lights. Shortly, he was winging his way to the Northeast.

40

Stone, Dino, Tommy and Annika sat in the nearly empty Key West Yacht Club. "Okay," Tommy said, closing his cell phone, "we've called every airport south of Palm Beach, and the state police are wiring the tail number all over the country."

"I don't think you're going to catch him," Stone said. "This guy is a pro. He knows you're looking for that airplane."

"What's he going to do, throw it away?" Tommy asked.

"Paint it, change the tail number. There are thousands of Cessna 182s in the country."

"Maybe we should notify paint shops, too."

"I wouldn't bother; you're not going to catch him. Look what he did today: we didn't expect him to hot-foot it out of there, and we *certainly* didn't expect him to double back to the airport and take off. He's good."

"Everybody gets caught," Tommy said.

"Except the ones that never get caught," Dino added.

"I'll bet the ballistics on that rifle would have matched the bullet that passed through, ah, Charley Boggs," Tommy said.

"Did you recover the bullet?"

"Yeah, but the report hasn't come back yet."

"I'd be willing to bet that the rifle you found was just to throw you off the track," Stone said. "The one in his duffel did the work."

"This guy will be back at work soon," Dino said.

"How does a man like this find his work?" Annika asked.

"He has an agent, just like an actor or writer," Stone replied. "My guess is it's Manny White."

"Then why would Manny alert us about a hit man?" Dino asked.

"He didn't, really. I mean, we weren't very alert, were we?" Stone said. "He didn't tell us enough to stop the guy."

"You think Manny is capable of that?" Dino asked.

"I think Manny is capable of arranging a hit on his mother," Stone replied, "if he still has one. Seems like Manny is the go-to guy for just about anything—skip tracing, murder, you name it."

"Of course, you can't prove that," Tommy said.

"I guess if you could convince the Miami or state cops to tap his phone and his cell phone, you might nail him," Stone said, "but you don't have enough on him to get a warrant for that, do you?"

"I guess not," Tommy said. "Well, the good news is, he's out of our hair. He'll never come back to Key West."

The man now known as Thomas Sutherland refueled his airplane at a small airport in South Carolina, then continued northeast. Shortly after two in the morning, he checked his GPS, picked up his microphone and pressed the talk button rapidly five times. Dead ahead, the runway lights at Johnnycake Airport came on. He landed and taxied to the fueling area. As his airport reference book had told him, there was a self-operated fueling station. He inserted a credit card into the slot, just as at a gas station, and filled his wing tanks; then he taxied to a remote area of the airport, shut down the engine and went to sleep, curled up in the rear seat.

He slept until nearly noon; then he walked up to the highway and found a diner, where he had a large breakfast. Back at the airfield, he found it pretty much deserted. An occasional airplane would take off or land, but there was no tower, not even an office, just a bunch of airplanes tied down, waiting for the weekend and their owners.

As he stood there a Mercedes station wagon drove up, and a man and a woman got out.

"Good morning," the man said, "or is it afternoon?"

"Barely," Sutherland said. "You off to somewhere?"

"Yeah, we're visiting some family in Maine for a couple of days." He opened the trunk to reveal four suitcases.

"Let me give you a hand," Sutherland said, taking one of the bags out of the trunk. "Which airplane?"

"The Bonanza over there," the man said, nodding. "Thanks."

Sutherland followed him to the airplane and watched him unlock the right-side front door. "Give me your keys, and I'll unlock back here," Sutherland said.

The man tossed him a heavy bunch of keys. As Sutherland opened the door, he managed to free the car's ignition key from the bunch; then he set the suitcase in the luggage compartment, leaving the keys in the lock.

After a preflight inspection, the man and his wife got into the Bonanza, and ten minutes later they were rolling down the runway.

Sutherland waited until the airplane had disappeared to the north; then he got his duffel and a tool kit out of his airplane, put them into the rear of the Mercedes, started the car and drove away.

He had his printed maps, and it took him less than

half an hour to find the home of his target. He cruised past the house, and as he did, he saw a woman leave by the front door, get into a pickup truck in the driveway and back out. She looked like the cleaning lady, and there was no other car visible at the house.

He drove a little farther down the street and saw a dirt track leading into some woods. He turned into it and drove to a clearing, where the land had been scraped clean. There was a sign advertising a construction company planted on the lot. Looked like someone was going to build there.

He got out of the car, taking his tool kit, and made his way through the woods back toward the house. When he arrived at where the trees met the lawn he stopped and watched the place for signs of life for a while; then he approached the house and began looking into windows. Plantings at the front of the property shielded him from the street.

At a rear corner of the house he found the dining room and the kitchen. At a breakfast nook beside the kitchen window, a place had been set for one person, and a bottle of wine left on the table. Apparently, his subject did not use the dining room when eating alone.

Sutherland stood with his back to the window and looked at the woods, some thirty feet away, as he pulled on a pair of latex gloves. He checked angles and heights and picked out a spot with a good line marked by the center of a row of azaleas planted at the edge of the woods. Perfect.

He removed a glass cutter and a set of suction cups, affixed the cups to the selected windowpane, then cut the edges of the glass repeatedly. Finally, he banged on the bracket of the cups with his fist, and the glass snapped out. It would have fallen into the dinette, but he was holding on to the suction cup bracket. Gingerly, he freed the glass from the suction cups, then turned the glass and drew it outside through the new opening. He put the suction cups and the glass cutter back into his tool kit and walked to the spot in the row of azaleas. He stood behind them, then sighted, then knelt and did the same. The kneeling position would be just right. He tossed the glass pane as far as he could into the woods, then shucked off the latex gloves and walked back to the car.

He drove downtown and found a movie theater with a double feature playing and bought a ticket. He saw both movies twice. He didn't want to be walking around town and risk being noticed by someone who could identify him later.

When Sutherland left the movie theater it was twilight, and he had forty minutes until he went to work. He drove back to the vacant lot, switching off his headlights before he turned down the dirt track. There had been lights on in the house when he passed and a car in the driveway.

He took a small flashlight from his tool kit, slipped it into his pocket, then opened the duffel and assembled the rifle, screwed in the silencer and loaded a magazine, though he expected to fire only once. You never knew.

He found his way to his firing position behind the azaleas and sat down cross-legged behind the row of bushes. He checked the rifle again, shoved in the magazine and racked the slide. He checked his watch: ten minutes to eight.

At five minutes to eight, the kitchen light went on, and a man walked to the refrigerator, took out a covered dish, put it into the microwave and pressed some buttons. He stood for two minutes while the dish warmed. Sutherland could have shot him then, but he would have had to break glass, which might distort the trajectory and even alert a neighbor.

Finally, the man removed the dish from the microwave, set it on the table, picked up a corkscrew and opened the bottle of wine left for him.

Sutherland rose to one knee, rested his elbow on the other knee and sighted through the space with the missing pane. It was a shot of only a little more than thirty feet.

His subject sat down at the table, lifted his glass, took a sip and set the glass down.

Sutherland thumbed down the safety and squeezed off the round.

His subject took the bullet in his left temple, spraying

blood and gore, and went down. Not even his wineglass was disturbed.

Sutherland put the rifle on safety and made his way back to the car, where he unloaded and disassembled the rifle and returned it to the duffel.

Half an hour later he drove into the darkened airport and parked the car where he had found it. He took a bottle of Windex and a cloth from his tool bag and wiped down every surface he might have touched, then shook out the floor mat to remove any dirt he might have tracked into the car. He took his tools and duffel and walked back to his own airplane.

Early the following morning, in the soft green light of the predawn, Sutherland set down his airplane on the Everglades strip, taxied to the ramada, refueled the airplane, then got into the Jeep Wrangler he kept at the little house and drove home to Jupiter and his wife.

Later that day, an unmarked envelope containing a large sum of cash was left inside the front screen door of his house.

41

Stone was packing his bags after a late breakfast when his cell phone buzzed. "Hello?"

"It's Eggers."

"Morning, Bill. I'm just packing for the return trip."

"Unpack," Eggers said. "You're back on my dime."

"What's up?"

"Warren Keating's attorney just called me. Early this morning, his housekeeper arrived and found him dead in his kitchen, shot in the head."

"Suicide?"

"The lawyer didn't have any other details."

"This just gets weirder and weirder," Stone said.

"Yes, it does. I want to know what's going on, and I want you to find out for me. Take another week if you need to."

"At my usual hourly rate?"

"I'll spring for a generous flat rate. We'll talk it over when you get home."

"Okay, Bill. I'll be in touch." Stone hung up and walked out onto the front porch, where Dino was drinking a second cup of coffee. "Ready for the latest?" Stone asked.

"Always."

"Warren Keating has died from a gunshot to the head."

"His own or somebody else's?"

"That's what I want you to find out. Call your buddy on the Connecticut State Police."

Dino dialed the number and pressed the speaker phone button.

"Robbery Homicide, Lieutenant Dan Hotchkiss."

"Dan, it's Dino."

"You again?"

"Me again. I heard about Warren Keating."

"Are you still in Key West?"

"Yes. News travels fast in this modern age."

"I want to know how you heard about it. The media don't know yet."

"Keating's lawyer called a lawyer I know, who called the lawyer I'm down here with. I am not a suspect."

"You are until I say you aren't."

"All I know is that he was shot in the head. Was it a suicide?"

"If it was, he managed to hide the gun after he was dead. Oh, and he removed a pane from the kitchen window so he could shoot himself through it without scattering glass everywhere and making a lot of noise. A very neat fellow, Mr. Keating. Quick on his feet, too."

"So the shooter removed the window and popped him from outside?"

"From the azalea bed behind the house. We found some impressions, but nothing so good as to give us a usable footprint. He cleaned up his brass, too, though it was only one shell. Clean shot to the left temple."

"Anybody hear a gunshot?"

"No, and it was dinnertime, so somebody in the neighborhood should have noticed. My guess is a silencer was used."

"Any other evidence?"

"Some tire tracks at a lot next door that was otherwise pretty clean, since a bulldozer had scraped it for a building site. Pirelli 210 snow tires that can be driven year round—expensive. The nearest Mercedes dealer is the only place anywhere around here who stocks them."

"Dan, this is a little off the wall, but we had a shooter like that in Key West who took a shot at somebody who was pretending to be Warren Keating's son. Didn't kill him, though; that's another story. The shooter left town in a bright red Cessna 182, headed north. You might check the local airports for an airplane like that." Dino gave him the tail number.

"Okay, I'll get it on the radio."

Dino gave him his cell number. "I'd appreciate hearing about anything else you come up with," he said. "Did you ever know Tommy Sculley, from the NYPD?"

"Yeah, I talked to him a couple of times."

"He's the lead detective on the investigation down here, so you might coordinate with him."

"I'll do that."

"Oh, by the way, did you find a slug?"

"We did, embedded in the drywall behind where Keating was sitting. It's in Hartford for ballistics tests."

"I'm sure Tommy would appreciate it if you faxed him the report for comparison."

"Will do."

"Thanks, Dan." Dino hung up.

"It's going to be from the same rifle," Stone said. "The one in Vernon's duffel."

"You know what this sounds like?" Dino asked.

"What?"

"Sounds like the grandfather, Eli, hired somebody to off his son and his grandson, leaving him with all of the eight hundred million from the sale of the business."

"That's nice and symmetrical, but what would a guy in his eighties do with eight hundred million?"

"Maybe he just hated his son and grandson enough to want them not to get any of it. It would be interesting to know who the money goes to if Eli kicks off soon."

"I'll ask Eggers next time we talk. Call Tommy and tell him about this."

Dino made the call while Stone listened in.

"That's an interesting turn of events," Tommy said.

"Tommy," Stone broke in, "were there autopsy photographs taken of the corpse you thought was Charley Boggs?"

"Yeah, I've got 'em in my desk drawer."

"See if there's a knife wound to the left rib cage."

Tommy took a moment. "No, nothing visible. Why do you ask?"

"The guy we thought was Evan Keating had a knife wound treated at Key West Hospital. Annika was his doctor, and she said he was clean-shaven."

"So the real Charley Boggs had been knifed, as well as shot?"

"Something else: he paid his hospital bill with a black American Express card."

"I've never seen one of those," Tommy said.

"It's their most elite card, limited to subscribers who spend a lot on their Amex cards."

"So?"

"The card was in Evan Keating's name. Do you think Evan Keating, during his identity swap with Charley Boggs, would loan Charley his credit card, one with no limit?"

"Well, let me put it this way," Tommy said. "If you and I swapped identities and I had one of those black cards, I think I'd hang on to it."

"So would I," Dino said.

"So I take it you're thinking that Charley Boggs might be Evan Keating instead of Charley Boggs?"

"It crossed my mind," Stone said.

"Then why would he come in and confess to killing the real Charley Boggs, but say it was himself?"

"Because I told him that somebody might have put out a contract on him, and he apparently thought it was his father. Maybe he figured that if he was dead, his old man might save the money on the hit man."

"That makes sense. Where is this guy now, do you know?"

"I do not. He checked out of this hotel three days ago."

"So he had time to visit Connecticut?"

"I guess he did at that."

Dino broke in and told Tommy about Dan Hotchkiss, and gave him his phone number. "Maybe you should consult with Dan," Dino said.

"Consult I will," Tommy said.

42

Stone and Dino were about to leave the hotel when a call came in.

"Hello?" Stone said.

"Stone, it's Chuck Chandler, at the tennis club."

"Hey, Chuck."

"I ran across something yesterday that might interest you."

"What's that?"

"My old boat, which now has no name."

"Where did you see it?"

"Out at Fort Jefferson."

"Where's Fort Jefferson?"

"It's at the very end of the Keys."

"I thought Key West was the very end of the Keys."

"No, they run out to the west from Key West for

about sixty miles—small uninhabited islands with no fresh water at all. There was a fort built out on the last one during the nineteenth century—that's Fort Jefferson. It was used as a prison during and after the Civil War, and Dr. Samuel Mudd, who was imprisoned for sheltering John Wilkes Booth and setting his broken leg, was sent there, where he performed heroically during a yellow fever epidemic."

"What's out there now?"

"Just the old fort, nicely preserved. There's no landing for a boat there, but you can swim ashore or take a dinghy in. The funny thing is that my old boat still had her dinghy aboard, and there was no one on her. We swam ashore and had a picnic in the fort, and there was no one else there."

"Well, if one took one's boat out there and abandoned it, how would one get back?" Stone asked.

"One would take another boat or a seaplane; those are the only choices. But why would anyone leave a very nice boat out there, where it might be broken into and plundered?"

"Good question," Stone asked. "And where would one get hold of a seaplane?"

"There are a couple for charter at the airport."

"Any idea how long the boat has been there?"

"I don't know, but I saw her three days ago, taking on fuel in Key West Bight."

"Any sign that the boat had been broken into?"

"Not that I could tell. I blew my horn a couple of times and tried to raise them on the radio, but no response."

"Thanks for letting me know, Chuck."

"You and Dino want some tennis?"

"I'm not sure how much longer we're going to be in town, but if we stay on, I'll call you."

"Take care, then."

Stone hung up. "Did you hear any of that?" he asked Dino.

"Enough to wonder if those two kids are dead on that boat," Dino replied.

"Let's find out," Stone said. He called Tommy Sculley and told him Chuck's story.

"I'll call the airport and pick you up in fifteen minutes," Tommy said.

The hired seaplane was an amphibian—it could land at the airport or on the water—and they were in the air within the hour. They flew west over the string of tiny islands, seeing only an occasional yacht anchored in the lee of one, its occupants picnicking or swimming. Stone, sitting in the copilot's seat, spotted the outline of the fort in the distance, and as they grew closer, he could see a solitary boat anchored off the fort.

The pilot circled the little motor yacht. "You want me to land?" he asked.

"Yeah, and taxi as close as you can to the boat," Tommy said. "Do you have a dinghy?"

"No, just a life raft."

"I'll have to swim, I guess," Tommy said, unbuttoning his shirt.

Stone started getting out of his clothes, too.

There wasn't much wind, and the pilot maneuvered to within a few yards of the boat, which seemed deserted. Tommy and Stone jumped, naked, into the water and swam for the boat. Stone was there first and hauled himself aboard, then gave Tommy a hand.

The two stood, dripping wet, in the cockpit, looking through the locked doors to the cabin below.

"Tell you what," Tommy said. "I'm worried that those kids are dead aboard, so I'm going to break in."

"I agree," Stone said.

Tommy found a boat hook and used it to pry the padlock hasp off the mahogany door. "They can send me a bill, if they're alive," Tommy said, sniffing the air inside. "Nobody smells dead." He started below, and Stone followed him.

Everything seemed to be in perfect order below, though it was hot. Tommy began opening the galley cabinets. "Let's search the place, as long as we're here."

Stone pitched in, and the two of them searched the cabin thoroughly, taking care to leave it as neat as they found it. "Let's take a look in the cockpit lockers," Stone said, and they went back on deck.

Stone pointed at the stern locker, which was fastened with a combination padlock. "Odd," he said. "The cabin door had an ordinary padlock, but this one has a combination."

"Why is that odd?" Tommy asked.

"Maybe it's so that someone who knew the combination could come aboard, leave something in the stern locker, then relock it and leave."

"We're going to need something more substantial than an aluminum boat hook to break into that," Tommy said.

"There's a tool kit below," Stone said. He went down and came back with a large screwdriver. It took a couple of minutes to break into the locker. Stone opened the locker and stood back. It was packed with plastic bags, taped shut.

They were about to open one when there was a sudden blast from a boat's horn. They looked up to find a small Coast Guard cutter standing a few yards off the port side.

"Ahoy, there," a woman's voice said on a loud-hailer. "We're boarding you."

Stone looked at Tommy. "We're not dressed for the occasion," he called back.

"There are some towels below," Tommy said, ducking into the cabin and returning with two skimpy bath towels.

The cutter's crew deployed fenders, and the female

captain, who was petite and attractive, stepped aboard, wearing a handgun and a name tag that read "Tabor." A crewman stood on the boat's upper deck with an assault rifle at port arms.

"Is this your boat?" Tabor asked them.

"No, Captain Tabor," Tommy said. "I'm Lieutenant Tommy Sculley, Key West PD."

"I don't see a badge," she said, suppressing a smile.

"Right," Tommy said. "It's on our airplane."

"What's going on here?" she asked.

"We're looking for the boat's occupants," Tommy said. "We got a report that the boat had been abandoned here, so we flew out for a look."

She nodded toward the broken lock on the cabin door. "I suppose you have a search warrant?"

"No, we were concerned for the safety of the crew," Tommy said, "so we had a look around." He opened the stern locker. "All we found was this."

Tabor looked into the locker and whistled. "Tell you what, Lieutenant: why don't you swim back to your airplane and bring me some ID. And if you try to take off, that seaman over there with the M16 will shoot you down."

"Yes, ma'am," Tommy said, dropping his towel.

43

Tommy swam back, holding his ID wallet out of the water, and handed it to the Coast Guard captain.

She looked at it suspiciously, then turned to Stone. "And who would you be?" she asked.

"My name is Stone Barrington," he replied. "If you want to see me without the towel, I'll swim back and get my ID, too."

Tabor blushed. "Okay," she said, "don't bother."

"We'd like to leave now," Stone said.

"We're going to tow this boat back to our base in Key West and impound it," she said. "How do I get in touch with you?"

"Call Lieutenant Sculley and Key West PD," Stone said. "Now, if you'll excuse me." He dropped the towel, hopped over the side and swam back to the airplane, followed by Tommy.

"Well," Tommy said, "that was interesting. I guess she just wanted to see me naked."

They flew back to Key West. Then, back at the hotel, Stone called Evan Keating's cell phone number and got his voice mail. "This is Stone Barrington; please call me immediately, very urgent," he said; then he hung up.

"Looks like he's going to need legal representation again," Dino said.

"Looks like," Stone agreed.

Stone was having a drink before dinner with Annika at Louie's Backyard when his cell phone buzzed. "Hello?"

"I got your message," a voice on the phone said.

"To whom am I speaking this time?" Stone asked. "Evan Keating or Charley Boggs?"

"Take your pick," he replied.

"Where are you?"

"Why do you want to know?"

"Tell me something: When you were knifed, how did you pay your hospital bill?"

Silence.

"Was Charley Boggs using Evan Keating's very exclusive credit card?"

"What's your point?"

"I guess I'll refer to you as Evan Keating from now on," Stone said.

"Okay."

"Once again, where are you?"

"I'm in Torrington, Connecticut."

"Oh? Why?"

"Look, Stone, I don't owe you any explanations."

"Evan, it would be wise of you, in a legal sense, to answer my questions."

"I don't get it."

"Where is your boat at this moment?"

"This is getting very strange," Evan said.

"It's even stranger that you're in Connecticut."

"My father is dead."

"I know."

"You know?"

"I know. How did you happen to find out?"

"I spoke to my grandfather, and he told me."

"When was that?"

"Early this morning."

"Where were you at the time?"

"On my boat."

"And where was the boat?"

"West of the Keys."

"And how did you get back to Key West?"

"I didn't go to Key West. I went by seaplane from the boat to Miami and got a plane there."

"Your boat is no longer at Fort Jefferson," Stone said.

"How do you know where it is?"

"Because I was aboard it this morning when the Coast Guard arrived, impounded it and towed it away."

"*What?*"

"Do I have your attention now, Evan?"

"You do."

"Someone saw your boat out there, unattended. I went out there with the police to find out if you were aboard, dead."

"Why should I be dead?"

"Well, during the past week or ten days, you've been knifed and shot. It's not too great a leap."

"But why did the Coast Guard impound the boat? It's not illegal to be anchored out there."

"Gee, Evan, I'm not sure. Do you think it could be because of the large amount of drugs in the stern locker?"

"There are no drugs on my boat."

"I pried the lock off the stern locker myself. The Coast Guard chose that moment to arrive, relieving me of the responsibility of calling them."

"The stern locker wasn't locked," Evan said. "The lock I had on it rusted out, and I threw it away. I haven't yet bought a replacement."

"Well, somebody did you the favor of buying a replacement, a very substantial combination lock."

"I don't know anything about that."

"Evan, I think you'd better return to Key West right away and answer some questions."

"I can't just yet. I'm dealing with my father's burial. My grandfather isn't up to it."

"I should tell you," Stone said, "that one of the theories being posited in all this is that your grandfather hired someone to kill both you and your father."

"That's preposterous!" Evan said. "No one who knows my grandfather would ever think that."

"Do you have another candidate for who might want both you and your father dead?"

A long silence. "No, I don't."

"Then answer me this: Who might have a *motive* for wanting you both out of the picture?"

"I don't know."

"A financial motive, maybe?"

"Do you mean the money from the sale of the family business?"

"I would have thought it was enough to kill for."

"For some people maybe, but not my grandfather."

"Well, on your flight back to Key West, you'll have time to consider who else might profit from your demise."

"Am I suspected of a crime?"

"You own a boat that was carrying drugs."

"There were no drugs in that locker when Gigi and I left," Evan said. "I know, because I got a rubber din- ghy out of the locker to move us and our luggage from the boat to the seaplane, and there was nothing else in that locker except fenders and mooring lines."

"Evan, are you coming back? What do you want me to tell the Coast Guard?"

"I'm coming back, and I'd like to retain you again."

"All right. When are you coming back?"

"My father's remains are being cremated tomorrow morning. I'll get the earliest plane I can after that. I shouldn't think it would be before tomorrow night, or perhaps the day after. It depends on how my grandfather is bearing up."

"All right, I'll call the Coast Guard and tell them that."

"Thank you. I'll call you when I get in. Goodbye." Evan hung up.

"You lead such an interesting life," Annika said.

44

Stone arrived back at the Marquesa near lunchtime the next day to find Dino on the phone. Dino punched the speaker button. "You might want to hear this; it's Dan Hotchkiss."

Stone sat down.

"Go, Dan," Dino said.

"Just a follow-up," Dan said. "We traced the Pirelli 210 tires to a Mercedes station wagon owned by a Dr. Ralph Peters, of Torrington. Dr. Peters left his car at the airport, and he and his wife went to Maine for a couple of days. When he was taking his baggage out of the car a man offered to help, a white male, fortyish, medium height, medium weight, wearing sunglasses and a yellow ball cap."

"That's our guy," Stone said.

"Dr. Peters said he saw a red Cessna there, too, one that isn't based there and wasn't there when he returned this morning. Also, when he got back he realized he was missing his ignition key from his key ring, and he found the key on the driver's seat. He figured it had fallen off when he was getting out of the car."

"Yeah, sure," Dino said. "I figure our guy borrowed his car for a while."

"The tire prints matched the Mercedes," Dan said. "We got back the ballistics report from our lab, too. The bullet we found in the kitchen wall was a .223. I've faxed the report to Tommy Sculley to compare with his slug."

"So now you know how the killer got to Torrington and out of town," Stone said. "He's probably having the airplane painted somewhere in South Florida as we speak."

"Probably," Dan agreed. "I don't think our chances of nailing this guy are very good, which is a shame, because I'd really like to know who hired him."

"Are you looking at Eli Keating for this?"

"God knows he's got a motive, but I can't see him hiring a hit man to kill his son and grandson. He's in his eighties, and very rich already. I could see how he'd be pissed off at his son for trying to lock him away, but he wouldn't have anything against the grandson. They were treating each other very warmly when I talked to them."

"Anything new on the poisoning of Harry Keating?" Stone asked.

"The FBI lab report came back; the poison was thallium, which is found in some insecticides, one of which was present in Warren Keating's toolshed. That one's a wash, since Warren is dead, too."

"Hey, Dan," Dino said. "Don't you guys ever catch a killer who's still alive?"

"Go fuck yourself, Dino," Dan said pleasantly. "Bye-bye." He hung up.

"Looka here," Dino said, nodding toward the pool as he closed his phone. Tommy Sculley, the Coast Guard cutter captain and a man they had not seen before were coming down the walkway toward them.

"Good morning, all," Dino said.

"Morning," Tommy replied. "Agent Corelli, this is Stone Barrington, an attorney, and Lieutenant Dino Bacchetti, of the NYPD. Fellas, this is Agent Rocco Corelli, of the DEA, and of course you know Captain Tabor, of the U.S. Coast Guard."

"Of course," Stone said. They pulled up more chairs, and everybody sat down.

"Coffee, anyone?" Stone asked.

Nobody wanted coffee.

"Mr. Barrington, I understand you represent one Charles Boggs, who owns the boat Captain Tabor impounded yesterday?"

"Actually, I represent the boat's owner, who is not Charles Boggs but one Evan Keating."

"Hang on," Tommy said.

Stone held up a hand. "Their respective identities are as we first thought them to be," Stone said. "I'll explain later, or at least, I think I will."

"All right, then," Corelli said, "you represent this Evan Keating?"

"I do," Stone replied.

"And where might I find Mr. Keating at this moment?"

"At this moment, he is, I believe, en route back from Connecticut, where he has been attending to his father's death for the past two days. The father is one Warren Keating, who was murdered a couple of days ago. Evan informed me that he will be back in Key West tonight or tomorrow sometime. He is anxious to speak with you about the drugs we found on his boat."

"There has been progress in the Warren Keating investigation," Dino said. "It appears that Mr. Keating was murdered by the same man who tried to murder his son, Evan, in Key West. The descriptions match, and when you get back to your office, Tommy, you should have the ballistics report for comparison with your bullet."

"Good," Tommy said. "I've sort of brought Tabor and Corelli up-to-date on all that."

"Agent Corelli," Stone said, "Evan Keating maintains that when he and his girlfriend left his boat, after hearing of the death of his father, the stern locker contained nothing but a rubber dinghy, which he took with him, and his mooring lines and fenders, and that it was not secured with a lock. He will tell you this himself after his arrival in Key West."

"And he has no idea why the locker was full of twenty kilos of pure cocaine, with a street value of millions?"

"None whatever. I should also tell you that Evan Keating is personally wealthy, and that he is anticipating a fifty percent share of the proceeds of the sale of his family's business, which will make him some hundreds of millions of dollars wealthier. I can attest to this, because I have reviewed the contract for the business sale. Thus, he has no motive to make money from the sale of drugs."

"That's very interesting, Mr. Barrington," Corelli said. "Does he have any other explanation for why the drugs were present on his boat?"

"No, but I can posit an answer to your question."

"Please do so," Corelli said.

"It seems likely that drug smugglers, who work regularly in and out of Key West, spotted Evan's boat, which is well known on the island, having been previously owned by the local tennis pro, Chuck Chandler. Perhaps this person or persons thought the drugs might arrive in Key West with less chance of being found if they entered the harbor on a well-known local boat instead of whatever drug-running rocket ship they were traveling in."

"I do know of a couple of cases where smugglers tried to move drugs on the boats of unsuspecting owners," Corelli said, "so your supposition is not entirely beyond reason. However, I will still need to question Mr. Keating and his girlfriend, Ms. Jones."

"If you'll give me your card," Stone said, "I'll arrange a meeting as soon as Evan arrives back in Key West."

"Tommy," Corelli said, "you know this gentleman. Is his word to be trusted?"

"Yes," Tommy said.

Corelli stood up, and so did everybody else. "In that case, I'll look forward to your call," he said, handing Stone his card.

They all shook hands, and Tommy and his party left.

"You up for some conch fritters?" Dino asked.

"Always," Stone replied.

45

Stone and Dino were polishing off their usual dessert of key lime pie.

"I think we should go to Miami," Dino said.

Stone blinked. "Why?"

"To talk to our erstwhile colleague Manny White."

"Why?"

"Because we don't have anything else to do, and visiting Manny will keep us busy."

"What do you hope to learn from Manny?" Stone asked.

"We already have our suspicions about Manny," Dino said, "but even if they aren't true, he probably knows more about all this than we do."

"That wouldn't be hard," Stone said. "But first I need to call Evan." He did so.

"Hello?"

"It's Stone. Where are you?"

"Still in Connecticut. We're taking a morning flight from LaGuardia tomorrow, and we'll land in Key West at two o'clock."

"Where are you staying?"

"At the Marquesa again. We can't stay on the boat, can we?"

"Not yet. A DEA agent came to see me earlier today. Naturally, he's anxious to talk with you about the drugs found on your boat."

"Naturally," Evan replied.

"I'll set something up with him tomorrow afternoon, and we'll go see him."

"All right. Not before four o'clock; you know how flights are these days."

"That will be good. See you then." Stone hung up, called Rocco Corelli and made the appointment. "All right," he said to Dino, "let's go to Miami. Do we have an address?"

"He'll be in the phone book," Dino replied.

On the way to the airport, Stone got a weather forecast and filed a flight plan. Half an hour later they were winging their way north.

They landed at Tamiami Airport and got Manny White's address from a phone book, then took a cab.

Manny White Investigations was housed in an elegant little Art Deco office building in South Beach, on the top floor. There was a nicely furnished reception room with a pretty receptionist, and they were shown into Manny's office right away.

Manny didn't rise to greet them. "Well," he said, deadpan, "to what do I owe the thrill of this visit?"

"We were in town and thought we'd drop by to say hello," Dino replied, offering himself a chair.

"Hello," Manny said. He turned toward Stone. "You too."

"Hi, Manny," Stone replied.

"So how long you been in business here?" Dino asked.

"Since I retired, seven years ago."

Dino looked around the office. "Business must be good."

"Not bad," Manny said. "It took a while to build it up."

"What sort of investigations do you do?" Stone asked.

"Skip tracing, employee embezzlement, divorce and child custody, you name it."

"How many operatives do you employ?" Dino asked.

"Half a dozen, all freelancers."

"Who are they?"

"Ex-cops, mostly. Now and then I run across somebody who's just smart, and I hire him."

"Manny," Dino said, "you were helpful to us when

a client of Stone's was in danger of getting shot. Suppose we wanted a little wet work done. Could you send me to somebody good?"

"What kind of wet work?"

"Do you really want to know?"

"How can I send you to the right guy if I don't know what kind of work you want done? Everybody's a specialist these days. You want somebody burgled, I recommend one guy; you want a debt collected, I recommend another guy."

"Suppose we wanted somebody's clock stopped," Stone said. "Could you handle that?"

Manny regarded him evenly. "You guys wearing a wire? Maybe you should be in your underwear for this conversation."

"I'll be happy to strip for you, Manny, but neither of us is wired."

"This is just an informal discussion," Dino said. "Very hypothetical. Could you handle a clock-stopping?"

"I don't handle nothing," Manny said. "I just pass along instructions."

"You sound like the Happy Hooker, Manny," Dino said.

"That's not an unfair comparison," Manny replied. "I'll need to know whose clock we're talking about and where he is, something about his habits."

"Maybe we should talk directly to your contractor," Stone said.

Manny shook his head slowly. "You never meet him; he's funny that way."

"What's the going rate for clock-stopping these days?" Dino asked.

Manny shrugged. "Depends on distance, difficulty and whether the guy has protection."

"Ballpark number?"

"Could be twenty-five big ones, if it's local and easy; two, three times that if travel is involved and if he has security. What part of the country we talking about?"

"Key West, maybe," Stone said. "Maybe Connecticut."

Manny became inert.

"Manny, you still there?" Dino asked.

"I'm still here," Manny said, "but you guys aren't." He nodded toward the door. "Take a hike."

"You're a little sensitive, aren't you, Manny?" Stone asked.

"What's the matter?" Manny said. "Don't you guys know when you're getting your chain yanked? I don't do that kind of business. Now get out of here—I got no more time for you."

"I'll bet you'd have time if I put twenty-five big ones on the desk right now," Stone said.

"Then do it, or hoof it," Manny said.

They hoofed it, thanking Manny for his time.

In the airplane on the way back, Stone tuned in a jazz station on the satellite radio, switched on the autopilot and sat back. "So Manny's the arranger, you think?"

"Oh, yeah," Dino replied. "Not that you could ever nail him. Not even if we'd been wearing a wire today."

"Manny's a shit, but he's not stupid," Stone said.

"Anyway," Dino replied, "we know how he's paying for that office space."

"You betcha," Stone said.

46

Stone met Evan Keating and Gigi Jones at the airport. Gigi rented a car and left for the Marquesa, while Stone drove Evan to the Federal Building in Key West, near the Monroe County Courthouse.

"Now, listen to me carefully, Evan," Stone said. "It's important that you answer all of Corelli's questions truthfully."

"Why not?" Evan said. He didn't seem concerned.

"I'll tell you why not. It's a federal crime to lie to an FBI agent, a DEA agent or any other federal law enforcement officer. Corelli is going to be investigating this incident with your boat from more than one direction, and if he finds something that contradicts your testimony, you'll find yourself doing jail time."

"Just for lying to a DEA agent?" Evan asked. "It doesn't seem all that important."

"Remember Martha Stewart? They didn't get her for insider trading; they got her for lying to an FBI agent. She did a year for that. You might keep that in mind if you start to fudge an answer."

"Why are you letting me talk to this guy?" Evan asked. "You're my lawyer."

"I'm letting you talk to him because I think you're innocent of a crime and you can be truthful with him without hurting yourself. If that's not the case, tell me now, and I'll cancel the appointment."

Evan was quiet. "Why is it to my advantage to talk to him?"

"Because you've been caught in possession of drugs—that's a felony. The amount found and its purity indicate intent to distribute—that's another felony. If you can truthfully convince Corelli that you're innocent, we may be able to make this go away. If I tell him you're not going to answer his questions, you're liable to find yourself charged and on trial, and they have a *lot* of evidence. Do you fully understand your situation now?"

"Yes, I think I do."

"Do you still want to answer Corelli's questions?"

"Yes."

"All right. Now, we're likely to be seated in a room with a mirror on the wall. Behind that wall is certainly going to be a video camera, and probably several other DEA agents, including Corelli's boss. Everything will be recorded, and they'll play it over and over again, so your demeanor will be important. Give full answers; don't be terse. It's not like you're taking a lie detector test; you'll be talking to human beings who will make judgments about you."

"Are they likely to give me a lie detector test?"

"It's a possibility. Does that make you nervous?"

"Of course."

"If they suggest it, I'll tell them no," Stone said. "That won't surprise them. If we feel they need more convincing, then we'll suggest a polygraph."

"How good are those things?"

"Pretty good, if the operator is experienced and neutral."

"I think I could pass it," Evan said. "Suggest it, if you feel it's in my interests."

"I'll keep that in mind," Stone said.

Rocco Corelli came to a reception room to get them, then put them in an interrogation room—just a table and four chairs. Another man joined them, and Corelli introduced him as John Myers.

"Are you a DEA agent, Mr. Myers?" Stone asked him as they settled at the table.

"I'm an assistant U.S. attorney," Myers replied.

Stone nodded as if that didn't bother him.

"Mr. Barrington," Corelli said, "first I have a few

questions for you for the record, given your presence on Mr. Keating's boat."

"That's fine with me," Stone said.

"Are you acquainted with a New York City police detective named Dino Bacchetti?"

"Yes, he was my partner when I was with the NYPD."

"Please explain the presence of the two of you in Key West."

"A law firm with which I am affiliated in New York was asked to send someone to Key West to find Evan Keating, in connection with a family business matter, and I was asked to go. Lieutenant Bacchetti came along as a sort of vacation."

"And how did you come to be aboard Mr. Keating's boat on the day in question?"

"I received a phone call from Chuck Chandler, a local tennis pro, who was the previous owner of the boat. He said that while cruising on his new boat, he saw Mr. Keating's boat anchored near Fort Jefferson. He didn't see anyone aboard, and he didn't find anyone ashore, and he was curious as to why the boat seemed abandoned.

"There had been a previous attempt on Mr. Keating's life by a person or persons unknown, and I became concerned for his safety. Lieutenant Tommy Sculley of the Key West PD came with Dino and me in a seaplane, which landed near the boat. Tommy and I swam to Mr.

Keating's boat, broke into it and searched it, fearing that he and his girlfriend might be aboard, injured or dead. We also broke into the stern locker of the boat and found what appeared to be a large quantity of drugs.

"At that moment, a Coast Guard cutter arrived and the captain joined us aboard. We had a conversation; then we left the boat in the charge of the Coast Guard, and they impounded it."

"Did you call Mr. Keating immediately?"

"No, there was no cell phone service that far out. I called him after we returned to Key West."

"Thank you, Mr. Barrington," Corelli said. "Mr. Keating, how did your boat come to be anchored and abandoned at Fort Jefferson?"

"My girlfriend, Gigi Jones, and I cruised out to the fort, where we snorkeled and went ashore to see the fort. We had dinner aboard and spent the night. The following morning I called my grandfather, Eli Keating, in Connecticut, and he told me that my father, Warren Keating, had been found shot to death a short time before."

"Mr. Keating, Mr. Barrington has just told us that there was no cell phone reception at Fort Jefferson. How did you call him?"

"I have a satellite telephone, which works very well at Fort Jefferson."

"I see. What did you do upon hearing the news of your father's death?"

"I called a seaplane service at Key West airport. They came and fetched us and flew us to Miami, where we got a commercial flight to New York, then rented a car for the drive to Connecticut."

"And you just abandoned an expensive boat anchored at Fort Jefferson?"

"I didn't feel I had a choice; my grandfather needed me. I locked it, and when the seaplane arrived, we took the small rubber dinghy from the stern locker and used it to paddle to the airplane. The plane couldn't come alongside without a wing hitting the superstructure."

"Did you lock the stern locker after removing the dinghy?"

"No, there was no padlock for it. The old one had corroded and was no longer workable, and I had not yet replaced it."

"What else was in the locker besides the rubber dinghy?"

"Just fenders and lines for the boat, and a second anchor. Miscellaneous boat stuff, nothing else."

"And you did not lock the stern locker before you departed?"

"No, I had no lock for that purpose."

"You didn't have a combination padlock?"

"No, I didn't."

"While you were anchored at Fort Jefferson, did another boat approach yours?"

"No, we didn't see another boat for the whole time

we were there, which was, I guess, around eighteen hours. We did see an airplane once, shortly after sunrise, flying low—sightseeing, I suppose."

"What kind of airplane?"

"A small Piper, I think, something like the Warrior."

"A seaplane?"

"No, I didn't see any floats. It circled the area a couple of times, then flew away in the direction of Key West."

"Did you see anyone at Fort Jefferson when you went ashore?"

"Not a soul. The circling airplane was the only sign of life we saw out there, until the seaplane arrived for us."

"What happened to your rubber raft?"

"It's still at the Key West Airport, I suppose. I haven't had time to retrieve it."

Stone was impressed with Evan's composure and the clarity of his responses. "Agent Corelli, Evan is willing to take a polygraph test, if it would be helpful to you."

Corelli glanced at Myers, who shook his head almost imperceptibly. "Thank you. That won't be necessary at this time," Correlli said. "Maybe later."

"Is there anything else, gentlemen?" Stone asked.

"Yes," said Myers, speaking for the first time. "I have some questions about Evan's relationship with Charles Boggs and the death of Mr. Boggs."

Stone didn't like this a bit. "How is that relevant?" he asked. "I haven't had time to consult with my client about that situation."

"Its relevance will become apparent," Myers said.

Evan spoke up. "It's all right, Stone," he said. "I'm willing to answer their questions about Charley."

Stone still didn't like it. "All right, gentlemen, but I reserve the right to stop the questioning and consult with my client, if I think it's necessary."

"Certainly," Myers said. Then he turned to Evan. "What is your full, legal name?" he asked.

Stone held his breath.

47

Evan Keating regarded Assistant U.S. Attorney John Myers calmly. "My name, since birth, is Evan Harold Keating. I was named for my great-grandfather, Evan, and my father's brother, Harry."

"Why did you approach the Key West police and the county attorney and tell them your real name was Charles Boggs?"

"I believed that my father, Warren Keating, had poisoned my uncle Harry, and that he might want to kill me as well."

Stone interrupted. "I should tell you that the FBI lab has confirmed that Harry Keating died of thallium poisoning, a source of which was found in Warren Keating's garden shed, and that prior to Evan's visit to the police, he received a gunshot wound from a sniper, so he had good reason to fear for his life."

"I thought that if my father heard that I had been killed, as Charley had been, he would stop trying to kill me," Evan said.

"How did you come to be acquainted with Charles Boggs?" Myers asked.

"We attended prep school together and were close friends until after we left college. After that, we lost track of each other, until I came to Key West and ran into him."

"Where did you run into him?"

"At a bar on Duval Street. I didn't recognize him at first, because he had grown a beard."

"Did you go into the drug business with Charley Boggs?"

"No, I did not. I realized early on that Charley was using cocaine, because he offered me some, which I declined, but I didn't suspect he was dealing until I saw him hiding something on his boat that appeared to be packets of drugs."

"How did you come to kill Charley Boggs?"

Stone interrupted. "Are you aware that Evan has received a guarantee of immunity from the county attorney which covers that incident?"

"I am," Myers replied.

"Will you guarantee that you will not prosecute Evan

for anything associated with the death of Charley Boggs?"

"Yes, since he has already told me that he was not dealing drugs. If he tells me anything to contradict that, I may reconsider."

Stone nodded to Evan.

"Gigi and I, perhaps foolishly, removed drugs hidden on Charley's houseboat and on his motorcycle and disposed of them in the sea off Key West. I had hoped to reason with him, to stop him from dealing. As you might imagine, Charley was upset with us, and an argument ensued. He seemed convinced that Gigi had persuaded me to get rid of the drugs, which wasn't so, and he produced a gun and pointed it at her. He racked the slide, and I could see that the safety was off.

"I picked up another gun of Charley's that was lying on a kitchen counter and pointed it at him. He fired a shot at Gigi, which missed, and I shot him before he could fire again. We disposed of both guns in the sea, off Key West."

"And you never, at any time, bought or sold any drugs?"

"We did not, at any time."

"Evan," Stone said, "did Charley Boggs earlier inflict a knife wound on you?"

"Yes, he did," Evan replied, patting his ribs on his left side. "I'll show you the wound, if you like."

Stone interrupted. "So you see, Evan had good reason to fear violence from Charley Boggs."

"Charley wasn't really a violent guy," Evan said. "It was the drugs. He was using a *lot* of cocaine, and it was making him crazy."

"Evan," Myers said, "do you have any idea why anyone would put drugs on your boat?"

"No, I do not."

Stone spoke up. "I have already posited to Agent Corelli that someone might have wished to use a boat familiar to the Key West authorities to move drugs into the harbor."

"Yes, I know," Myers said.

"Is there anything else, gentlemen?" Stone asked.

Myers looked at Corelli, who shook his head. "Not at this time," Myers said.

"Will you release Evan's boat?" Stone asked. "He lives aboard it, and he's being put to the expense of staying in a hotel."

"I'll direct the Coast Guard to do so," Myers said, "but I must tell you that if evidence surfaces that indicates the involvement of Mr. Keating in drug dealing, his boat will be subject to impounding again."

"I understand," Evan said.

Stone and Evan rose, everybody shook hands, and they left the building and went to Stone's car.

"That seemed to go well," Evan said.

"Yes, it did. I'm greatly relieved," Stone replied.

"I have your fee back at the Marquesa," Evan said.

"Thank you," Stone said. "If you see any other sort of trouble coming down the pike, I'd appreciate it if you'd tell me now."

"What sort of trouble?"

"Do you expect to be stabbed, shot at or charged with any crime?"

Evan laughed. "No, I don't. I hope to lead a more peaceful life from here on."

"Good," Stone replied.

48

Late in the afternoon, Stone and Dino were having a drink on their front porch when Evan Keating came down the walkway and stopped.

"Good afternoon," he said, offering Stone an envelope. "There's your fee for your day's work."

"Thank you," Stone replied, tucking it into a pocket.

"I wonder if I could ask a favor of the two of you," Evan said.

"What can we do for you?" Stone asked.

"Gigi and I are being married tomorrow morning, and since we don't know anybody in Key West, we need a couple of witnesses. Would you stand up for us?"

Stone looked at Dino, who shrugged. "Sure," Stone said.

"Thank you. We're in the cottage at the end of the walk, and the hotel arranged for a justice of the peace at noon."

"We'll be there," Stone said.

"There'll be lunch in the restaurant after that, and I hope you can join us."

"Sure, we'd like that," Stone said.

"We'll look forward to seeing you at noon, then," Evan said, and with a wave, he walked back toward his cottage.

"You mind staying another night?" Stone said.

"Not at all," Dino replied. "It's funny, but usually, when I go on vacation, I'm antsy to get home. Something about this place, though—I hate to leave."

"Why don't you buy a house, and I'll come to visit?" Stone said.

"Funny, I was going to ask you the same thing."

They were just about to order their second drink when Tommy Sculley ambled up to their cottage and accepted a rocking chair and a drink.

"I thought you'd like to know that your client is clear with the feds," Tommy said. "And the Coast Guard has released his boat. It's being towed to the yacht club. They'll put it in my berth, since my boat is out of the water for some work."

"That's good to hear," Stone replied, "and I'll pass the news about the boat on to Evan."

"And the ballistics report the Connecticut cops sent

me matches the bullet that was recovered from Evan's boat, so the same assassin was after both Evan and his father."

"That doesn't make any sense," Stone said. "The only person with any kind of motive to kill *both* of them is Evan's grandfather, and his motive would be purely financial. Since he's a wealthy man anyway, and since he's in his eighties, he doesn't seem a likely candidate. The Connecticut state cops have already looked at him and eliminated him as a suspect."

"What can I tell you?" Tommy said, accepting a drink from the room service waitress. He raised his glass. "Here's to unsolved murders; what would cops do without them?"

"Maybe you're underestimating old Eli Keating," Dino said to Stone. "Just because he's old doesn't mean he can't hate, and God knows, he must have hated Warren for stashing him in that nursing home."

"I'll give you that," Stone said, "but remember, Evan was shot at first, and even your Connecticut cop commented on how warm the relationship was between Evan and his grandfather."

"Okay, but there's one other solution to this, although it may seem improbable," Dino said.

"I'll take improbable, if it works," Tommy replied.

"First, Warren hires the hit man to kill Evan. The guy takes his shot but doesn't get the job done. Then either Evan or Eli, or both in collusion, hire the hit man to kill

Warren, and that one takes. And both Eli and Evan had motive to kill Warren, you'll admit."

"And they hired the same hit man?" Tommy asked.

"That's the improbable part," Dino said.

"But how would two of them, or all three, know about the same hit man?"

"The answer has to be, they both, or all three, knew Manny White, in Miami, or knew about him."

"How's that?" Tommy asked.

Stone spoke up. "The law firm I work with, which was representing Warren, got in touch with Manny for a skip trace on Evan. Warren needed Evan's signature on the contract to do the deal on selling the family business. Dino and I paid a visit to Manny, and we think he's the middleman, the connection to the hit man."

"Okay, so Warren, after he uses Manny for a skip trace, also uses him to find the hit man," Tommy said. "I'll buy that."

"Manny was the one who warned us—well, sort of—that Evan was a candidate for a hit," Dino said. "He said somebody had called him about some dirty work, but that he had hung up on him."

"But he didn't hang up," Tommy said. "He arranged for the guy to come to Key West and plug Evan. I buy that. What I don't quite buy is how Evan or his grandfather managed to hire the same hit man to go after Warren. Did either of them have a connection through the law firm, Stone?"

"No," Stone replied. "Evan doesn't know anybody at the law firm, and there's no reason for him to know Manny White. His grandfather knows the managing partner at the law firm, Bill Eggers, but Bill would never help Eli find a hit man. He wouldn't even put Eli in touch with Manny; if he needed Manny for something, Bill would deal with him himself."

"Are you saying that this Eggers guy is involved?"

"Of course not. He'd have no motive to have Evan killed. He did the legal work on the sale of the family business, and he'd want it to go through."

"All right," Tommy said, "we're agreed that both old Eli and young Evan would have motives for killing Warren—Eli because he got locked away in the nursing home, and Evan because his father tried to have him killed. Are we all agreed on that?"

"Agreed," Stone said.

"Yeah," Dino chimed in.

"But," Stone pointed out, "how did one of them get in touch with Manny White? How did they know about him?"

"You got me," Dino said.

"You got me, too," Tommy agreed. "Why don't we ask Manny?"

"We sort of already did," Dino said. "Stone and I went to see him and talked like we wanted a hit man. He didn't throw us out at first, but eventually he did. I don't think he'd look forward to another visit from us, since he never liked us much in the first place, when we were all NYPD."

"Maybe he'd talk to me," Tommy said.

"Does he know you from New York?" Dino asked.

"Yeah, I was around. He'd know my face, if not my name."

"Does he know you know us?" Stone asked.

"That wouldn't be hard to figure out," Tommy replied.

"Then we're fucked," Dino said.

"Not if we can think of somebody else to approach Manny, somebody with a plausible story of who recommended him, and somebody with a bunch of cash to wave at him."

"You got somebody in mind?" Dino asked.

"No, but I'm thinking," Tommy replied.

"Well, that's a relief," Stone said. "Let us know when you've figured it out."

49

Stone and Annika sat up in her bed, watching a DVD of *An American in Paris*.

"Isn't Gene Kelly wonderful?" Annika said.

"Absolutely wonderful. He's America's best dancer ever, in any discipline."

"You know about dancing?"

"No, but I still have an opinion."

"You think Kelly is better than Fred Astaire?"

"Astaire was great, but he was a ballroom and tap dancer; he didn't have Kelly's balletic training and sense. Kelly could do everything, often at the same time."

"Better than Baryshnikov?"

"Baryshnikov is a product of Russia, although I think he's Latvian or maybe Estonian by birth."

"Good point."

"Would you like to go to a wedding tomorrow?" Stone asked.

"Oh, Stone, are you proposing?"

"I'm just proposing that you accompany me to the wedding of Evan Keating and Gigi Jones."

"They're getting married?"

"That's why I'm inviting you to their wedding. It's at noon, at the Marquesa, in their cottage, and there's lunch afterward in the restaurant there."

"I'd love to. Let me see if I can swap shifts with someone."

"Would you like me to put the movie on hold?"

"Yes," she said, reaching for him.

"I thought you were going to make phone calls."

"Later."

Stone thought later was a good idea.

Later, she made the calls and swapped her shift; then she snuggled next to Stone. "When are you leaving?" she asked.

Stone looked at his watch: past midnight. "Tomorrow morning," he said. "We'll get an early start."

"Is there room in your airplane for me?" she asked.

He turned and looked at her. "Are you really thinking about moving to New York?"

"I have an interview for a job in three days," she said. "It sounds good. Of course, I'll have to let my house and find an apartment in New York."

"You won't have to find an apartment; you'll be staying with me."

"In your apartment?"

"In my house."

"You have a whole house?"

"I do. It was left to me some years ago by my great-aunt, and I renovated it, did much of the work myself."

"Tell me about it."

"It's simpler just to show you."

"How much luggage can I take on your airplane?"

"Two bags, not gigantic. Anything you need more than that, ship it."

"Okay," she said. "This is exciting."

"Yes, it is."

"We have had a great deal of lovemaking since you've been here, haven't we?" she asked.

"More than I've ever had before," Stone said.

"And you aren't tired of me?"

"Not in the least. I'm not sure how long I can keep up the pace, though. I may need a little rest now and then."

"Maybe now and then," she said, throwing a leg over him.

Stone went back to the Marquesa in the morning, had breakfast and called Bill Eggers.

"Morning, Bill."

"Good morning."

"I thought you'd like to know that Evan Keating and his girlfriend, Gigi Jones, are getting married today."

"Congratulate them for me," Eggers said.

"I'll do that."

"You can tell Evan, if his grandfather hasn't already, that the sale of Elijah Keating's Sons closed yesterday, and that I've wired his share of the proceeds to his bank in Miami. And it's more than he expected, because old Eli got another fifty million out of the buyers."

"So Evan's share is four hundred and twenty-five million dollars?"

"How'd you know that?"

"Because Evan showed me the contract."

"Oh."

"What does a kid his age do with that much money?"

"He'll think of something," Eggers said.

50

Stone picked up Annika, who looked fetching in an actual dress, something he hadn't seen her in, and they drove back to the Marquesa.

"Do you go to a lot of weddings?" she asked.

"Not if I can help it," he replied. "I had to go to one last year that I couldn't avoid. How about you?"

"My only family is a sister, Greta, who lives in Washington, D.C., and she's not married yet, so I've been to fewer weddings than most, I suppose. Once in a while one of the girls at the hospital gets married."

They picked up Dino at the cottage and walked up the path to Evan and Gigi's cottage, where Evan was seated on the front porch with a man in a suit. He greeted them and introduced the justice of the peace. Stone introduced Annika.

"We've met," she said.

"Of course, in the hospital," Evan replied.

"I'm glad you recovered so well."

"Thank you. Gigi's inside doing God knows what," he said. "She'll let us know when we can go in. I'd offer you some champagne, but Gigi says we have to wait until after the ceremony."

Stone whispered in his ear, "I just heard that the deal for the sale of the business closed yesterday, and there's four hundred and twenty-five million dollars in your Miami bank account."

Evan laughed, the first time Stone had seen him do so. "Well, that's a nice wedding present. Oh, I forgot." He pulled an envelope from his pocket. "I've made a will, and I'd like for you and Dino to witness it, if that's all right."

"Of course," Stone said, reaching for his pen. "Ask the JP to sign, as well. Three signatures is good."

Evan put the last page of the handwritten will on the porch table and signed it; then Stone, Dino and the JP added their signatures and addresses.

"Be sure and initial all the pages, too," Stone said.

Evan did so, then put the will into the envelope. "I'd like you to continue as my attorney, so will you put this in your safe?"

"Of course," Stone said; then he handed him his

card. "Here's my New York number, if you should need me."

Gigi stuck her head out the door. "All right, you can come in," she said.

Everyone filed into the living room of the cottage, where she had placed flowers here and there. She was wearing a white lace dress, and Stone thought she looked lovely.

The JP arranged everybody, then read the standard wedding ceremony, while Evan and Gigi made the appropriate responses. Stone noticed that Gigi didn't have a problem with vowing to obey. The JP pronounced them man and wife, they kissed, and then Evan opened a couple of bottles of Dom Pérignon, while Gigi distributed champagne flutes. They toasted and drank for a few minutes; then they went off to lunch in the hotel's restaurant.

The JP accepted an envelope, then excused himself, leaving the five of them at a round table in a far corner of the restaurant. More champagne was drunk.

"Where are you going to live?" Stone asked Evan.

"Here, in the winter," Evan replied. "We like living on the boat, but I expect I'll buy a house pretty soon. The rest of the year we'll just wander, until we find someplace we like for the summers."

"Sounds like an interesting life," Stone said.

"Stone," Gigi said, "I want to apologize for hitting

you when we first met. I thought you were some sort of threat to Evan, and I just reacted."

"Thank you, Gigi," Stone said. "I seem to have recovered, and if not, I know a doctor who can help me." He kissed Annika on the ear. "Where are you from, Gigi?" he asked, changing the subject.

"I'm from Coral Gables," she replied.

"And what did you do before you were married?"

"Oh, lots of things," she said. "I sold real estate. I sold boats. I started a couple of small businesses. I was even a private investigator for a while. That's how I met Evan."

The waiter interrupted them to present a huge crown roast of lamb, which, apparently, was the wedding feast. Everyone applauded and then, when the lamb had been served, began eating.

"Have you spent your whole career as a lawyer?" Evan asked Stone.

"No, I was a police detective, which is where Dino and I met; we were partners."

"Are you still a cop, Dino?" Gigi asked.

"I certainly am," Dino replied.

"Dino is the lieutenant in charge of the detective squad at the Nineteenth Precinct, on the Upper East Side of New York City," Stone explained. "That's how we both knew Tommy Sculley, who moved down here when he retired."

"Sculley seems like a good guy," Evan said.

"He is," Stone replied. "We hadn't seen him in years, until we came down here looking for you."

"Well, I'm glad you found me," Evan said.

"By the way," Stone said, "you should see somebody right away about investing the proceeds of the sale; you're losing a lot of interest every hour you wait."

"My grandfather is already dealing with that," Evan replied. "He's been heavily into investing ever since he retired from the company, nearly twenty years ago, and he's done very well. He just has more to play with now. He's put me on an allowance."

"I hope he hasn't been too strict with you," Stone said.

"No, very liberal. And I don't have to mow his lawn to earn it, the way I used to."

Stone laughed. "I used to have to sweep out my father's woodworking shop every day to earn mine."

Annika, who was sitting next to Evan, reached for the bread basket and knocked over Evan's champagne, some of it into his lap. "Oh, I'm sorry," she said, half rising and bending over to use her napkin on the spill.

There was a sound of breaking glass, and Annika fell sideways into Evan.

Stone turned and saw blood on Evan's jacket. "Gun!" Stone yelled. "Everybody down!" He threw himself at Annika and Evan, while on the other side of the table Dino got Gigi to the floor.

Stone lifted his head and looked out the shattered window behind him but saw no one. He turned his attention to Evan, who was covered in blood. "Somebody call 911 for an ambulance and the police!" Stone yelled, as he reached to pull Annika away from Evan. He couldn't believe that Evan had, once again, been the target of an assassin.

Then he realized that the blood on Evan's jacket was not Evan's. It was Annika's.

51

Dino put his head up and caught a glimpse of a motorcycle turning the corner from Simonton Street. "Motorcycle!" he yelled, pointing. He got a glimpse of a black helmet, before the machine disappeared down the block.

Stone tossed him the car keys. "Go!" he yelled. "I'll call Tommy!" Dino ran, as Stone grabbed his cell phone. Evan was giving Annika CPR.

Dino got out of the restaurant in time to see the bike turn left at the next corner. He leapt into the rental car, which was parked in front of an antiques store across the street, and burned rubber. He was turning the corner when his cell phone rang. "Yeah?"

"It's Tommy. Where are you?"

"The motorcycle turned left a block from the restaurant."

"Elizabeth Street?"

"Yeah, that's it," Dino said, checking the sign at the next corner. "Now he's turning right on that busy street, what is it?"

"Eaton."

"Yeah."

"I'm going to block the bridge from the island," Tommy said. "I'll call you back as soon as I've given the order."

"Okay." Dino slapped his phone shut and made the turn onto Eaton, scaring the life out of a woman trying to cross the street. He could see the motorcycle, three or four blocks up the straight street, passing cars with abandon. His phone rang again. "Yeah?"

"I've got two cars on the way to the turnoff for U.S. One. Anybody leaving the island has to go that way."

"The bike is red, looks Japanese," Dino said. "I can't get close enough for a plate, but he's wearing a green Windbreaker and a black helmet. He'll be at the entrance to the Navy base in a few seconds."

"I've got another car headed to the intersection of Eaton and Roosevelt Boulevard," Tommy said. "I've told them to ram him, if possible."

"He's past the Navy entrance," Dino said, "headed toward the bridge over Garrison Bight, where the sports fishermen dock."

"My car is at the light he's coming up to," Tommy said.

"I'm closing in on him just a little," Dino said. He whipped around a car and jammed the accelerator to the floor as he ran up the bridge. He had to slow for a curve after leaving the bridge, and he looked up to see the intersection ahead. A police car on the other side of Roosevelt was plowing through the intersection as the motorcycle reached it. The rider braked, slid sideways, then regained balance, missing the cop car by inches. He turned onto Roosevelt and accelerated.

"Your guy at Roosevelt missed him," Dino said. "He's headed up the boulevard now, and he must be doing eighty. Your car is backing up to get onto Roosevelt." Dino turned on his flashing caution lights and began using his horn.

"Don't kill yourself or anybody else!" Tommy said. "We'll head him off at the pass."

Dino eased off and got stuck behind a line of traffic. Ten seconds later, he was in oncoming traffic, blowing his horn over and over. Now he was free and up to ninety miles an hour. He saw the bike make the curve to the right. By the time he got to the turn, he was in the wrong lane again, signaling for a left turn onto U.S. 1. He made the corner with a great screeching of tires and saw two cop cars blocking the bridge. The motorcycle was on the sidewalk, getting past them.

"Shit!" Dino yelled, slamming on his brakes. He held

his badge out the window, blowing his horn, but he had to come to a complete stop. "That's the guy!" he yelled at the two policemen, who were watching the motorcycle disappear down the road. The cops dived into their cars and got them turned around; then Dino was bringing up the rear of a procession, as the two police cars headed up U.S. 1.

"Tommy," Dino yelled into the phone, "the bike got past the cops on the bridge, and he's headed north." Then, as they passed a wide street forking to the right, Dino thought he caught a glimpse of a motorcycle down that road, turning a corner. He put his car into a four-wheel drift and made the fork. What the hell, he thought, the cops have got the main road covered.

Dino was still driving fast, but he slowed at every corner, looking for the motorcycle. Then, a quarter-mile down the road, he saw it, lying on its side in the gutter. Two small boys were standing over it, looking at it. Dino slammed on his brakes, reversed and turned into the street.

He got out of the car and ran over to the motorcycle, which was still running. That, he supposed, was what was fascinating the two boys. "Kids," he said breathlessly, "did you see the rider get off?"

They both nodded.

"Which way did he go?"

They pointed down the street.

"Is he on foot?"

"Naw," one of the kids said. "He got in a car and drove off." He pointed at the rubber the man had left behind.

"Straight down the road?"

"Naw, he turned that way at the corner," the boy said, pointing right.

"What kind of car?"

"Ford," one kid said.

"Toyota," the other said. They began to argue.

"Shut up!" Dino said. "What color?"

"Black," one said.

"Green," the other said.

"Shit," Dino muttered to himself, running back to his car. "Tommy," he said into the phone, "you still there?"

"Yeah," Tommy said.

"The bike took a right at a fork in the road."

"I know where that is."

"He took another right, abandoned the bike and took off in a car, turned right at the next corner. He could be headed back toward Key West."

"Holy shit!" Tommy yelled. "Call you back."

Dino went back to the motorcycle and turned it off. There was a long leather scabbard buckled to a knee guard. His phone rang. "Yeah?"

"We're searching the whole island now," Tommy said.

"The bike is . . ." Dino looked for a street sign and

gave him the name. "It's got a scabbard for a rifle strapped to it. Get somebody out here; there may be prints."

"Right," Tommy said, and he hung up again.

"Listen to me, kids," he said, showing them his badge. "Don't you touch that bike, and don't you let anybody else touch it. More cops will be here in a minute." He gave each of them a ten; then he got back into his car and turned around.

There was no point in continuing his search, since he didn't know what he was looking for. He drove back to the Marquesa restaurant.

As he reached the corner he saw a pair of EMTs wheeling a gurney out into the street. Nobody was holding an IV bottle over her, and the sheet was pulled over her head. He went into the restaurant and found Stone, sitting on a bar stool, talking into his cell phone.

Stone hung up. "That was Tommy. They've lost the son of a bitch," he said. "They're setting up another roadblock at the Seven Mile Bridge, but he could be back in Key West now, or on a plane."

"Annika?" Dino asked.

"The bullet went in here," Stone said, pointing to a spot over his left ear, "and came out over her right eye. She had a pulse for a couple of minutes, but I lost it. The EMTs said there was never a chance." Stone slumped over the bar. "Now what do I do?" he said, disconsolately.

52

Stone was stretched out on his bed, half asleep. Dino had contacted Annika's sister, who was on her way to Key West, and he was now on the phone, making arrangements with a funeral director whom Tommy had recommended.

Stone felt as if he had been beaten up—stiff and sore and slightly nauseated. He sat up and put his feet on the floor and his head in his hands; then he got up, went into the bathroom and vomited. He wiped his face with a cold washcloth and went out to the porch. Dino and Tommy were sitting there.

"How are you feeling?" Dino asked.

"Lousy, but we have things to do."

"Everything has been done that can be done," Dino said. "Go lie down."

"I can't," Stone said. "There's more to do."

"What?" Dino asked.

"We've got to keep Evan alive," Stone said.

"He's okay for the moment," Tommy said. "Dino and I are both carrying, and you should be, too."

"That's not what I'm talking about. Dino. Did you hear my brief conversation with Gigi in the restaurant, right before the shooting?"

"I heard her apologize for hitting you over the head, that's all."

"I asked her where she was from, what sort of work she did before she met Evan."

"I didn't hear that part, I guess."

"She said she had sold real estate and boats and that she had started a couple of small businesses. She also said she had been a private investigator for a while, and that's how she met Evan."

Dino stared at him. "You're thinking . . ."

Stone nodded. "All this time we've been trying to connect the dots, trying to figure out who had motive and the connection with Manny White, and we forgot about Gigi."

"Well," Dino said, "she's certainly got motive now, and if she worked for Manny . . ."

"If she knows Manny well, she'd know about his little sideline," Tommy said.

"I think we're all on the same page now," Stone said. "Except Evan."

"And the guy's still out there," Tommy said. "And so's Evan." He nodded toward the walkway.

Stone looked up to see Evan coming down the walk, and they pulled up another chair for him.

"How are you feeling?" Evan asked Stone.

"I'm all right."

"I want to tell you how sorry I am," Evan said.

"Thanks," Stone replied, "but I'm afraid you've got more problems than I have."

"You think he'll try again?"

"Yes, but there's more to it than that."

"What else?"

Stone took a deep breath. "Have you ever heard of Manny White Investigations?"

"Yeah," Evan replied. "Gigi used to work for them."

"Evan, all three of us knew Manny White when we were on the NYPD, years ago."

"I never met the guy," Evan said. "Gigi quit after we met."

"We think Manny White was the middleman who hired the guy who shot you last time."

"That's quite a coincidence," Evan said.

"There are more coincidences," Stone said. "We think he also sent the man who killed your father. The bullets from your shooting and his are a match; they were fired from the same gun, and when Tommy gets back the ballistics report on today's shooting, we think there's going to be another match."

"This is bizarre," Evan said.

"There's still more," Stone said. "The first person to come under suspicion for both shootings was your grandfather."

"That's ridiculous."

"Probably so, but he was the only one with a financial motive for both shootings. Or at least he was at the time."

"Who do you suspect now?"

"There's only one other person with both a motive and a connection to Manny White," Stone said, then waited for it to sink in.

There were clearly wheels turning in Evan's head. Then the penny dropped. "No, that's crazy."

"Think about it," Stone said. "Killing your father gave you a much larger share of the proceeds from the sale of the business, didn't it?"

"Yes, but Gigi would have had no claim on that."

"Not then," Stone said, "but she was planning ahead, and now things are different. I haven't read your will, but I'm just guessing that Gigi is the principal beneficiary."

Evan stared at him. "She's the *only* beneficiary," he said.

"When your father tried to have you killed, she must have been very angry."

"She was. Very."

"So she called Manny White and arranged for Warren to be killed."

Evan was looking at his feet and shaking his head.

"And when the two of you were married and you signed that will . . ."

"Where is the will?" Evan asked.

Stone got up, went inside, got the will from his pocket, came back to the porch and handed Evan the envelope.

Evan stared at it but said nothing.

"I know how hard this is," Stone said.

"No, you don't," Evan snapped. "I wish you'd never told me this. I would rather have . . ." He trailed off.

"You'd rather have remained fat, dumb and happy and let her have you killed?"

"It would have been easier," Evan said.

"No, it wouldn't have. You'd have figured it out eventually, but with that shooter still in Key West, he might have gotten to you before you did."

"She couldn't have done this," Evan said.

"Evan, how many people knew where you were having your wedding lunch today?" Dino asked.

Evan thought about it. "Just the people at the table and the JP," he replied.

"And whose idea was it to have the lunch at the Marquesa restaurant?"

"Gigi's."

"And who chose the table by the Simonton Street window?"

"Gigi," he replied.

"I think you've just narrowed the list of suspects," Stone said.

Evan tore the will into small pieces.

"I'm afraid the will doesn't matter anymore," Stone said.

"Why not?" Evan asked.

"Because there's a marriage certificate. The JP would have filed it, and you'll be mailed a copy. Under Florida law, she stands to inherit everything you have."

"I just can't believe this," Evan said, shaking his head.

"If not for Annika's move toward you at lunch, Gigi would now be a very rich widow."

"Can you prove all of this?" Evan asked.

"No," Stone said.

"If you're right, this guy is just going to keep coming after me, isn't he?"

"Yes."

"What should I do?"

"First, let me find you a Key West attorney and file for an annulment."

"How long will that take?"

"I don't know, perhaps several weeks."

"And what am I going to do for that time?" Evan asked.

"Well, for a start," Stone said, "don't consummate the marriage."

"What else?"

315

"Only one person can connect Gigi to the shooting today," Stone said. "So we've got to find a way to persuade Manny White to tell us everything."

"How are you going to do that?" Evan asked.

"I don't know," Stone said, "but you can't go back to your cottage. We're going to have to move you to someplace safer."

Tommy spoke up. "My department has a little house we use to stash witnesses sometimes," he said. "I could take him there."

"Where's Gigi at the moment?" Stone asked Evan.

"She went for a walk."

"Then let's go move you out of that cottage right now," Stone said.

"You want me to just disappear?"

"You have to."

"What am I going to tell Gigi?"

"Not a thing. You can leave her a note saying you had to go to Connecticut; your grandfather has had a stroke. That might even buy us some time, since she knows that if he dies, she could inherit even more money."

"We're wasting time," Dino said.

53

The house was down a little lane a few blocks from the Marquesa, and it was tiny: two small bedrooms and a sitting room with an old TV.

"Don't worry," Tommy said to Evan. "You've got cable. And by the way, don't use your cell phone."

"I left it in the cottage, at Stone's insistence. Gigi is supposed to think I forgot it."

"Good idea. Got everything you need?"

"Oh, it's great," Evan said, tossing his suitcase on the bed in the larger of the two bedrooms. "I hope you don't mind, I'm going to take a nap," he said; then he closed the door.

Stone, Dino and Tommy sat down in the living room.

"Tommy," Dino said, "can you put a guard on him, or do we have to do it ourselves?"

"We're not going to be here long," Stone said, "and since nobody knows where he is, a guard won't be necessary."

"You know something we don't know?" Dino asked.

"Look, our only shot is to get Manny White to agree to arrange a hit on somebody, then nail him, right?"

"Right," Dino said.

"Well, you, Tommy and I are out; he knows us all, and he won't trust any of us."

"When you're right, you're right," Dino said.

"So who are we going to get to do this?"

"I don't think my boss would go for sending a Key West cop up there," Tommy said, "so don't count on any of my people."

"Okay," Stone replied. "How about a Miami cop?"

"The interdepartmental thing is complicated," Tommy said, "and it could take a while to set it up."

"And Miami would get the collar," Dino pointed out.

"Oh, I don't give a shit about that," Tommy said.

"Who do we know who could pull this off that Manny doesn't know?" Dino asked.

"I can think of one guy," Stone said.

"Yeah, who?"

"Evan."

"And why do you think Evan could pull this off?" Dino asked.

"He's a very calm guy," Stone said. "He doesn't rattle easily."

"I'll give you that," Dino replied.

"And he's motivated," Tommy pointed out.

"That too," Dino said.

"Okay, let's say he'll do it," Stone said. "Who's the target? Who does he want killed and where?"

"Somebody in South Florida," Tommy said, "not Key West."

"Good," Stone said. "Who and where?"

"You guys ever know Mike Levy, who was an investigator for the DA's office?" Tommy asked.

"No," Stone and Dino said simultaneously.

"He's retired, lives on the inland waterway, somewhere between Stuart and Palm Beach. Is that too far north?"

"Is it near the interstate?"

"Yeah. It's only a couple of hours' drive from Miami, and being on the waterway, it could be approached by boat. That might appeal to the shooter."

"Does Levy have any family?"

"His wife died last year; I went to the funeral. He's got kids, but they're both in the New York area."

"So he's all alone there?"

"Yeah, and Mike might find something like this entertaining."

"Who do we get for backup?" Stone asked.

"The local sheriff might play," Tommy said. "I worked on something with him a while back."

"We're going to need a lot of cash for bait," Dino said.

"Evan can supply that," Stone said.

"We're going to have to get him some fake ID," Dino said. "Manny's going to be careful. He'll search him for a wire, maybe even check him out."

"Let me work on that," Tommy said. "We've done that kind of thing for undercover drug buys."

"There's something else," Stone said. "We need a connection to Manny White that can't be traced back to us. Evan's going to have to say that somebody sent him, somebody Manny would trust."

"Wally Millard," Dino said. "Wally's sent him business before; Manny would trust him."

"You think Wally would do it?" Stone asked.

"Let me talk to him about it," Dino said.

"What else haven't we covered?" Stone asked.

"I think that's about it," Stone said. "I'll talk to Evan."

"Talk to me about what?" Evan asked.

Stone turned to see him standing in the bedroom door, in his shorts, rubbing his eyes.

"Evan," Stone said, "go back in the bedroom and use the phone to call your grandfather's house. Tell his secretary that if anyone calls for you to say you're on your way there, or if it's tomorrow, that you're in town, but not in. Tell her to confirm that your grandfather has had a stroke, if anybody questions that. Then put on some clothes and come sit down for a minute," Stone said.

Evan went back into the bedroom and closed the door.

"You think he'll do it?" Dino asked.

"We're about to find out," Stone said.

Dino took out his cell phone. "I'm going to go call Wally," he said, going out onto the screen porch.

Tommy stood up. "And I'm going to go call Mike Levy."

Evan came back into the living room and sat down. "I made the call; the secretary and my grandfather are both on board."

"Evan," Stone said, "have you ever done any acting?"

"Yes, in high school and university theater. I played both leads and character parts."

"Well," Stone said, "we've got an important role for you."

"Oh?"

"How much cash do you have on hand?"

"Do I have to pay to play?"

"Only temporarily."

"I've got about sixty thousand in my briefcase. You may remember that I've given you forty thousand over the past week. Why don't we use *your* money?"

"I've already wired it to New York," Stone lied. "Unlike you, I don't like to travel with a lot of cash."

"To each his own," Evan said. "I've always found cash on hand comforting."

"It just makes me nervous."

"What kind of role do you want me to play?"

"It's the lead," Stone replied.

54

Manny White opened his desk drawer and picked up the throwaway cell phone that was ringing. "Yeah?"

"You know who this is?" she asked.

"Sure," he said. "I wish you every profitable happiness."

"Gee, thanks."

"So how's the new life?"

"On hold," she said. "The old, old man has had a stroke, and he's flown north. You should pull our friend off. He's very hot here, anyway."

"Okay. Shall I send him north in pursuit?"

"No. I don't know how long he'll be there; he hasn't called me yet."

"Call him, then."

"I can't; he left in a hurry when I was out, and he forgot his phone."

"Okay, I'll pull our guy out."

"Tell him to avoid the airport. They'll be checking cars on the highway, too."

"You've got a boat, haven't you?"

"Yes."

"Take him up the road someplace, where he can rent a car."

"They'll be watching up there, too."

"Then take him up to Key Largo. I'll meet you there and drive him home."

"I guess I could do that."

He gave her the name of a marina. "You know it?"

"Yeah."

"When will you be there?"

"I can leave first thing in the morning," she said. "Tell him to call me on this number, and I'll tell him how to find the boat."

"Okay, I'll call him now. We should be in Key Largo by late tomorrow afternoon. I'll call you a couple of hours out and give you a better ETA. Hey, since you got some time off, you want to do a little work?"

She laughed. "Are you kidding? I'm never going to work again."

He laughed, too. "Can't blame you. Call me tomorrow." He hung up.

She hung up, too, and she didn't have to wait long for the call. "Yes?"

"Hi, it's Larry Lee," he said.

"That's the name these days, huh?"

"Always has been."

"Manny told you what he wants to do?"

"Yeah, and it sounds good to me; I don't like being holed up like this."

"You know where the Key West Yacht Club is?"

"Yeah, I've driven past it."

"There's a thirty-two-foot motorboat with no name on the stern—an old one, mahogany and white—just inside the main gate. Meet me there at seven a.m. tomorrow morning, and ditch your car somewhere else first. If you get there before I do, let yourself onto the boat; the lock is broken on the cabin doors."

"Okay, see you at seven."

"Call me ten minutes before you get there, so I'll know you're on the way. I'll call you if anything changes." She hung up, happy for something to do with herself. She liked being on the water.

A few blocks away, late that evening, Tommy sat down with Evan next to a phone. "Here's what we're going to do," he said. "I've made some arrangements with the phone company. You're going to call your grandfather's number in"—he looked at his watch—"two minutes.

There'll be a click, and then you'll get a dial tone. Dial Gigi's number. She'll see the Connecticut number on her caller ID. Don't be too definite about when you're coming back."

"I get the picture," Evan said. He waited until Tommy cued him; then he dialed the number, got the dial tone and dialed Gigi's number.

"Hello?"

"Hi," he said.

"There you are," she replied. "Where are you?"

"I just got to Grandfather's house," he said. "I'm sorry to run out like that, but it was an emergency."

"How is he?"

"Hanging on by a thread, apparently. I sat with him for a couple of minutes, but he's in a coma. His doctor didn't want to take him to the hospital, said there was no point. He has a living will and a do-not-resuscitate order."

"Maybe that's best, then."

"It's what he wanted. How are you?"

"I'm okay. I think I'll move back onto the boat tomorrow, though; I miss being on the water."

"Good idea."

"I may even cruise around some. You can reach me on my cell."

"Another good idea."

"Do you know how long you'll be there?"

"No way to tell; it could end tonight or in a couple

of days, according to what the doctor said. I'll arrange a small graveside service. Most of his friends are dead, so there's no point in doing the whole church thing."

"Come back to me soon," she said. "I love you, and I miss you."

"Same here, babe. You take care."

"You too." She hung up.

Evan hung up.

"Did she buy it?"

"Sure she did," Evan replied. "She has no reason not to. Does this plan you and Stone and Dino are working on provide for putting her away?"

"Not directly, but if we get Manny in a tight enough squeeze, he'll implicate her."

"I hope so," Evan said.

55

Gigi was already on the boat when her cell phone buzzed. "Yes?"

"It's Larry. I'm across the street—I've ditched the car."

"Come ahead, then."

"Okay." He hung up.

She started the engines and checked the gauges. A moment later there was a knock on the hull, and Larry Lee stepped into the cockpit. "Good morning," she said.

"Good morning. We ready to head out?"

"We've got to stop at Key West Bight for fuel, so you go below and stay there, until I call you up. I can handle the fueling."

"I'm afraid you're going to have to handle everything," he said. "I know nothing about boats. I'll try and do what you tell me, though." He threw his bags below and took a seat.

Gigi tossed the lines ashore and edged out of the berth and into the channel. In an hour they'd be on their way to Key Largo. Larry looked pretty good, she thought. She had fucked him a couple of times before; maybe she would again. It would make an interesting change from Evan.

Evan sat in the living room with Stone, Dino and Tommy while they briefed him.

"Okay," Dino said, "Wally Millard is on board; he's the guy who's recommending Manny to you. If it should come up in your conversation with Manny, Wally is medium height, stocky, gray hair. He's ex-NYPD, now a PI. A lawyer friend referred you to him; you had all your meetings with him at Elaine's. Be vague about what kind of work he did for you."

"Okay," Evan said. "What's Elaine's?"

Dino looked at Evan as if he felt sorry for him. "It's a very popular restaurant in New York, at Eighty-eighth and Second Avenue."

"Got it."

Tommy handed Evan a typed sheet of paper and a map. "My friend Mike Levy has agreed to be the target," he said. "I want you to commit all this to memory, except the map, which you can show Manny. There are written directions to Mike's house, both from I-95 and from the Intracoastal Waterway, but I want you to strongly suggest an approach from the water. Mike has a Boston Whaler at a little marina just south of there; it's marked on the map. Tell Manny the shooter can use the boat, then leave the keys in the locker under the steering wheel."

"Why do you want an approach from the water?" Evan asked.

"Because it's easier to see the shooter coming. If he comes by land, he could leave his car anywhere and sneak through the woods. Mike's making a dummy that he'll put on the back porch, which overlooks the waterway. There's a floating dock there with the initials M.L. on a sign. He can shoot from the boat or from the dock."

Evan read the instructions over carefully. "All right. Why do I want Levy killed?"

"A business partnership gone wrong—there's some insurance money. Don't try and give too much detail; you don't want a guy like Manny to have any more information than he actually needs to accomplish the hit. The more you tell him, the more he'll ask."

"Okay."

Stone handed Evan an envelope. "Here's your money back. We've wiped all the fingerprints off, and all the bills have been marked with a tiny dab of a fluid that won't show except under ultraviolet light. Also, we've left the bands from South Beach Security in place; that will lend credibility. Offer him forty grand, and go as high as sixty if you have to. You'll give him half the money up front and let him propose how you give him the second half. That's probably when the state cops will bust him, so you have to call us and give us a location. Otherwise, they'll have to put a tail on you."

Tommy gave him a wallet. "You've got a driver's license, a Social Security card and some miscellaneous ID, all in the name of Howard Worth. It's an identity we did for a drug cop; all we did was make a new license with your photo from my cell phone camera."

Evan put the wallet in his pocket. "Do you want me to identify myself by that name?"

"No, that stuff is just in case he searches you. Tell him your name is Joe, just Joe. All he should know about you is that name and the number for this phone." Tommy handed him a phone. "Memorize the number. It's a throwaway. Don't call anybody but Manny from this phone."

Stone handed him another phone. "Use this for general purposes, like calling us."

"Am I going to have to wear a wire?" Evan asked.

"No," Tommy said, handing him a well-used briefcase. "The briefcase is wired, so keep it within about eight feet of you and Manny. It'll pick up everything and record it. It's a solid-state recorder, very small, and it's concealed under the lining of the case. We've put a few pens, paper clips and other junk in there, just to look like you use it every day, but there's room for the money, too."

"Got it," Evan said.

"It's okay if you're a little nervous," Stone said. "Anybody would be, under the circumstances. Try and stick to the script we've talked about, but you can improvise, if you think it will help. Just don't talk too much; you might make mistakes."

Stone described Manny's office, so he would know what to expect. "Okay, you ready to make the call?"

Evan took a deep breath and let it out. "Okay."

Manny's secretary buzzed him. "There's a man who says he needs to talk to you, says it's urgent."

"What's his name?"

"Joe, just Joe."

Manny picked up the phone. "Manny White."

"Mr. White, my name is Joe. I'd like to speak to you about a job, a very important job."

"So speak," Manny said.

"Not on the phone," Evan said. "I can meet with you around midday today, if you're available. In your office or wherever you choose."

"Give me some sort of idea about what you want," Manny said. "I may not do your kind of work."

"Wally Millard, in New York, says you might be able to help."

"Oh, okay, then. How about one o'clock, in my office?"

"Then we're good."

"You have the address?"

"No."

Manny gave it to him, then hung up and called Wally Millard.

"Millard."

"Hey, Wally, it's Manny White."

"Hey, Manny, how you doin'? Funny you should call. I sent you some business yesterday."

"Yeah, he just called. Who is he?"

"He doesn't want to do names. Calls himself Joe. But I've done a couple jobs for the guy, and he's always been straight with me. Pays well and on the dot, too."

"Okay. If you're vouching for the guy, he can't be all bad."

"I was never sorry I worked for him," Wally said.

"Thanks, pal," Manny said; then he hung up.

"We're on for one o'clock," Evan said.

"Then we'd better get started," Stone said. He called the airport and asked for his airplane to be refueled and pulled out of the hangar.

56

Stone landed at Tamiami Airport, rented a car and drove to South Beach. When they were a block from Manny White's office building, he stopped. "Okay, you take the car from here," he said to Evan. "Put my cell phone number in your personal phone on a speed-dial button, so if you get into trouble you can call us. When you're done, drive back to this point and pick us up."

"Okay," Evan said.

"There's parking behind his building, and you can go in the rear entrance."

"Got it."

Stone had the feeling he was a lot more nervous than Evan. "Don't hurry it; he'll think you're panicky."

"When do I want this hit done?"

"As soon as possible. Tell him you're under some

time pressure, but don't tell him why. Tonight is okay, tomorrow. Don't agree to anything later than that, and insist on knowing when they're going to do it. Tell him you want to be well away from the action."

"Okay. Can I go now?"

Stone and Dino got out of the car, and he drove away.

Manny White's secretary buzzed him. "Mr. White," she said, "your appointment is here."

"Send him in," Manny said, and he rose to meet the young man who entered his office. They shook hands, and Manny indicated a chair. "Have a seat, Joe."

"Thank you. Wally Millard sends his best regards."

"How did you meet Wally?" Manny asked.

"My New York lawyer sent me to him when I needed some work done."

"What sort of work?"

"We don't need to go into that," Evan said.

"Tell me about your problem," Manny said.

"I'm in business with a man, and it's not working out. I want to sell the business, and I have a buyer, but my partner wants a lot more out of the deal than he put in."

"So you want a sort of business divorce?"

"You could put it that way."

"And it won't be amicable?"

"No, and I'd like it to be permanent."

Manny stood up and walked around the desk. "Stand up, Joe," he said, "and take off your jacket. I need to take some precautions."

Evan stood up and watched as Manny went through his coat pockets and felt along every seam.

"Unbutton your shirt and pull out your shirttail," Manny said.

Evan did as he was told.

Manny lifted his shirt and inspected his chest and back, then made sure there were no wires attached to the shirt. He patted Evan down carefully, paying particular attention to his crotch. "Drop your pants to your knees," Manny said.

Evan did so and stood still while Manny pulled down his shorts and parted the cheeks of his ass. After Evan had pulled up his pants, Manny checked his shoes and socks.

"All right, you can get dressed," Manny said. "You're clean." He picked up Evan's briefcase and opened it.

Evan took out the envelope with the cash. "We're not ready to get to this yet," he said.

Manny emptied the briefcase onto his desk, then felt the inside for lumps; then he raked the detritus from the case back into it and set it on the desk.

Evan put the money back into the case.

"All right," Manny said, "tell me what you want."

Evan took a pad from the briefcase and wrote, "I want him dead," then showed it to Manny.

"I understand you. What's the man's name?"

Evan wrote "Michael Levy" and the address.

"Where is this?"

"North of here a couple of hours, about eight or nine miles south of Stuart, on the Intracoastal Waterway."

"How far from I-95?"

"Six or seven miles, but your best opportunity would come from a boat, which I will provide." Evan took the map from his pocket and spread it on Manny's desk. "There's a little marina up this creek, right here. It's private and untended, and I have a Boston Whaler tied up there. It's black and has the name *Waverider* on the bow. The key is in a little locker under the steering wheel, and the outboard has a push-button starter."

"Okay, and this map gets my guy there from the interstate?"

"Right down this little road," Evan said, pointing. "All he does is start the boat, untie it and go down the creek a hundred yards or so to the waterway, then turn north. There's a powerful spotlight in the boat, if they go after dark, but I'd suggest starting at dusk and approaching the place after the sun is well down. The house is here, marked by an X, and there's a dock. There's a sign on the dock with the initials M.L."

"Will my guy need to go inside?"

"Maybe, but probably not. Mike has a drink or two on his back porch at sunset. Your man can approach him down the dock, as if to ask for directions, or if he's good with a rifle, shoot from the end of the dock."

"He's good with everything. Is your friend armed?"

"He has a shotgun, but he keeps it locked in a cabinet in the kitchen, so it won't be at hand. When the job's done, your man should just take the boat back to the marina and tie it up, then drive away."

"You understand, something like this will be expensive?"

"What did you have in mind?"

"Fifty thousand dollars, half up front, the rest when the job is done."

"I can manage forty, twenty now."

"You'll have to manage fifty."

Evan pretended to think it over for a few seconds; then he nodded. "All right," he said, "but there are time constraints. I need it done tonight if possible."

Manny looked at his watch. "That may be possible. If not, then tomorrow night."

"No later than that," Evan said. He took the envelope from the briefcase and removed three bundles of $10,000 each. He removed five thousand from one bundle, then slid the stack toward Manny.

"I don't give receipts," Manny said, raking the money into a desk drawer. "How can I reach you?"

Evan wrote down the number of his throwaway cell phone and handed it to him.

"I'm expecting a call from my man soon," Manny

said. "I'll call you when I know. Here's how we do the final payment: You and I will meet for a drink around the time of the work being done. When I get a call that it's complete, you pay the rest."

"How will I know he's dead?" Evan asked.

"You can drive up there and take his pulse if you want to, but you pay when I get the call. Wally will tell you that I don't welsh on deals. Anything goes wrong, you get all your money back."

"I'd rather be out of the state when it happens," Evan said.

"We'll be in a public place where I'm known. The waitress and the bartender will remember you, but not me. You'll have a solid alibi."

A cell phone rang, and Manny took it from a drawer. "Yeah?" He listened for a moment. "Good news." He covered the phone and said to Evan, "It's my guy," then he continued. "What's your ETA?" He listened some more. "Are you up for something good tonight? It's a couple of hours north of here. The usual price. Good. Instead of my picking you up, rent a car. Call me when you're on your way, and we'll meet at that place we met last time, say four o'clock? I'll have all the details and the first payment. See you then." Manny hung up. "He's available tonight," he said to Evan.

"Good."

"You and I will meet at a restaurant called the Steak

Shack. It's on this street, about two blocks down." Manny pointed.

"Good."

"Seven-thirty and bring the rest of the money."

"I'll see you then," Evan said. The two men shook hands, and Evan left.

Manny stood at the rear window and watched Evan get into a car and drive away; then he called Larry again.

"Yes?"

"Listen, the job is going to involve a boat."

"I don't do boats."

"Put Gigi on."

"Hello?"

"Listen, kiddo, I need your help for an important job tonight. It needs to be done from a boat, and Larry doesn't mess with boats."

"I already found that out," she said. "He's useless. How long is this going to take?"

"You'll be done by nine tonight. Larry's renting a car, and we'll meet at a place he knows, where I'll give you the details."

"How much?"

"Ten grand for very little work in advance. All you have to do is get him to a dock in the boat."

"All right, I'll see you later." She hung up.

Manny sat down at his desk, pleased with himself. This one was going to be a piece of cake, and it would make up for the failure in Key West.

57

Stone and Dino looked up to see Evan and the car coming. He stopped, and they got inside, Stone behind the wheel. "How'd it go?" he asked.

"Perfectly," Evan replied. "He searched me and the briefcase for a wire, but he didn't find anything. While I was there he got a call from his hit man, and we're on for tonight."

"Hey, that's quick service!" Dino said.

"I told him to use the boat, as we'd planned."

Stone got on the phone to Tommy Sculley. "Hey, Tommy, we're on for tonight."

"*Tonight*? I'd better get my ass in gear. I've alerted the county sheriff, and they're standing by. I guess I'd better seaplane it up there and land on the waterway. It's the fastest way to Mike's place from Key West."

Evan spoke up. "Put it on speaker."

Stone did.

"Tommy," Evan said, "I told him Mike has a drink on his back porch at sunset every night, so you need to be there while it's still broad daylight."

"Okay, I'll alert everybody."

"Something else: I'm going to meet Manny White at a place in South Beach called the Steak Shack, at seven-thirty. He's to get a call there when the job is done, and I'll give him the rest of the money. The bartender and the waitress are supposed to be my alibi."

"You done good, kid," Tommy said. "The sheriff's guys will bust the hit man when he brings the boat back to the marina, and the state cops can bust Manny as soon as the money changes hands."

"Tommy," Stone said, "for God's sake tell the state cops to be careful. This is apparently a restaurant where Manny is well known, and we don't want to spook him by having cops at half the tables. Have them look in from outside, or Evan can phone them when it's done. They can bust Manny on his way out of the place."

"Okay, okay, I get it," Tommy said. "Where are you two guys gonna be?"

Stone looked at Dino. "What's your preference?"

"We're here. Let's stay here," Dino said. "We can go in with the state cops after the money changes hands. Anyway, I'd like to see the look on Manny's face."

"Me too," Stone said. "You get that, Tommy?"

"I got it. Just don't let Manny spot you, or he'll walk out."

"Evan recorded their whole conversation," Stone said, "so we'll have him, anyway."

"Wait a minute," Evan said, "I just thought of something."

"What?"

"I didn't get everything recorded."

"What are you talking about?"

"I'm afraid I got a little too clever. I wrote down part of it on a pad, the part where I tell him I want the guy killed, and showed it to him instead of speaking."

Stone groaned. "You get that, Tommy?"

"Yeah, I got it. Evan, you've got to get it all recorded tonight when you meet Manny. Don't write things down this time, okay?"

"Okay, Tommy," Evan said. "I'm sorry."

"Just do a good job tonight, and we'll bag everybody."

"I swear I will," Evan said.

Suddenly, Dino yelled, "Everybody duck!"

Everybody ducked.

"What's this about, Dino?" Stone asked.

"It's Manny. He just drove past us."

"Did he see us?"

"I don't think so, but man, was that close. He's way up the street now, so you can sit up."

Everybody sat up.

"I heard that," Tommy said. "Did you guys just blow this whole deal?"

"I think we're okay, Tommy," Dino said. "He didn't see us."

Manny White drove down Collins Avenue and onto the mainland, toward Florida City. An hour later he pulled up at a diner, near where the Florida Turnpike started, and went inside. Larry Lee and Gigi Jones were at a corner booth.

Manny slid in beside them and laid his briefcase on the table.

A waitress approached. "What can I get you?"

"A Diet Coke," Manny said.

"Same here," Larry said.

"Iced tea," Gigi said.

The woman left, and Manny opened his briefcase and took out the map Joe had given him. "This is gonna be easy," he said. He showed them the marina and told them about the boat, then gave them every detail he could remember about the cottage and the dock. "The guy has a drink on his back porch every evening at sundown," he said. "That's your time to hit him. Just get the boat near the dock in decent light. There's a sign on the dock with his initials, M.L."

"Is the guy going to be armed?" Larry asked.

"He keeps a shotgun locked up, so he can't get at it in a hurry," Manny replied. "If you can use your rifle from the end of the dock, that's best."

"Why can't we approach from the landward side?" Gigi said.

"Too many neighbors to see you come and go."

"What about people at the marina where the Whaler is?"

"It's private and unmanned. You can sit in the car and see whether anybody is around."

"This all sounds good," Larry said. "It just came up today?"

"Yeah, a friend of mine in New York sent the guy, says he's okay and . . ." He opened the briefcase and gave Larry and Gigi ten thousand dollars each. "He brought gifts," Manny said.

The two tucked their money away.

"You two had better get going before rush hour starts up," Manny said. "Take the turnpike north; there'll be less traffic than on I-95, and no trucks. I'll get the check."

"You're a prince, Manny," Gigi said.

"What are you going to do about the car?" Manny said.

Gigi spoke up. "I'll drop Larry off at his house in Jupiter and return the car to Key Largo tonight. To-morrow, I'll head back to Key West. I'll let you know when Evan gets back from Connecticut, and we'll get him taken care of."

"I don't want to go to Key West again, if I can help it," Larry said. "I've missed twice there; it's bad luck."

"I'll see if I can get him to Miami," Gigi said. "You'll have a very nice payday when we get that done."

The three split up and went their separate ways.

58

Tommy Sculley sat in the right seat of the amphibian Cessna 182 and watched the Intracoastal Waterway a thousand feet below them.

"You gotta get lower," Tommy said, looking at the map, "and right now."

"Okay," the pilot replied, reducing power. The airplane, with the drag of the floats, slowed immediately and began to descend.

"Man, everything looks different from the air," Tommy said.

"Always," the pilot replied. He pointed at the map. "Is that the creek right before we get to your buddy's house?"

"That's gotta be it," Tommy said. "That's where the marina is."

The pilot reduced power further and put in a notch of flaps. "Then we better get down fast; we're nearly there. Watch for boats and other obstructions."

Tommy peered ahead. The sun was low in the sky, and the western half of the waterway was in shadow. "Damn, we're really cutting it close," he said.

"We had headwinds," the pilot replied, putting in another notch of flaps. "I see a dock up ahead. We clear of traffic?"

Tommy checked ahead. A large cabin cruiser was moving south on the waterway, but was not a factor for them. "You're all clear, as far as I can see," he said.

The pilot touched down smoothly and slowed. "How can we tell if this is the right dock?"

"It's the first one up from the creek," Tommy said. "Can you turn around and come in with my side to the dock? Then I can hop out and hold the plane. Leave the engine running, so you can take off immediately if this is the right place."

The pilot made a wide turn, set the engine at idle and approached the dock. As he did a man came jogging down the dock.

"That's Mike!" Tommy yelled. "He'll catch us."

The pilot maneuvered closer until the wing was over the dock. The man reached out, grabbed the strut under the wing and pulled them until the floats brushed the fenders attached to the dock.

Tommy opened the door and tossed his overnight

bag onto the pontoon, then hopped out and closed the door. He gave the pilot a thumbs-up and, with Mike's help, pushed the airplane away from the dock. A moment later the airplane was picking up speed, and a moment after that it lifted off and headed south, climbing.

"Hey, Mike!" Tommy said, shaking his hand and clapping him on the shoulder. "How you been?"

"Not too bad," Michael Levy replied. He was a little over six feet tall, on the slim side, wearing shorts, sneakers and a polo shirt. He grabbed Tommy's bag and started up the dock. "C'mon," he said. "I'll show you what I've got done."

Gigi drove the rental car down the paved road, with Larry Lee, which was his real name, in the passenger seat. "Look at that," Larry said, pointing to an airplane climbing above the tree line, headed south.

"It's just an airplane," Gigi said, checking their map. "Here's the road to the marina coming up."

"It's against the law in Florida to land an airplane on a beach or on the inland waterway," Larry said.

"Does anybody pay attention to that?" she asked.

"The cops don't," he replied.

"Did the airplane have any official markings?"

"No, it looks ordinary enough," Larry said, "but I still don't like it."

She reached the road with a sign pointing left to the Osprey Marina—PRIVATE.

"Slow down," Larry said. "Slow way down." They came to a bridge. "Stop at the top of the bridge," he said.

"All right."

The bridge gave them a little elevation to see above the trees, which weren't very tall.

"We've got a nearly empty parking lot, a shack and a floating pontoon," she said. "No more than a dozen boats, and I don't see any people."

"There's one," Larry said. A man had stepped onto the pontoon from a small motorboat with a cabin and was walking toward the connecting footbridge that rose and fell with the tide. He was carrying a sailing duffel. "Let's just wait here a minute," Larry said.

The man walked ashore, tossed his duffel in the back of a pickup, got in, started it and drove toward the road.

"Go ahead slowly," Larry said. "Let him get past us, then stop before you get to the parking lot."

The truck passed them going the other way as they drove off the bridge.

"He looks like a regular guy with a boat," Gigi said.

"Yeah, he does. Just pull over about fifty yards ahead at that wide spot. I want to take a look on foot."

"Larry, the place looks deserted." She sighed.

"Gigi, did I ever tell you that I've never been arrested, not even for a speeding ticket, let alone a kill-ing?"

"Yes, Larry."

"Well, that's because I'm careful, and I always listen to my own brain, and right now, my brain is a little nervous."

Gigi pulled over and stopped. "You want me to wait here?"

"Turn the car around and keep the motor running," he said.

She did so, and Larry got out of the car. He crossed the road, entered the woods, which was mostly smallish live oaks, and began running lightly through the trees. He slowed down when he could see the edge of the parking lot, then approached the pavement cautiously. From a few feet into the trees he could see everything. The parking lot was empty, and so was the pontoon. The sun was low in the sky, big and red, with the light filtering through the pollution from I-95. It was dead quiet.

Larry looked around the perimeter of the parking lot, checking for men in the tree line, but he saw noth-ing. He retraced his steps to the road and went to the car. As he put his hand on the door handle he heard something. *Whomp-whomp-whomp.* He got quickly into the car. "Chopper," he said. "Let's go, but don't drive over thirty."

"Which way?"

"Back the way we came," Larry said.

"I don't see the chopper," she said, and then she crossed the bridge and turned right, and there it was.

"State police," he said.

"But it's headed away from us, toward I-95."

"Look," he said, pointing. "Stop here."

Ahead of them, several miles away, a column of black smoke was rising, and the helicopter was flying toward it.

"Accident on I-95," Larry said. "That's what the chopper is for. We're okay; let's go back to the marina."

Gigi made a U-turn and retraced her route.

"This time park in the parking lot," Larry said.

"Are you feeling less nervous?" she asked.

"I'll tell you in a minute," he replied.

She pulled into the lot.

"Turn around and back into a spot, near the bridge to the pontoon," he said. When she stopped, he got out of the car and looked around, listened. "Pop the trunk."

She did, and he walked to the rear of the car, still looking around, and got his duffel with its equipment inside. He waved for her to follow him.

Gigi got out of the car and padded down the bridge to the pontoon. "There's the boat," she said, pointing to the end of the float. It was a black Boston Whaler, and the name on the side registered.

Larry was already climbing in. He opened the small

locker under the steering wheel and came out with a key attached to a plastic float. "Looks like we're in business," he said.

"And not a moment too soon," Gigi replied, checking the sunset and untying the mooring lines. She stepped into the boat, inserted the key into the ignition lock and turned it. The fifty-horsepower outboard purred to life.

"Let's get out of here," Larry said. "This place gives me the creeps."

59

Stone and Dino stood with Evan beside the rental car, a few blocks from the restaurant.

"It's seven twenty-five," Dino said. "You'd better get going. Park as close to the restaurant as you can."

"Have you got the money?" Stone asked.

"I have."

"Don't give it to him until he confirms the hit," Stone said, "and make him say it out loud, for the recorder. My guess is, he'll leave the second he gets the money, and then he's the state police's problem."

"Where are they?" Evan asked.

"Already in and around the restaurant for some time, I should think," Stone replied. "Don't look for them in the restaurant; they'll spot you—don't worry.

And when Manny gets up and leaves, don't try to stop him or follow him."

"Got it," Evan said.

"You've been pretty cool through this so far," Dino said to him. "Now is not the time to get nervous. A little, maybe, that would be normal, but not much."

"I'm not excessively nervous," Evan said.

"Then get going."

Stone opened the car door for him. "Just stay at the restaurant until it's all over," he said. "We'll come find you."

Evan got into the car and drove away.

"You think this is going to work?" Dino asked.

"Nothing we can do about it," Stone replied. "It's in the hands of other people now."

As Tommy followed Mike up the fifty yards of catwalk from the dock, he saw a man sitting on the front porch, rocking and sipping a drink.

"We got company?" Tommy asked.

"We've got two deputies with rifles in the house, but have a look."

They approached the porch, and they were ten yards away before Tommy got it. "It's a dummy," he said.

"Made it myself," Mike said.

It was wearing Mike's clothes, with a floppy fishing hat. Tommy could see a string tied to the rocker and another that held the dummy's left hand in place, holding a glass. When the string was pulled, the glass went to the dummy's lips. A deputy was standing inside in the living room, pulling the strings.

"That's sweet work, Mike," Tommy said, looking at his watch. "But we'd better get off the porch; it's nearly dark."

As Gigi put the outboard in gear, a light suddenly came on behind them. Larry spun around, alarmed; then he took a deep breath and let it out. "Spotlight on the shed," he said. "Comes on automatically when it gets dark enough."

"That'll help us find our way back," Gigi said, pushing the throttle a bit forward and starting down the creek toward the waterway.

"Switch off your running lights," Larry said, "and keep it at idle, so we make as little noise as possible."

Gigi did so. "Larry, what is this thing you have about boats?"

"I don't have a thing about boats. I like riding in them; I enjoyed the trip to Key Largo from Key West. I just don't have any experience operating them. I don't like the wind and tide doing things to them, either. I feel like I'm not in control."

"Oh."

"We've got a buoy dead ahead," Larry said, switching on a small but very powerful flashlight.

"I see it," Gigi said. "It just marks the creek."

"Seems like there ought to be a light on it," Larry said.

"There is," Gigi said. As they passed the buoy it came on, flashing green.

"Let's get out into the middle of the waterway until we see the dock," Larry said. "And keep a lookout for other boats."

"Okay." Gigi steered for the center, keeping the motor at idle. The boat steered sluggishly going so slowly, but it was manageable.

Larry turned his flashlight to his duffel. He held the light in his teeth as he quickly assembled his rifle and screwed on the silencer and telescopic sight.

"Will the guy be able to see any muzzle flash?" Gigi asked.

"No, the silencer is also a suppressor. You'll hear a *ffft* noise, and he won't even hear that. He'll never know what hit him."

"I see a light up ahead," she said. "It seems to be on shore, not on a dock."

They were both whispering now, aware of how voices carried over water. "I can see a porch," Larry said. "Go past the house and upstream a hundred yards or so, then make a U-turn and go south, close to the dock."

Larry took a small pair of binoculars from his pocket. "I have the porch," he said. "The porch light isn't on; the light is coming from inside."

"Can you see anybody?"

"I see something, but . . ." They were fifty yards from the dock now. "I have a man in a rocking chair."

"That's gotta be our guy," she said.

Larry pressed a magazine into the rifle and worked the bolt action slowly to make as little noise as possible. "Is this as slow as you can go?" he asked.

"Yes," she whispered, "but we've got a little tide against us. When you're ready, I can take it out of gear and we'll slow nearly to a stop."

Larry sat cross-legged in the bottom of the boat, looking through the telescopic sight. "He's got a drink in his hand," he said. "Get ready to stop."

Gigi steered the boat to a point three feet from the dock.

As they came abreast of the pontoon, Larry said, "Stop."

Gigi pulled the gear lever to neutral, and the boat slowed immediately. "I won't be able to steer," she said.

"Don't worry," Larry said, squeezing off a round.

60

Evan found a parking space a couple of doors from the Steak Shack and parked. He got out of the car, took his briefcase and began walking up the sidewalk. To his surprise, someone fell in beside him.

"Evening," Manny White said.

"You startled me," Evan said. "I thought you'd be inside."

"I've already been inside," Manny said, "checking out the place, and I wanted to be sure nobody's following you."

"Who would follow me?" Evan said. "Nobody knows I'm here but you."

"Yeah, sure, kid. Get the door, will you?"

Evan opened the door and held it, but Manny stood, turning slowly, having a last look at the street.

"You first," Manny said.

Evan went into the restaurant, followed by Manny, and they were immediately met by a maître d'.

"Good evening, Mr. White," the man said smoothly.

"Good evening, Marty," Manny replied. "This is my friend Joe; he's going to be a good customer, so treat him right."

"Of course, Mr. White. How do you do, Joe?"

"Just fine, thanks," Evan said. "Nice place you have here."

"Mr. White, your regular booth is ready, but if you wish to have a drink at the bar first . . ."

"No, thanks, Marty," Manny said. "We'll sit down now."

They were shown to the booth, and Manny took the seat facing the door.

Evan noticed him scanning the faces of the other diners. "See anybody you know?"

"A couple of people," Manny said. "I'm more interested in who I don't know."

"You're a careful man, Manny," Evan said. "I like that; it means we're less likely to have problems tonight."

"You have the money?" Manny asked.

Evan patted the briefcase on the seat beside him. "Right here. It's yours as soon as we get that phone call."

A pretty waitress approached. "Hi, Mr. White, what can I get for you and your guest?"

"Scotch," Manny said.

"Same here."

"Two Chivas Regals coming up," she said, then left.

Evan noticed that Manny was sweating. "Do we have any problems, Manny? Is everything all right?"

Manny mopped his face with his napkin. "Don't worry. I have good people on this," he said.

"People? More than one?"

"One to handle the boat, one to shoot," Manny said.

"Oh, okay." Evan looked out a side window. "It's almost dark," he said.

"Dark is good," Manny said as their drinks arrived.

Tommy Sculley sat on Mike Levy's living room floor, with Mike and two deputy sheriffs on the floor nearby. One deputy was pulling a string in a rhythmic fashion, controlling the rocker. The other occasionally pulled the other string, controlling the drinking hand of the dummy.

"So, Mike, how you been?" Tommy asked.

"Not bad. I still miss Ruth, but I've been seeing somebody."

"Good for you."

"I hear a boat," one of the deputies said. "Going slow."

Everybody got very quiet.

"Listen to me," Tommy said softly. "If there's shooting, stay on the floor; we don't want the shooter to see anybody inside."

"Aren't we to fire back?" a deputy asked.

"Absolutely not," Tommy replied. "We want the guy alive, and your boss and a bunch of deputies will be waiting for him at the marina."

As if to confirm this, a radio came alive. "Eddie, you there?"

A deputy picked up the handheld. "We're in place," he said.

"We're ready at the marina. No shooting back, you hear?"

"Yes, Sheriff." He set down the radio, and as he did, there was the sound of shattering glass, and a broken pane spattered the room with shards.

"I didn't hear a shot," Mike said.

"And you won't," Tommy said.

From outside, they heard an engine rev, then quickly the sound faded as the boat moved away.

Tommy stood up. "We're okay," he said, looking at the picture window, which was spattered with what seemed to be gore. "Jesus, Mike, what's all that stuff?"

"Sponge cake and ketchup," Mike replied. "It was all I had."

They got to their feet and went outside to inspect the dead dummy.

"Got me right through the forehead," Mike said.

The motorboat could no longer be heard.

Gigi throttled back as they approached the green flashing buoy at the mouth of the creek leading to the marina. "Are you happy with your shot?" she asked.

Larry was sitting on the seat beside her, disassembling his rifle. "Don't worry. His brains are spattered all over the front of the house," he said.

Manny and Evan finished their drinks and Manny ordered two more.

"It's getting kind of late, isn't it?" Evan said.

"I trust my people," Manny replied. "Don't sweat it."

"Should we order some dinner?" Evan asked.

"You can, if you like," Manny replied. "I'm not going to be here that long."

Gigi drove slowly past the buoy and into the creek.

"Throttle back to idle," Larry said.

Gigi did so, and the boat was barely making headway against the current from the creek. They made another fifty yards, and Gigi could see the pontoon and the other boats in the dim light.

Larry reached over and switched off the ignition.

"Why did you do that?" Gigi asked.

"The light on the shed is off," Larry said.

As he spoke, they both saw the beam of a flashlight

on the trees above the pontoon; then it went off. They were now drifting backward with the current, and the boat began to turn sideways.

"Something's wrong," Larry said. "Just let the boat go where it wants to."

The boat drifted toward the south shore of the creek and brushed against some mangrove. Larry reached overboard, grabbed at the mangrove and propelled the boat downstream. From behind them they heard an unintelligible shout and an equally unintelligible reply; then the engine of a boat started.

"Get us out of here!" Larry hissed. "Go north."

"Back past the house?"

"They won't be expecting us there."

Gigi started the engine and eased the throttle forward.

Larry pushed her hand forward. "Don't worry about the noise; they won't be able to hear it over their own engine. We're only a few miles from Stuart; head for there, as fast as you can."

Gigi swung the boat north as they passed the buoy and aimed for the opposite shore. "You're awfully jumpy, Larry," she said.

Larry looked over his shoulder and saw the running lights of a boat leaving the creek, then another and another. "We're being pursued," he said. "Make it wide-open now."

He took a small black box from his pocket, extended a six-inch antenna and pressed a button.

There was an explosion from behind them, and Gigi looked back in time to see a large fireball rising. She moved the throttle all the way open. The boat leapt forward, its big outboard pushing the small hull. "What was that?" she yelled.

"Our rental car; a little something in the gas tank." Larry looked back and watched the boats hesitate as they came out of the creek, no doubt debating which way to go. "Good thing our boat is black," he said.

"I didn't see anything at that marina that could out-run us," Gigi said, peering through the darkness ahead, looking for other boats.

They raced past the small house on the other side of the waterway, and Larry saw people standing on the dock. "This was a setup," he said. "They were laying for us."

"Then why is nobody shooting at us?" Gigi asked.

"Because they want us—*me*—alive," Larry replied, looking at the chart in his hand. "There's a flashing buoy where we turn left for Stuart. When we get there, stick with me; they're not looking for a couple."

Gigi got out her cell phone and pressed a speed-dial button.

61

Manny felt his cell phone vibrate, and he pressed a button on his Bluetooth earpiece. "Yes?" he said.

"It's Gigi," she shouted over the whine of the outboard motor. "It was a setup; we're running for Stuart Harbor, and we'll make our way home from there."

"I understand." Manny hung up, reached into his inside coat pocket, extracted a sheet of paper and handed it to Evan.

Evan unfolded the sheet and read: "There's a gun on you, so don't say a word or do anything I don't tell you. The job is done. Open your briefcase on the seat beside you, and hand me the money under the table. Don't be obvious. Then leave the briefcase there, get up and go to the men's room, down the hall ahead of you, to your right. Stay there for five minutes, then do anything you like. Nod to tell me you understand."

Evan nodded, opened the briefcase and handed over the envelope with the money. Manny checked it without lowering his head, then put the sheet of paper back into his pocket and nodded.

Evan got up, and went to the men's room.

As soon as he left, Manny slid out of the booth, walked around the screen behind him, opened the back door to an alley and got into a waiting car, driven by his secretary. "Go," he said. She drove fast down the alley, made a right, then a left, and stopped.

"Go straight home; you've been there all evening. There'll be people at the office tomorrow. Play dumb, and hang on to the box I gave you." He took a bundle of cash from the envelope and handed her the rest. "Put this in the box and seal it; I'll call you in a couple of days on your cell with instructions on where to send it. See you later," Manny said. He got out of the car and into a dark blue sedan, not his own. Five minutes later he was off the island, headed for Miami International Airport and a flight to Mexico, where he owned a house.

Half a block from the Steak Shack, Stone and Dino watched as two carloads of men poured onto the sidewalk and ran inside the restaurant.

"That's it for Manny," Dino said.

Stone's cell phone buzzed, and he opened it. "Yeah?"

"It's Evan. Manny got the call, I gave him the money and he sent me to the men's room. What's going on?"

"The state cops are all over him," Stone said. "We'll be there in a minute." He hung up. "Let's go," he said to Dino. They arrived inside the restaurant to see a lot of men standing around, talking on cell phones.

"Look for a gray Toyota," one of them within earshot was saying. "Woman driver."

Stone went over to the booth where Evan was talking with a man in a suit. "What happened?" he asked. "Where's Manny?"

Evan gave him a big shrug. "He handed me a note with instructions, I gave him the money and went to the men's room. When I came back he was gone. The note said the job was done."

"Shit," Stone said.

Gigi motored into Stuart Harbor faster than the law allowed.

"Head for the Pirate's Cove Hotel Marina," Larry said, pointing at a sign. "Pull up next to a ladder."

She did so and climbed up the ladder.

Larry switched off the engine, and while holding on to the ladder with one hand and his duffel with the other, pushed the Whaler under the dock. "Walk. Don't run," he said. "Hold my hand, and make conversation. Laugh."

She did as she was told. They walked ashore and to the hotel's garage.

"Look for something older, something eighties or nineties," he said.

She pointed at an elderly Lincoln Continental, and she followed his directions and got behind the wheel.

It took Larry less than half a minute to hotwire the car. "Back out and go slowly up the driveway," he said. "Take your first left, then your first right."

Shortly, they were on A1A, driving south. Larry produced a cell phone and made a call. "Hello, sugar," he said, "Plan B. Meet me at the place in fifteen minutes." He hung up. "That was my wife," he said. "We're going to dump this car a few miles down the road. Then we'll head south in our car. We'll drop you in Florida City, where you can get a cab to Key Largo and your boat."

"Okay," she said. "Nobody knows where I am, so I can just say I've been on the boat the whole time."

"That's the girl," Larry said.

Fifteen minutes later he said, "Turn right, and drive behind the filling station." The station was dark, having been closed for months.

She followed his instructions.

"Stop here," he said, "and flash your lights. Then shut it down."

She did so, and a car across the street flashed its lights.

"You've got your money, right?"

"Right here in my bag," she said.

Larry raised his hand and shot her once in the head; then he opened her bag, removed the money and put it into his duffel. Taking her bag with him, he got out of the car, wiped down the areas he had touched, ran across the street and got into the car.

"Hey, sugar," he said, kissing her. "Stop at the first Dumpster you see; I want to get rid of something." A couple of minutes later she did, and he tossed Gigi's bag away. "Okay," he said, "let's head for the Everglades."

"Is the girl not coming?" his wife asked.

"She didn't make it," Larry said. "She knew my name."

"So does Manny," she reminded him.

"If he got out, it won't matter," he said. "We'll watch the news for a while before we go home."

An hour later, they were comfortably ensconced in the little cabin in the swamp.

Manny abandoned the car in long-term parking, after wiping it down, and took the bus to the terminal, wheeling the suitcase he had in the trunk.

He approached the AeroMexico counter.

"May I help you, señor?" the young woman asked.

"Are there still seats on the ten o'clock flight to Mexico City?"

She tapped a few computer keys. "We have only one first-class seat," she said.

"That will do nicely," Manny said, taking out his wallet. "Oh, God," he said, sliding the license across the counter, "I've left my credit card at home. Will cash be all right?" He slid his fake passport across the counter.

"Of course, señor," she replied.

He took some hundreds from the packet of Evan's money in his inside pocket and counted out the money.

She gave him his change and printed out the boarding pass. "Any luggage to check?" she asked.

"Just my carry-on," he replied.

"Your flight will be boarding in forty minutes, señor," she said. "Gate sixteen, to your right."

"Thank you, señora," Manny said. He grabbed the handle of his bag and made his way through the crowd. He stood in the security line for ten minutes, then emptied his pockets of everything metal and set his carry-on on the conveyor belt for X-raying. At a signal from the security guard, he stepped through the metal detector. A soft beep sounded.

"Sir," the guard said, "please step back, remove your shoes, put them on the conveyor belt and step through again."

Swearing under his breath, Manny followed his instructions. On his second trip through the metal detector it beeped again.

"Sir," the guard said, "please remove your jacket and hand it to me."

Manny did so, then realized the problem. "It was my belt buckle," he said to the guard, unbuckling his belt and taking it off.

But the guard was already searching his jacket, finding his passport and the bundle of hundreds in his inside pockets.

"Sir," the security guard said, "did you fill out and sign the federal form declaring this cash, which appears to be more than five thousand dollars?"

"Gosh," Manny said, "I forgot about that. Can I fill it out now?"

"Of course, sir," the guard said. He beckoned to his supervisor and whispered a few words in his ear.

The supervisor smiled. "Will you come with me, please, sir?"

Manny put on his shoes and belt, collected his carry-on and followed the man. How could he have forgotten about the form?

The supervisor opened a door and ushered him into a small room, where a man in a business suit with a plastic ID clipped to the pocket waited. The supervisor gave him Manny's passport and money, then left. "Sit down, please," the man said.

Manny sat down. "I'd like to fill out the proper form, please," he said. "My flight leaves in half an hour."

The man was leafing through the passport. "Let me compliment you Mr., ah, Bernstein," he said.

"What?"

"This is the best example of a counterfeit passport I've seen for some time. Show me some authentic ID, please."

Manny sighed, produced his wallet and handed the man his driver's license.

"Thank you, Mr. . . . Manfried White?"

"That's me," Manny replied. "I can explain about the passport. You see . . ."

The man held up a hand. "No explanation will be necessary, Mr. White," he said. "We've been expecting you." He pressed a button under the table and two other men in suits entered the room. "This, gentlemen," he said, "is the Manny White your colleagues phoned about. Mr. White, may I introduce Detectives Marino and Copeland, of the Florida State Police?"

Manny sagged. "I can explain all this," he said.

The two men stood him up and began handcuffing his hands behind his back. "And we're looking forward to hearing your explanation, Mr. White," one of them said.

62

Stone shook the hand of Greta Swenson, Annika's sister, and walked her to the departures door at Key West International.

"I want to thank you for your courtesy, Stone," she said. "Annika spoke highly of you."

"She was a wonderful person," Stone replied, handing her the package containing Annika's ashes. "I hope you have a comfortable flight home."

She kissed him on the cheek.

Evan, who was on the same flight to Atlanta, where they would both change planes, shook Stone's hand. "I can't thank you enough," he said. "I'm sorry I gave you such a difficult time."

"Will you return to Key West?" Stone asked.

"Maybe, eventually. I'd like to spend some time with my grandfather now. We have a lot to talk about."

"They'll want you to come back to Miami for Manny White's trial," Stone said.

"That will be a pleasure," Evan replied.

"Have you heard anything from Gigi?"

"No, nor the boat. She's not answering her cell phone; I've left several messages."

"Good luck to you, then." They shook hands again, and Evan walked Greta into the terminal.

Stone returned to the car, where Dino was waiting, and got in.

"Nice lady," Dino said.

"Yes," Stone replied, "she is."

"Can Tommy and I buy you a drink?" Dino asked, pulling away from the terminal.

"You certainly can," Stone said.

The three of them sat at the bar at the Key West Yacht Club and raised their glasses.

"To complicated cases," Tommy said. "They're the most fun."

They drank.

"I have news from the state cops," Tommy said. "This afternoon the cops in Hobe Sound found a woman in a stolen car behind an abandoned service station, one bullet in the head. No ID, but she fits the description of Gigi Jones Keating."

"That's interesting news," Dino said.

"There's more: She had an apartment in South Beach, and they searched it. Found a stash of mixed drugs, too much for personal use. They figure that she was in business with Charley Boggs in some way, and that's how the big stash got left on Evan's boat."

"She was a piece of work," Dino said.

"Sounds like her hit man didn't trust her," Stone said. "Any word on him?"

"The state cops tell me Manny lawyered up right away. My guess is he'll make a deal before he goes to trial, and then we'll find out who the guy is."

Dino shook his head. "Not Manny," he said. "He knows that at his age he'll die in prison, deal or no deal. He won't rat the guy out."

"By the way," Tommy said, "the state guys said the only reason they caught Manny was he forgot to take off his belt at airport security, and the buckle set off the metal detector. Except for that, he'd be in Mexico now."

Everybody had a good laugh.

"Are you guys really leaving tomorrow morning?" Tommy asked.

"At long last," Dino replied, "though I hate to go."

"We've loitered long enough," Stone said.

AUTHOR'S NOTE

I am happy to hear from readers, but you should know that if you write to me in care of my publisher, three to six months will pass before I receive your letter, and when it finally arrives it will be one among many, and I will not be able to reply.

However, if you have access to the Internet, you may visit my Web site at www.stuartwoods.com, where there is a button for sending me e-mail. So far, I have been able to reply to all my e-mail, and I will continue to try to do so.

If you send me an e-mail and do not receive a reply, it is probably because you are among an alarming number of people who have entered their e-mail address incorrectly in their mail software. I have many of my replies returned as undeliverable.

Remember: e-mail, reply; snail mail, no reply.

When you e-mail, please do not send attachments, as I *never* open these. They can take twenty minutes to download, and they often contain viruses.

Please do not place me on your mailing lists for funny stories, prayers, political causes, charitable fund-raising, petitions or sentimental claptrap. I get enough of that from people I already know. Generally speaking, when I get e-mail addressed to a large number of people, I immediately delete it without reading it.

Please do not send me your ideas for a book, as I have a policy of writing only what I myself invent. If you send me story ideas, I will immediately delete them without reading them. If you have a good idea for a book, write it yourself, but I will not be able to advise you on how to get it published. Buy a copy of *Writer's Market* at any bookstore; that will tell you how.

Anyone with a request concerning events or appearances may e-mail it to me or send it to: Publicity Department, Penguin Group (USA) Inc., 375 Hudson Street, New York, NY 10014.

Those ambitious folk who wish to buy film, dramatic or television rights to my books should contact Matthew Snyder, Creative Artists Agency, 9830 Wilshire Boulevard, Beverly Hills, CA 98212-1825.

Those who wish to make offers for rights of a literary nature should contact Anne Sibbald, Janklow & Nesbit, 445 Park Avenue, New York, NY 10022. (Note: This is not an invitation for you to send her your manuscript or to solicit her to be your agent.)

If you want to know if I will be signing books in your city, please visit my Web site at www.stuartwoods.com, where the tour schedule will be published a month or so in advance. If you wish me to do a book signing in your locality, ask your favorite bookseller to contact his Penguin representative or the Penguin publicity department with the request.

If you find typographical or editorial errors in my book and feel an irresistible urge to tell someone, please write to Penguin's address above. Do not e-mail your discoveries to me, as I will already have learned about them from others.

A list of my published works appears in the front of this book and on my Web site. All the novels are still in print in paperback and can be found at or ordered from any bookstore. If you wish to obtain hardcover copies of earlier novels or of the two nonfiction books, a good used-book store or one of the online bookstores can help you find them. Otherwise, you will have to go to a great many garage sales.

Read on for an excerpt from
Stuart Woods's thrilling novel

HOTHOUSE ORCHID

On sale now

Holly Barker arrived at CIA headquarters, in Langley, Virginia, at her usual seven thirty a.m., parked the car in her reserved spot and took the elevator to her floor. She set her briefcase on the desk, hung her coat on the back of the door and sat down, ready to do the work she always did before her boss, Deputy Director for Operations, or DDO, Lance Cabot arrived. To her surprise, the door between their adjoining offices opened, and he stood there, looking at her in his wry way.

"Good morning," he said, "and no cracks about how early I'm in."

Holly smiled. "Good morning," she replied.

"Come in." He stood aside and let her pass into his office, which was much larger and more luxuriously furnished than hers. Rumor was that Lance had furnished the office out of his own pocket, but Holly knew him better than that. He was much more likely to have found a way for the Agency to pay the tab. He waved her to a seat.

"Coffee?" he asked, picking up a pot from the paneled cupboard that contained a small kitchenette and a fully stocked bar.

"Yes, thank you."

Lance poured them both a cup and sat down at his desk. "Have I ever told you how good you are at your job?" he asked.

Holly blinked. "Not in so many words."

"We've both been working on this floor for three years," he said, "and, quite frankly, I think you could do my job as well as I do."

Holly blinked in astonishment. Lance had always been miserly with praise, apparently believing that a "well done" sufficed.

"Except for the politics," Lance said.

He was right about that, she knew. "Well . . ."

"You're hopeless at the politics."

"I'm working on that," she said.

"Yes, but you're still hopeless."

"Not without hope of improvement," she said, contradicting him.

Lance smiled a little. "Well, you can hope."

"Lance," she said, "I hope this is all a prelude to a

384

big promotion, a larger office, a huge increase in salary and a company Cadillac." This was said less than half in jest.

"As I said, Holly, you can hope." Lance pushed back from his desk, crossed his legs and sipped his coffee. "Actually, you have to leave us."

Holly clamped her teeth together to keep her jaw from dropping. "I don't know how to respond to that," she managed to say.

Lance's eyebrows went up. "Oh, it's only for a time, say a month."

Holly stared at him, uncomprehending.

"I'm not firing you," he clarified.

"Good. Then I won't have to kill you," she replied. "Now what the hell are you talking about?"

"I'm not doing the talking; other people are."

"Talking? Not about you and me, surely."

"Well, maybe that, too. What they're talking about is Teddy Fay."

Teddy Fay was a name never mentioned at Langley, a great embarrassment to everyone in the building, except to those who secretly rooted for him. Teddy was the former deputy chief of Technical Services, the division that supplied operational officers with everything they needed to accomplish their missions: a weapon, a wardrobe, an identity or a cyanide capsule. Whatever, Tech Services obliged. But Teddy Fay, after retiring, had gone off the reservation, had started killing right-wing political figures, Middle Eastern diplomats—anyone who Teddy felt did not have the best interests of his country at heart—and no combination of the Agency's and the FBI's resources had been able to stop him or even find him. Holly was the only CIA employee who had ever even seen him since his retirement and then only when he was disguised.

"Am I getting blamed for Teddy Fay?" she asked.

"Not exactly," Lance replied. "It's just felt that you've had a number of opportunities to kill him and you haven't done so."

"Lance, I've seen the man only once when I knew who he was, and, on that occasion, I managed to put a bullet in him."

"Yes, but not in the head or the heart," Lance pointed out. "And given that, during your schooling at the Farm, you ran up the highest scores with a handgun of any trainee ever, some wonder why you didn't do just a little better. In fact, I myself have wondered."

Holly had wondered about that, too. "I won't dignify that with a response," she said, by way of saying nothing. She almost said that she was not an assassin but thought better of it.

"Be that as it may, you are just a little too hot around here at the moment, so take some leave. The director has had a word with the higher-ups around here, complaining about the unused leave time that some officers have allowed to pile up, and you're high on the list.

You've got nine weeks coming, and it's time you took some time."

"Lance, I've got an awful lot on my plate right now."

"You need a change of diet," he said. "And, you might recall, we've made a few modifications in that house of yours in Florida."

Holly had nearly forgotten about that, and she had not visited the house since. "That wasn't my idea."

"Go there. E-mail or call, if you can't stand being out of touch, but go."

Holly sighed. "Well, I guess I could clean up my desk in a few days," she said.

"You've got two hours to write me a memo on what's pending so I can reassign the work. Then you're out of here." He paused for a reaction and got none. "Are you hearing me?"

"I'm doing that job for the director," she said. She had grown fairly close to Katharine Rule Lee, the director of Central Intelligence, and she wanted to further that relationship.

"This request comes from the director. I'm only passing it on. Give me the file. I'll handle it."

Holly threw up her hands.

"Why are you still sitting there?" Lance asked.

"All right, all right," Holly said, then slouched out of the big office and to her desk. Her work was neatly filed, and she made a stack of folders as she wrote her memo. She was done in exactly two hours. She knocked on Lance's door.

"Come in."

She walked into the room to find the director sitting where she herself had sat earlier that morning.

"Good morning, Holly," Kate Lee said.

"Good morning, Director," Holly replied. She set the bundle of file folders on Lance's conference table, then handed him the memo and watched while he read it through.

"I thought I'd stop in and reassure you before you leave," the director said. "It's not that we're trying to get rid of you. It's just that we're . . . well, trying to get rid of you for a little while. We needn't go into why."

"I understand," Kate said. "At least I think I do."

"This will pass," the director said. "After all, Lance has assured me that Teddy Fay is still dead."

Holly nodded as if she agreed.

"Oh, by the way, Lance probably hasn't told you this, if I know him, but we're bumping you up to executive grade, and, in addition to the salary increase and a few perks, you now have a new title: Assistant Deputy Director of Operations—ADDO—effective immediately."

"Thank you, Director," Holly said with real appreciation, "and no, Lance didn't tell me." She shot him a glance.

Lance tossed her memo on his desk. "Oh, get out of

here," he said. "Let us know your whereabouts." He tossed her an envelope. "You'll need this."

The director stood up and offered her hand. "Congratulations, Holly. Now go and buy yourself a very nice present."

Holly flew.

Also Available from
New York Times Bestselling Author

STUART WOODS

The Stone Barrington Novels

L.A. Dead

Cold Paradise

The Short Forever

Dirty Work

Reckless Abandon

Two Dollar Bill

Dark Harbor

Fresh Disasters

Shoot Him If He Runs

Hot Mahogany

Available wherever books are sold or at penguin.com

New York Times bestselling author

STUART WOODS

MOUNTING FEARS
A Will Lee Novel

President Will Lee is having a rough week.
His vice president just died during surgery.
Confirmation hearings for the new vice
president are under way, but the squeaky-clean
governor whom Will has nominated may have
a few previously unnoticed skeletons in his
closet. And Teddy Fay, the rogue CIA agent
last seen in *Shoot Him If He Runs*, is plotting his
revenge on CIA director Kate Rule Lee—
the president's wife.

Plus there are some loose nukes in Pakistan
that might just trigger World War III if Will's
diplomatic efforts fall short. It's up to President
Lee—with some help from Holly Barker, Lance
Cabot, and a few other Stuart Woods series
regulars—to save the world, and the
upcoming election.

**Available wherever books are sold or at
penguin.com**